THE
BILLIONAIRE'S
ANGEL

The Winters Saga
Book Seven

IVY LAYNE

GINGER QUILL PRESS, LLC

The Billionaire's Angel

Find out more about the author and upcoming books online at www.
ivylayne.com

CONTENTS

THE BILLIONAIRE CLUB

Chapter One

Sophie

My hands shook as I measured a short length of tape. Staring down at the black cockroach in my hand, I wondered again how I'd gotten myself into this mess.

It's not what you're thinking. The cockroach wasn't real. I've learned how to be brave in the past few years, but not brave enough to carry around live bugs. Yuck. No, this cockroach had been carefully cut out of black construction paper, along with the selection of spiders and crickets spread across the seat of the leather couch.

It was after two in the morning, and I was in my employer's library, fumbling in the dark to tape the fake bugs to the inside of the white silk lampshades. The next person to flip on the lights would be treated to the illusion that huge bugs lurked inside the lamps. I could already imagine the screams that would echo through the house.

It wouldn't be the first time.

I really had to find a way to keep my charge off the internet. Boredom plus an active mind equals trouble. At least it does when your name is Amelia Winters.

Since Amelia was seventy-eight and her hands weren't as nimble as mine, I got roped into carrying out the pranks she dreamed up. I was supposed to be her nurse, and I was when she needed one.

High blood pressure and type two diabetes meant she needed some supervision, but not enough to require live-in care. Since most of the family had moved out of the enormous house, and Amelia's great nephew Aiden traveled often for work, I was there to keep her both healthy and entertained.

It could have been a lonely job, if not for Amelia. Her pranks aside, she was a blast to work for - funny and loyal and sweet. Her body was slowing down, but her mind was sharp, and she had a wicked sense of humor. Sometimes too wicked.

The pranks, case in point. At least once a week she came up with a new one, sending me out for materials and instructing me on the details of her plans.

At first, I'd worried she was going to get me fired. Since my husband had died, I'd been bouncing from job to job. I'd been more than ready to settle down when I'd been hired here, and I hadn't wanted to be kicked out for lining the hallway with tiny cups filled with water.

Amelia might be almost eighty, but her sense of humor was a lot more frat-boy than elderly matron.

Fortunately for me, the family was well versed in Amelia's ways. Aiden, who'd scared the heck out of me when he'd hired me, adored his great-aunt. She could probably set the house on fire, and he'd laugh and kiss her on the cheek. The rest of them were the same—affectionate and amused by Amelia's antics. The only two exceptions were the housekeeper, Mrs. Williamson, and Aiden's cousin, Gage.

Mrs. Williamson and Amelia were chalk and cheese. Mrs. W was far too proper to admit she didn't love *every* member of the Winters family, but we all knew Amelia drove her nuts. Amelia, for her part, delighted in pestering Mrs. W. More than once I'd heard her mutter under her breath that Mrs. W had a stick up her you-know-where.

She'd never say it, but I'm pretty sure Mrs. W thought Amelia should give in and act her age. I'd only been with the family for six months, but I could have told her that was a lost cause. By all accounts, Amelia Winters had never acted her age, and at seventy-eight, she wasn't about to start.

I adored Amelia, and I had to admit, some of her pranks were funny, but I liked Mrs. W too much to let her think her beloved Winters House was infested with six-inch cockroaches. As soon as I'd taped the last fake insect in place, I pulled out my phone to shoot Mrs. W a warning text.

Sometime tomorrow she'd come into the library on a made-up pretext and let out a very convincing scream. Amelia would get her laugh, and Mrs. W wouldn't have to kill her. Everyone would be happy.

I tapped SEND on my text and went to shove the phone in the pocket of my robe when two arms closed around my chest like steel bars, pinning my hands to my sides.

My phone tumbled from nerveless fingers, bouncing off my bare toes and skidding across the carpet. I froze where I was, my heart thumping in my chest so hard I heard the whoosh of blood in my ears.

Panic shot ice down my spine.

My nerves screamed: DANGER! DANGER!

Head spinning with fear, I tried to think. The long, hard body pressed to my back made that impossible. Eyes squeezed shut, memories flashed against my closed lids, a newsreel of everything I wanted to forget.

Hard hands grabbing me in the dark, dragging me from my bed. Pain.

It isn't Anthony, I told myself. *Anthony is dead.*

Summoning every ounce of courage I had, I said, "Let me go."

A low, husky voice rumbled in my ear. "Not until you tell me what the hell you're doing in here in the middle of the night."

A hitch in my voice, I said, "Amelia. Amelia sent me."

The words tangled in my throat. I couldn't say more. The heat of a male body so close to mine, the strength of his arms trapping me, his warm breath against my cheek - it was too much.

I hadn't been this close to a man—any man—since my husband had died.

After Anthony, I'd never wanted to be this close to a man again.

In a rush of awareness, I knew this wasn't Aiden. Aiden had always been careful to preserve a polite, formal distance between us. If he caught me skulking around the house in the middle of the night, he'd never grab me from behind. Heck, with the way Aiden adored Amelia he'd probably volunteer to finish the prank himself.

If it wasn't Aiden. It had to be Gage. Aiden's cousin had arrived two days before, when Amelia and I had been out on a shopping trip, picking up construction paper and tape. I met him briefly at the family dinner to celebrate his home-coming, but I hadn't seen him since. Hoping my guess was right, I said, "I'm Sophie. Amelia's nurse."

A grunt in my ear, but the arms around me didn't loosen. Shoot. I knew better than to struggle. Fighting back only made them hurt you more. My breath shallow, body still, I tried again.

"I'm allowed to be here. I'm not doing anything wrong. Please let me go."

I felt his head drop to my shoulder, the heat of his forehead pressing into my bare neck. He drew in a deep breath.

Was he *smelling* me?

Panic sliced through me again.

No. Please, no. Please don't make me have to leave this place.

I'd thought I was safe here. For the first time in years, I was safe. I didn't want to have to leave.

His heart jackhammered, the echo of its frantic beats fluttering against my back where his chest pressed tightly to me.

"Please," I whispered. The arms around me loosened. I stayed frozen. I was too cautious to move until I'd truly been set free. This could be a trap, and I was too smart to fall for it. Anthony had trained me well.

Warm lips brushed the side of my neck. Another deep inhale. He *was* smelling me. The urge to flee was almost impossible to resist, but I knew in my gut running was the worst mistake I could make.

I wracked my brain for everything I knew of Gage. He was the oldest son of James and Anna Winters, Aiden's aunt and uncle. James and Anna had been brutally murdered when Gage was a child. When Aiden's parents had been killed in an identical crime eight years later, Gage had been eighteen. The day after their funeral he'd joined the army. Until today, he'd never really come home.

Details of his military service were scarce, but Amelia had told me everything she knew. He'd enlisted, gone to college, then through officer training school, before he'd joined the Rangers. After that he'd moved into special forces, his missions and teams so top secret his family hadn't been sure he was still with the army until they'd called to tell Aiden that Gage was missing.

For months the family had been stuck in limbo, swinging between grief and hope, right up until a second call had informed Aiden that Gage had escaped captivity. He was coming home as soon as the military hospital released him, but they'd warned Aiden that the months of imprisonment had taken a toll.

Gage was no longer the man his family remembered.

Aiden had commented dryly that Gage had been gone so long, they barely knew him at all. No matter what the circumstances of his homecoming, to his family, Gage was a stranger. As my panic ebbed, I realized the man holding me captive might possibly be more freaked out than I was.

He probably had some form of post-traumatic stress if he'd been held captive for months. Finding an intruder in his home was just the kind of thing that would set him off, especially when his home must seem like a foreign place after so many years away.

Logic told me that a former special forces soldier suffering from PTSD was *more* dangerous, not less, but my guess at what might be going through his head put me back in control. As a woman alone in the dark, I was terrified. As a nurse, and a woman used to dealing with volatile men, I knew what I needed to do.

"Gage?" I asked, careful to keep my voice low and soothing. "Gage, it's okay. You can let go. I'm Amelia's nurse. I'm allowed to be here. It's okay."

I kept talking in the same soothing voice, feeling the tension slip from his body. Eventually, he lifted his head and stepped back, setting me free. With an odd sense of triumph, I crossed the room before I turned around. I thought he was steady, but I wanted some space between us, just in case.

"I'm going to turn on the lamp," I warned just before I reached beneath the shade and turned the knob. Light flared, blinding me for a moment. A deep chuckle rumbled from across the room.

"Whose idea was it?" he asked.

His voice distracted me for a second, so deep and calm, at odds with the tension that had seized his muscles only a few minutes before. I glanced at the light and saw the shadow of an enormous spider lurking on the inside of the shade.

I stepped away with a shiver before I realized what I was doing. Silly, since I was the one who had taped the bugs in place, but I hadn't expected them to look so real. Amelia was good.

Clearing my throat, I said, "Amelia's. It's always Amelia's idea." I wanted to ask if he was okay, but I held my tongue.

"Clever," he said.

"That's Amelia," I agreed.

"Is this the only room you did?"

"It is." Judging it safe to move, I began to gather up my materials, tucking my phone back in the pocket of my robe and making sure I had all the extra bugs and the tape. A prank was no good if I left the evidence sitting around.

"Mrs. W won't be happy."

I smiled. It was sweet the way the family doted on Mrs. W. I'd always imagined a family as wealthy and powerful as the Winterses would be stuffy, far above those they'd consider the help. Instead, they treated Mrs. W like family and had welcomed me as an equal, insisting I join them for meals and giving me a room in the main house that was bigger than my apartment when I'd been in nursing school.

"I already texted her," I reassured Gage. "She'll make a big fuss tomorrow when she turns on the lights. Unless Aiden does it first."

"Aiden doesn't know?"

I shook my head, picking up the last scrap of construction paper. Suddenly without anything to do, I crossed my arms over my chest. Gage stood in shadow, his features hard to make out, but I was uncomfortably aware I was in my robe, my hair down, looking like an unprofessional mess.

In the six months I'd been living in Winters House, I'd never encountered another soul awake in the middle of the night.

Clearing my throat, I said, "No, Aiden likes to be surprised."

Gage let out a grunt I couldn't decipher. He took a step forward, leaving the shadows of the corner. Light bathed his features, and my breath caught. I'd heard Gage and Aiden were like twins. Everyone else must be blind. To my eyes, they looked nothing alike.

Sure, they both had the same build - tall, broad shoulders, lean hips. The same dark hair. Even their features were superficially similar, with sharp cheekbones, aristocratic noses and full lower lips. Where Aiden's hair had the same auburn tones as his little sister, Charlie, Gage's was a true brown, not a hint of red to be seen.

I'd always thought soldiers wore their hair short, but Gage's was a little long. Shaggy. As if he hadn't had it cut in months. Which of course, he hadn't. I imagined his hairstyle hadn't been a priority when he'd been trying to escape his captors.

He'd probably cut it now that he was home. Maybe with

8

shorter hair, he'd look more like Aiden. I took in the tension in his shoulders, his hands curled into fists.

No. The obvious aside, Aiden looked nothing like Gage.

Aiden was cool. Refined. Controlled.

Standing in the pool of light, his faded grey t-shirt stretched around his biceps, hugging his well-defined chest, Gage was raw, his power barely leashed. Despite his stillness, he vibrated with energy.

I sensed it was taking everything he had to remain where he was. His vivid blue eyes were the least of the differences between Gage and his cousin.

Those eyes were leveled on me, pinning me in place as effectively as his arms had a few minutes before.

Clearing my throat, I said, "Are you going to spoil it for her?"

"The prank?" Gage asked. At my nod, he said, "No."

"Thank you." I started for the door to the library, careful to give Gage a wide berth. I didn't think he was going to grab me again, but it seemed smarter to stay out of arm's reach.

"Tell me next time," he said.

"What?" I stopped at the door, confused.

He was silent for a long moment before answering in a halting voice. "I don't do well with surprises these days. The next time Amelia decides to mess with us, fill me in."

Instantly, I understood. Amelia's plan to duct tape an airhorn to Aiden's desk chair would be a nightmare to a man newly home from a combat zone, even if he *didn't* have post-traumatic stress, and I was betting Gage did.

"Do you have a cell?" I asked.

Gage raised his eyebrows in question. I explained, "I text Mrs. W to warn her. I'll try to talk Amelia out of a few of her plans that might be a problem, but I can text you, too. That way you know what's coming."

"So, Amelia hasn't slowed down. Good to know some things don't change," he said, his voice heavy with something I couldn't quite identify. Regret? Whatever it was, Gage Winters sounded sad.

I had the absurd urge to comfort him.

Absurd because not only did I not know what was wrong, he was a Winters. Yes, he'd been through a terrible experience. But he was alive. He was home with his family, living in this enormous mansion, with a job waiting for him at Winters Incorporated, and more money than he could count stashed away in the bank.

Gage Winters didn't need my comfort. He didn't need anything from me.

He might remind me of a wounded animal, but wounded animals were dangerous. And I'd been bitten enough.

The only person in this house who needs you is Amelia, I reminded myself. *Stay away from Gage Winters.*

"Are you in Vance's old room?" Gage asked.

"I am. Across from Amelia. I guess her room used to be Holden and Tate's?"

Gage nodded. "If you're done with your bugs, I'll walk you back."

"It's just down the hall," I protested.

"All the same. I'll walk you back."

I didn't bother to argue. Gage followed me out the door, turning off the lamp before we left the room. The short stretch of hall outside the library was dark, the doors to the wine room and Aiden's office lost in the shadows.

We turned the corner to the main hall where silvery moonlight streamed through the tall, arched windows, casting the walls in dreamlike shades. Outside, in the center courtyard of Winters House, a fountain burbled, the water flashing black and silver.

I loved this fairy tale of a house. I completely understood why Mrs. W was so devoted to it. How could Gage have left this place and not come back for so many years? In the six months I'd been with Amelia, Winters House had become a haven.

Why had Gage left it just when he'd needed it most?

I couldn't imagine the losses this family had suffered. Not really. I'd lost my mother to cancer when I was a teenager, but Gage had not only lost both his parents as a child, he'd lost the aunt and uncle who'd raised him when he'd barely been a man.

More than once since he'd gone missing I'd wondered what had happened to make the eighteen-year-old Gage flee his family home.

Now that he was back, was he going to stay? None of it was my business, but I couldn't help my curiosity.

Gage kept his distance as we walked down the hall, following just slightly behind me. Our feet shuffled along the polished hardwood floors, almost silent in the sleeping house. This wasn't the first time I'd wandered Winters House in the middle of the night, but it was the first time I'd done so with company.

We reached the door to my bedroom, across the hall from Amelia's. I reached for the handle, and Gage's fingers closed over mine. I started in surprise, letting out a little squeak. I was grateful for the dark as I felt my cheeks turn red.

"I'm sorry about earlier," Gage said in his low rumble. "I wasn't expecting to see anyone in the library and I reacted on instinct. I didn't mean to scare you."

"You didn't," I lied. "It's okay."

Gage dropped his hand and stared at me, his blue eyes gleaming in the moonlight, seeing everything. He knew I was lying, knew I'd been scared. Lips pressed together and eyes wide, I silently begged him to let it go.

Gage took a step back and dropped his hand.

"Sleep well, Sophie," he said, his low voice sending shivers down my spine.

"You, too," I whispered, and escaped into my room.

CHAPTER TWO

GAGE

Aiden was avoiding me. It took me a while to figure it out. He worked so much, sometimes it seemed like he was avoiding everyone. I'd been home for two days, and we hadn't spent more than twenty minutes alone together since I'd walked through the door.

Don't get me wrong, Aiden was glad I was home. Everyone was. And I was relieved as hell to be here. There'd been times, too many of them, when I'd been certain I'd never see home again. Somehow, I'd imagined things would go differently if I ever got here.

Always the dutiful head of the family, Aiden had met my plane. I'd seen him here and there over the past thirteen years, but I hadn't really noticed him growing older until I'd come home for good.

Fuck, we'd both gotten old. We were the same age, pretty much. We even looked alike. And now we had the same grooves drawn into our faces, the same lines around our eyes.

Once, we'd been inseparable.

Now, Aiden could barely meet my eyes.

He was pissed at me. Still. Or maybe, again. For what, I wasn't sure, and Aiden wasn't talking.

There was a long list of possibilities; I'd run out on all of them after Olivia and Hugh had died. None of them really knew why. I'd been eighteen, lost in grief and guilt and fear and I'd abandoned my family. I had to live with that, but the last six months seemed like enough penance to me.

I didn't know if Aiden was mad that I'd left, or mad that I'd come home. Or pissed that I'd spent the last thirteen years throwing myself into danger when I didn't have to. Shit, if I really wanted to make a list of all the reasons Aiden had to be mad at me, it would take all day.

Unfortunately for him, I was back, and he was going to have to deal with me. So far, he'd proven adept at dodging me, leaving the house early and working late. The night he'd been home for dinner, we had been surrounded by the rest of the family and Aiden had been careful to preserve his distance. So far, I'd let it go. Now, I was done.

Aiden stepped out of the dining room, a folded newspaper in his hand, and stopped short when I blocked his path.

"Gage. You're up early," he said in a politely distant tone. "Mrs. W is still serving breakfast if you're hungry."

He moved to walk around me. When I stepped to block him, his eyes narrowed briefly before he raised one eyebrow and gave me the look he used when he wanted to send people scurrying in the other direction.

It didn't work on me.

I was a soldier. And I'd shared a room with him when he still wet the bed. It took a lot more than Aiden's glare to send me running.

"I'll eat in a minute," I said. "I want to talk to you about the company."

Aiden checked his watch in a show of impatience and said, "Can we do this later? I have an early meeting."

"You can spare two minutes," I said. "I want to come to work. I'm not expecting any favors. We can talk about the skills I have and how we can use them, but I have a stake in Winters Inc., and I'm tired of sitting around, doing nothing."

An undefinable emotion ghosted over Aiden's familiar features. Regret, or grief, tinged with anger. I'd been right. He was pissed.

Checking his watch again, he said, "Gage, you just got home. You need to take it easy. Relax, settle in. I'm happy to have you at the company, but why don't we table this until after the holidays? The next few weeks are going to be busy between Charlie's wedding, and then Tate's. You've been gone thirteen years. You can wait another few weeks."

"Aiden," I tried again, "we need to talk."

"Later, Gage."

Aiden skirted around me and was gone, heading past the kitchen to the garage. Temporarily defeated, I entered the dining room to find it empty. It was still early, just after seven. Aunt Amelia and Sophie were probably still asleep. Considering that Sophie had been up half the night, I hoped she was still asleep. I wasn't ready to face her in daylight.

The door leading from the butler's pantry into the dining room swung open, and Mrs. Williamson's familiar face appeared. "Scrambled eggs with cheese, sausages, and black coffee?" she asked with a wink.

"That would be great, thanks, Mrs. W."

I sat at the table, smiling to myself. I hadn't expected my homecoming to be easy. I'd spent too much time away for that. But Mrs. W was just as I'd remembered her. She alone seemed to bear no resentment over my absence. She'd welcomed me with a firm hug and a kiss on one cheek, only saying, "I missed you, and I'm so glad you're home."

We'd both pretended to ignore the shine of tears in her eyes, and mine.

Even Aunt Amelia had given me shit after she enfolded me in a fierce hug. She hadn't been able to stop herself from scolding me for getting captured in the first place. Like that was the plan. At least I'd gotten my team out of harm's way before I'd gone down. But did I get any credit for that? Not from my family.

I knew they'd been scared. After so much death and loss, learning that I was missing must've been awful. I got it. I did. But I was home. I was even in one piece, which was a miracle, all things considered.

Mrs. W came in, setting a steaming cup of black coffee in front of me, along with a woven silver basket covered with an embroidered napkin, the crimson 'W' standing out against the snowy linen.

Steam wafted up, smelling of biscuits and butter. I'd missed a lot of things about home, but the food had to be at the top of the list.

Mrs. W squeezed my shoulder and left. From her, that was the equivalent of a long embrace. Mrs. W had firm ideas about her place in the family. Mostly that she wasn't family. The rest of us disagreed, but we'd long since learned not to bother arguing with Mrs. W.

Now that our parents were dead, Helen Williamson was the closest thing we had to a mother, and every one of us loved her like one.

I thought of the bugs taped on the insides of the lampshades in the library and mentally corrected myself. Almost all of us loved her like family. Aunt Amelia, not so much. I'd never really understood why those two didn't get along.

Since Mrs. W would rather die than admit she disliked a member of the Winters family, she refused to talk. When I'd asked Amelia, she'd only narrowed her sharp eyes and shook her head saying, "I have my reasons."

I didn't envy Sophie the job of keeping the peace between those two.

Sophie.

I wasn't sure if I was dreading or anticipating seeing her again. Both. It was both.

Dreading, because I owed her an apology. I still couldn't believe I'd grabbed her in the dark like that. I'd terrified her. It killed me to know I'd scared any woman, but especially this one.

And anticipating... Fuck, once I'd gotten a good look at her, how could I not anticipate seeing Sophie again?

When I'd first walked into the library, all I'd seen was a shadow, moving in the dark in a room that should be empty. In that room. The library carried too many memories. More than memories, nightmares of the last time I'd walked into a scene that didn't belong.

My head wasn't screwed on right these days. I'd come back in one piece physically, but mentally—let's just say I was doing better than expected, but I wasn't quite back to normal. Not yet. Maybe I never would be.

Bad dreams. Insomnia. Jumping at loud noises. I'd been around long enough to know what post-traumatic stress looked like. I'd seen it in other guys. Even talked to them about it, encouraged them to get some help.

So easy, when it wasn't me.

I laid in bed at night and closed my eyes. All I could see were things I wanted to forget. The fucking flashbacks were the worst. I knew they weren't real. In my mind, I knew I wasn't back there, locked in a cage.

My body disagreed. When they hit, I broke out in a sweat, my heart raced, and every part of me was convinced I was in mortal danger.

I knew what was wrong with me, but I wasn't in control.

If I had been, I never would've grabbed Sophie like that.

At first, my arms had closed around her, and I'd been ready to throw her to the floor, to restrain her as if she'd been the intruder I thought she was.

Then, I'd smelled her.

Such a simple thing, scent. It sneaks into your brain, provoking a response before you can process. My instincts told my body to relax before my brain got in gear. Nothing that smelled like Sophie could be a threat.

I kept trying to figure it out, but I couldn't break it down. Her scent was a contradiction. Sweet and sultry, like flowers and spice. Innocence. Seductive, sensual innocence.

I'd grabbed her because I thought her an intruder, but I held on because I wanted more.

Her body was soft, rounded and warm against me. It wasn't until I realized how fast her heart was beating, how short her breath was, that I let go.

Fuck, I owed her an apology.

I'd wanted to comfort her, but I was aware enough to realize that as the person who'd scared the crap out of her, my comfort wouldn't be welcome.

And, if she realized I was half hard after holding that soft body against me, it would've made everything worse.

I could've stayed in the library with her all night. Just her scent and her low, soothing voice had been enough. But when she turned on the light, the sight of her was a punch to the gut.

Sophie was a tiny thing, at least compared to me. There was no way she was much more than 5' 3". In her tightly belted white robe, silvery blonde hair spilling over her shoulders, she'd looked like an angel. Except no angel should have a body like that. The robe hid everything, but I'd held her against me.

The feel of her ass would keep me up at night, not that I'd complain. Remembering her soft curves was a much better reason for insomnia than flashbacks and nightmares.

I wanted to see her again. Hopefully, she wasn't one more person in this house who was pissed at me.

Reminding me that not everyone was mad, Mrs. W returned with a plate filled with cheese eggs and sausage. If I kept eating like this, I'd have to get back into the gym. I planned to do that anyway. Physically, I was ready. I wasn't made for idleness.

Aiden was nuts if he thought I was just going to sit around for the next three weeks. I'd find a way to get what I wanted, one way or another.

I ate my breakfast, savoring every bite, and headed down to the lower level of Winters House. Smaller than the main level of the house, the lower level had only three rooms, but all of them were huge.

I passed the cavernous space Mrs. W used for kitchen storage. I didn't even think about opening that door. No one went in that room without Mrs. W's express permission. I have no idea what she kept in there, but I suspected it was some combination of extra food and the many linens and place settings she used in the dining room.

Whatever. I didn't want to know. A little further down the hall was the gym. It probably wasn't getting much use these days.

I swung open the door to see that Aiden had upgraded since I'd last been home, adding a brand-new rowing machine and a new treadmill. The free weights and

Nautilus looked the same. Someone had set up an area with yoga mats, probably Charlie when she still lived here.

Grateful for the distraction, and something productive to do with my day, I headed for the treadmill. I'd get in some miles while I planned the rest of my workout. Six months of captivity, followed by weeks in the military hospital, had left me ridiculously out of shape. I was headed to a desk job at Winters Inc., but that didn't mean I was going soft.

I ran for an hour before I hit the free weights. By the time I was done, my muscles were wrung out, fatigue pulling at me. I couldn't remember the last time I'd slept well, and the night before was no exception. After walking Sophie to her bed, I'd gone to my own.

I'd fallen asleep right away, for once, but woken an hour later, my heart thudding in my chest, covered in a cold sweat, my hands shaking from a nightmare I couldn't remember.

Fucking flashbacks.

I had a theory that if I exhausted my body, my mind would shut down and let me sleep. Putting it to the test, I jogged up two flights of stairs to my bedroom suite, took a quick shower, and climbed into bed. Closing my eyes, I willed myself to fall asleep.

I might have slept. Mostly, I drifted in a light doze, the sounds of the house creeping through the heavy wooden door of my suite. A vacuum running. Female voices. A scream that shot adrenaline through my veins before I remembered the construction paper insects in the lampshades in the library.

I almost gave up on sleep after that, but I hadn't gotten more than a few hours a night for months. If I couldn't get past this, I'd never get my shit together.

I closed my eyes again, breathing in deep, slow inhalations. Gradually, my nervous system went off high alert and my muscles relaxed. I rolled over and doubled up my pillow, trying to get comfortable.

My surroundings were unfamiliar, the house I'd grown up in strange. Alien. As a teenager, I'd shared these rooms with Aiden, his parents in the suite that was now his. Sometime after they'd died and I'd left home, Aiden had moved into their rooms. I didn't care about that. Aiden was the oldest, just as his father had been. Those rooms were his by right. I didn't want them.

It probably seemed logical to redecorate our old room after he moved out. I was gone, and we weren't kids anymore. Our double beds had disappeared, along with the identical dressers covered with trophies and cork boards pinned with concert tickets and snapshots taken with friends.

Everything of our shared childhood had been stripped from the room and packed away.

Now, the suite was elegantly decorated with a bedroom set in dark wood, one I might have chosen for myself if I hadn't preferred that everything stay the same. The sitting room where we'd hung out and studied had a new flat screen TV and a comfortable couch.

As teenagers, we'd begged for a TV in our room more times than I can remember. Now that I had one, bigger than anything I'd dreamed of at seventeen, I just wanted it gone. That TV was one more reminder of how much things had changed.

How everyone but me had moved on. I'd left home to escape my memories, but they haunted me all the same.

It felt like I lay in that bed for hours, half asleep, lingering just on the edge of dreams. I finally got up and stretched out on the couch to watch a movie. I must have slept for a while because I woke to find the sun setting.

Instead of refreshed, I was slow. Groggy. The house was empty when I left my suite. At the sound of my feet on the stairs, Mrs. W came out of the kitchen to tell me that Aiden had a dinner meeting and Aunt Amelia was at her bridge club with Sophie.

I ate alone. I could tell Mrs. W felt badly about it, and I didn't know how to tell her I was relieved.

I loved my family. Maybe it didn't seem like it after I'd left home and rarely come back, but I did. It's just that there are a lot of them.

After six months in a cell, I wasn't ready for crowds. In the airport on my way home, the press of people had left me feeling as if my skin wanted to crawl off my bones.

I wanted to be with my family, that's why I came home, but the collected mass of my relatives and their significant others was a crowd, loud and rambunctious. I craved them and wanted to flee at the same time.

After a solitary dinner, I went back to my suite and sat at the desk to make a list. I needed to get in gear, to get my life back. At eighteen I'd walked away from my future, from the life I'd planned for myself, and if Aiden's attitude was any indication, no one was going to hand it back to me.

That was fair. But if Aiden thought I was going to sit back and let him push me out of my own company, he'd learn he was mistaken. I could give him time. I owed him that. But I wasn't going to sit around and wait for him to get over himself.

I needed the basics. A new phone. A laptop. A wardrobe that consisted of more than athletic shorts and cargo pants. I wasn't flying to London for my suits like Aiden - the thought of sitting through a crowded flight twisted my gut in a knot - and I wasn't asking Aiden for access to the company plane. Not yet.

I'd talk to Vance. My little brother wasn't so little anymore, and he had good taste. He also wore clothes aside from suits, had little patience for shopping, and was speaking to me. All things I couldn't say about Aiden. I made a note to call him in the morning.

The phone and laptop were easy enough. A quick trip to a big box electronics store and I'd be in business. I added a tablet to my list. Mine had broken shortly before the mission that had derailed my career and my life, and I hadn't had a chance to replace it.

Setting down my pen, I stood from the desk and stretched. Once I had the laptop, I could get to work. I had a lot of catching up to do on Winters Inc., and I could start with everything available in the public record.

I shoved my hands in my pockets and paced the sitting room of my suite. I needed something to do. Even after my nap, I should be tired. I had months of broken sleep to make up for.

I was tired. There was a part of me that was so deeply exhausted, I doubted I'd ever sleep enough to fill the well.

Still, after months of insomnia, I knew I wasn't close to tired enough to sleep. Another workout wasn't the answer. I thought about a movie but rejected that idea. Maybe later. What I really wanted was a book.

The library was deserted, a single lamp lit in the corner of the room. I went straight to the built-in shelves on the right side of the fireplace, to the bottom where Uncle Hugh always kept his mysteries. Aunt Olivia made him hide them below eye level, the brightly colored spines clashing with the more formal leather-bound volumes that made up the bulk of the collection.

I'd read most of Hugh's books when I'd been a teenager. I'd always gotten along well with my uncle Hugh, even before my own father had been killed. Our shared love of mysteries was just one of the things that bound us together. It burned that his death was still unsolved, not unlike the central plot to one of the books we'd loved. He deserved better.

I forced my thoughts off that path. If I started thinking about what Hugh and Olivia deserved, it would be a short jump to remembering what I should have done. How I might have saved them if I hadn't been an immature, selfish asshole the night they'd died. If I was going to dwell on the past, I might as well pick up the decanter of whiskey in the corner and drain it dry.

I owed my family better than that. I'd run from my problems once. I'd run and stayed away. Thirteen years was long enough. I was home, and I was sticking. Alcohol was just another way of running. I was done with running.

Gritting my teeth against the desire to pour just one glass, I grabbed a book at random and settled into the couch. A click of the remote on the end table and the fireplace came to life, bathing the room in a soft, warm glow.

I'd read the book before, in high school, but I didn't mind. Stretched out on the library couch, with one of Uncle Hugh's favorite books in my hands, I felt at home for the first time in years.

At home, but not relaxed. A shuffle of bare feet in the hall reached my ears, and every muscle in my body drew tight, prepared to act, only moments before a shadow fell in the doorway to the library.

CHAPTER THREE

SOPHIE

I couldn't sleep. I was used to it. Years had passed since I'd had a decent night's rest. Before my marriage I'd been a champion sleeper, able to ignore the bright light of morning streaming into my bedroom and sleep until noon, then take a nap a few hours later. I used to love to sleep.

Marriage to Anthony cured me of that indulgent habit. I didn't usually have trouble falling asleep. It was staying asleep that caused me problems. Like clockwork, I'd jerk awake in the middle of the night, my heart pounding, my mind caught in a nightmare.

I'd sit in bed, gasping for breath, the memory of hard hands on my legs, dragging me from sleep, alive in my mind.

Anthony is gone, I'd remind myself. You're safe now. Everything is okay.

I knew that was true. I was safe. Anthony was dead. In the six months that I'd been living at Winters House, those words were even more true. The Winters family had a high-tech security system. No one was getting into this house uninvited. I had nothing to fear here.

I knew that. Well, the logical part of my brain knew it. The animal part of me, the part that knew what terror was... that part was afraid to trust in safety.

Once, I'd thought I was safe. I'd thought I was marrying the prince from a fairytale and had ended up in a nightmare. Two years had passed, and I still woke almost every night shaking in remembered terror.

To be honest, I was sick of it. I was ready to move on. I was done with being damaged Sophie. Scared Sophie. Most of all, I was finished with victim Sophie. I'd made a mistake, trusted the wrong man.

How many other women could say the same? A ton. Anthony was dead, and I'd moved on. I had. I just needed my subconscious to move on with me.

For now, I strode down the halls of Winters House, my path lit by the moonlight streaming through the tall windows, considering whether I wanted to try the new tea Amelia had recommended for insomnia. I adored Amelia, but that tea smelled like something better left in the bottom of the trash can. Insomnia might be a better option if it tasted anything like it smelled.

Flickering light caught my eye, for a second sending a bolt of fear through my chest. Fire. Winters House was on fire. Then I realized the smoke alarms would have gone off if it had been a real fire. At the very least, I would have smelled smoke. This was nothing more than someone forgetting to turn off the gas fireplace in the library before heading to bed.

I took a detour, intending to turn off the gas and the lights on my way to the kitchen, and stopped short. Gage Winters was stretched out on the leather sofa reading a book, the light of the fire flickering over his cheekbones. My heart kicked into a thumping beat at the sight of him.

Unlike our first meeting, this time he was relaxed, or as relaxed as I imagined Gage Winters ever was. Even at ease, lounging in front of the fire with a book, he gave off the same sense of barely leashed energy he had the night before. This was not a man who knew what it meant to chill out.

His blue eyes pinned me in place, scanning me in a slow pass from the top of my head to my bare feet, heating as they moved. His full lower lip curved into a smile.

"Do you have more paper bugs?" he asked in that deep, smooth voice.

I shook my head, *no*.

"Another prank Amelia dreamed up? I heard the screams this afternoon. She must have been happy."

I cleared my throat. "She was. Mrs. W has a very convincing scream. And she pretended to scold Amelia, which I think she secretly enjoyed."

Gage chuckled, the sound floating across the room, drawing out my own, small laugh.

"If you're not setting up another of Amelia's pranks, what are you doing awake in the middle of the night?"

I was suddenly conscious of how I must look, wrapped in my oversized robe, my hair in a loose braid down my back. I dressed casually at Winters House—the family didn't want me to wear a uniform—but a robe and bare feet were inappropriate. It hadn't occurred to me that I'd run into anyone, despite my encounter with Gage the night before.

Tightening the belt on my robe, I smoothed stray wisps of hair back from my face and said, "I'm sorry to interrupt you, I thought someone left the fireplace on. I was just going to make some tea. I'll get out of your way."

Cheeks pink with embarrassment, I was ready to flee to the kitchen when Gage said, "Can't sleep?"

I turned back, shaking my head. "I wake up in the middle of the night a lot and have trouble falling back to sleep." My curiosity took hold of my tongue, and I asked, "Is that why you're awake in the middle of the night again? Trouble sleeping?"

Gage took a second to answer, a second during which I lectured myself on asking him personal questions. I wasn't his friend. I worked here. And asking a virtual stranger personal questions was rude.

I took a step back toward the door, expecting him to dismiss me. He didn't need to explain why he was up reading in the middle of the night. It was his house. I was an employee.

When he spoke, Gage's voice was so quiet I had to strain to hear, the words a vibration in the air I felt more than heard.

"I haven't been sleeping much lately..." He trailed off.

"Trouble falling asleep or staying asleep?" I asked.

"Both," he admitted. "I have nightmares."

My training kicked in, and without thinking I said, "That's normal, considering what you've been through. Did they talk to you before you left the military hospital? Tell you what to expect?"

Gage's face shut down, his eyes flicking away and his mouth going hard, that lush lower lip compressing into the top in a thin line.

Shit. None of my business. I took another step back and shook my head in apology.

"I'm sorry, sometimes I forget everyone isn't a patient. I'll let you get back to your book."

"Wait," Gage said, his voice carrying a demand I knew better than to ignore.

Men like Gage Winters were used to being obeyed. I'd

had enough of obeying men to last me a lifetime, but I worked for his family, and I liked my job. More than that, I realized I wanted to hear what he was going to say next. I fought the urge to give myself another lecture and stopped, turning back to face him again.

The hard line of his mouth had softened, but those blue eyes were still sharp and on guard. "The tea—does it help?" he asked.

"I don't really know," I said. At his raised eyebrow, I explained. "The tea I usually drink when I can't sleep helps a little. But this is a new one. Amelia ordered it for me off the internet. I have no idea if it's any good, but I promised her I'd try. Do you want me to make you a cup?"

I expected him to refuse. I have no idea why I even offered. I was usually good at watching my words but with Gage my tongue out-ran my brain. Something about him made me speak without thinking. I tried not to remember that speaking without thinking could be dangerous. I was safe here. If Gage ended up being a problem, nothing was stopping me from leaving.

"I'd love a cup of tea," Gage said, something warm drifting through his eyes. "Do you need any help?"

"No," I said, the sound almost a yelp, before fleeing to the familiar comfort of the kitchen.

They say a watched pot never boils but the electric kettle in Winters House didn't get that memo, because it was happily boiling away long before I was ready to face Gage again.

I should get an electric kettle for my room, I thought. Then I wouldn't have to come to the kitchen at night and wouldn't risk running into Gage in my robe again. I could do that. It would be convenient, but I'd miss my nightly trips through Winters House.

There was something about traversing the sleeping house in the dark, alone, the way the moonlight turned the house into a fairytale, that made me feel as if I'd stumbled into my own happy ending. I loved this house. Loved to be alone in it.

Though, I wasn't alone now. I poured steaming water over the tea bags in matching mugs, wincing at the odor as the hot water hit the tea. Yuck. I couldn't imagine something that smelled this bad could possibly help me sleep. The stench alone would keep me awake.

I'd promised Amelia I'd try the tea, so I dutifully carried the two mugs down the hall to the library, thinking wistfully of a nice mug of honeyed chamomile instead.

Gage was sitting up on one side of the sofa when I returned, leaving the other side open for me. I wasn't sure about sharing the sofa with him, but it was wide enough to give me space, and sitting in one of the arm chairs by the fire would have been weird when he'd moved to leave me a seat.

I felt awkward enough with Gage; I didn't need to make a point by sitting across the room and make it even worse.

I handed him one of the mugs, warning, "It's hot."

Holding my breath, I raised my own mug to my lips, blew across the top, and took a hesitant sip. I have no words to describe the taste that hit my tongue.

Acrid and yet organic. Organic the way a rotten stump is organic. This tea was not about fresh fruit and flowers. It tasted like old gym socks and wet leaves from beneath a dead animal.

Gage took a sip and choked. Wiping my hand across the back of my mouth, I watched as he gritted his teeth and forced himself to swallow. It was a good thing he hadn't spit it out. I wasn't sure Mrs. W would be able to get the stench out of the carpet. It would have been a shame to abandon the library because it smelled like this tea.

"What the fuck is in this stuff?" Gage asked, his eyes narrowed on his mug as if he was plotting the best way to destroy it.

"I have no idea, but it's horrible," I said. Saliva pooled in my mouth and I swallowed. I needed something to get rid of this taste.

"Are you sure she's not pranking you?"

I thought about it. It was possible. "No, I don't think so. I control Amelia's access to cookies. I don't think she'd risk cookies to tease me."

"You control her access to cookies?"

"She's diabetic. It's not severe, but she has to limit sugar. Amelia is serious about her sweets. And sneaky. I search her room every day for contraband. I don't think she'd risk dessert just to see me squirm. Especially since she missed the show."

"Good point." Gage stood. "I'm going to pour this out. Want to come find something to wash the taste away?"

"Yes, please."

I followed Gage down the hall to the kitchen, holding my breath so I didn't inhale the steam wafting off the tea. Whatever was in this, it was the foulest brew I'd ever smelled. I tipped my mug over the sink with relief, turning on the faucet to wash the tea away.

Gage picked up the box on the counter and turned it over, looking for the ingredient list. "It's all in Hanzi," he murmured. Then, louder, "It's in Chinese. I can read some Chinese, but I don't know any of these characters."

"Herbal medicine wasn't included in your Chinese lessons?" I asked, rummaging through the cabinets for something to clear our palates. There was no way I'd sleep tonight if I couldn't get the taste of this tea out of my mouth.

"Not exactly," Gage said with a wry smile. "I don't need to know what they put in this tea. All that matters is it tastes disgusting."

Gage handed me his cup to pour out in the sink and crossed the room to rummage in the cabinet above the electric kettle. Pulling out a box of tea, he handed it to me, saying, "Here, make two cups of this. I'll be right back. I've got an idea."

He strode out of the kitchen, making a face as he swallowed hard, trying to get the taste of that tea out of his mouth. I did the same. I should've known anything that smelled so bad would taste worse.

Again, I filled and started the electric kettle. Gage had given me a box of decaffeinated English breakfast. I wondered what his plan was. Decaf English breakfast wouldn't be my first choice to cure insomnia. I usually drank a chamomile based blend that was supposed to be relaxing. It wasn't bad, but it didn't do much to help me sleep.

Gage was back a minute later, a bottle of whiskey in his hand. He went to the pantry and returned with a jar of honey.

"Tell me that's not your brother's whiskey," I said, eyeing the bottle cautiously. Just a few weeks ago Charlie Winters's fiancée, Lucas Jackson, had stopped by to ask Aiden's blessing for his proposal to Charlie, and after receiving it had made off with Aiden's best bottle of whiskey.

Though, apparently, that had actually been his second best bottle. His best bottle had been stolen by Charlie six months before. Aiden Winters was not easygoing on the best of days, and he was not happy about losing two bottles of expensive liquor. Secretly, I thought it was funny, and suspected that deep down he might too, but I was an employee. The last thing I wanted was to get caught raiding the liquor cabinet.

Gage turned the bottle over in his hands and his lips quirked up. "I heard about that," he said. "It'll be a while before he finds something good enough to replace the bottle Lucas took. This is just the company whiskey from the library. I usually try not to drink when I can't sleep, but I don't think tea alone can scrape the taste of Amelia's tea off my tongue."

"Good point," I said. I watched as he poured hot water over the teabags in our mugs, added a generous dollop of honey to each, and a much bigger slug of whiskey than I would have. Almost to myself, I said, "I don't usually drink when I can't sleep either. I'm not much of a drinker anyway, and I'm up almost every night—" I trailed off.

"I know what you mean," Gage said. "It feels like asking for trouble. Because if it works—"

"Then you're just trading insomnia for a drinking problem," I finished.

Gage nodded, his blue eyes meeting mine in understanding and sympathy. He gave a final stir to my mug and handed it over. Still cautious after the last sip of tea, I took a careful taste. Whiskey was not my favorite drink, by far, but the thick honey and familiar English breakfast smoothed the edges just enough. It was delicious, and even better the bite of the whiskey washed the taste of Amelia's tea from my mouth. Heaven.

"Have you always had insomnia?" Gage asked. I looked up to see his eyes on me, measuring and curious. I didn't want to answer. Alone with him in the dark and cozy kitchen, sipping the tea he'd made, I'd been lulled into a sense of safety.

I didn't realize how far my guard was down until I heard myself say, "No. I was always a good sleeper. My mom used to say I was sleeping through the night at two months old."

"Me too," Gage said. "I got even better in the Army. Nothing teaches you to catch sleep where you can like the Army." He took a sip of tea and looked at me over the rim of his mug. "We both know why I can't sleep. What about you? How long have you had trouble sleeping?"

How to answer that question? Was there any way I could tell the truth without giving away too much? Stalling, I took another sip of the tea.

"Sophie?" Gage asked. He was being nosy, and I could've told him it was none of his business, but I could hear the concern in his voice.

Maybe the whiskey loosened my tongue, because I said, "It started after I got married."

Gage's eyes went hard and flashed to my left hand. I knew what he was looking for and I said, "He's dead. He died in a car accident almost two years ago."

Eyes narrowed on my face, Gage said slowly, "You must've been young when you got married, or you weren't married very long."

I took another sip of tea and wished I'd told him to mind his own business. "Both. I was young. Just finished nursing school. I was working my first job, in the ER, when he came in with a broken arm. We were only married three years."

"It wasn't good?" he asked, his words so gentle they drew tears to my eyes.

It hadn't been good. It had been very, very bad. And I wasn't going to tell Gage Winters about any of it.

I shook my head, my eyes on my tea.

"Have you talked to anyone about it? A friend? Or a therapist?"

I almost laughed at the irony of Gage asking me that question. Blinking away the moisture in my eyes, I met his gaze and challenged, "Have you?"

Gage looked away. I wasn't surprised. I could fall back on the easy explanation that macho guys like Gage didn't want to talk about their feelings. But the truth was, a lot of people didn't like to talk about their feelings. I wasn't beating down the door of the closest therapist to spill my guts about my horrible marriage.

Both of us knew better. I was a nurse for heaven's sake. I knew exactly why I wasn't able to sleep, and I knew that therapy would probably help. Still, two years had passed since Anthony had died and set me free. I'd managed to sell our house and move away. I'd had four different jobs with different families until I'd ended up at Winters House, and during none of that time had I made a single appointment with a therapist.

Gage surprised me when he said, "I know I should. I have a buddy who went through a bad time after an IED blew up under his caravan. Some of the guys gave him shit for it, but he said talking to someone helped."

I drank the rest of my tea in three long gulps and set the mug in the sink. "I'd better get to bed," I said.

I moved to walk past Gage when he stopped me with a hand on my arm. "Sophie, you know you're safe here, right?"

Surprised that he could read me so well, I looked up expecting to see compassion, or sympathy, in his blue eyes. I didn't expect heat. Interest. The desire in his eyes was at odds with his gentle question.

Testing him, I asked quietly, "Am I?"

Gage tightened his hand on my arm and drew me closer until my breasts brushed his hard chest. We were separated by inches of fabric. His T-shirt, my robe, and my nightgown beneath. My body didn't care. My nipples tightened, and my breath grew short.

Gage dropped his head until his lips brushed my temple. His hold on my arm loosened, his hand stroking up and down, fingers circling my wrist, then letting go to slide to my elbow before trailing down again. The warmth of his fingers, even through the sleeve of my robe, was soothing. Soothing, and something else. Something dangerous that sparked my nerves and set my heart beating faster.

His breath brushing my skin, smelling of honey and whiskey, he whispered into my ear, "You'll always be safe with me, Sophie. I promise."

His hand left my arm, and he took a step back. If he was waiting for me to speak, he was going to be disappointed. I had no idea what to say.

I was a coward. Crossing my arms over my chest, I whispered a hasty, "Good night," and fled the kitchen.

For a second, my breasts pressed to his chest, his mouth at my temple, I'd been sure he was going to kiss me.

I'd wanted him to. I wanted Gage Winters to kiss me.

I don't think I needed to list all the reasons kissing Gage Winters was a terrible idea.

Laying in bed, staring at the ceiling, I did it anyway.

First, I worked for his family.

Second, third, and fourth, he was newly home, was working through a trauma, and was in no position to start a relationship.

Fifth, I didn't do one night stands.

Sixth, I had pretty much zero sexual experience.

Anthony had been my first, and sex with him had been

brief and dull. I was pretty sure sex involved more than laying there with my eyes closed, but that's what Anthony wanted from his wife. I'd learned quickly to give Anthony what he wanted.

Gage Winters would expect more than an untutored girl in his bed.

At that thought, I stopped listing all the reasons kissing Gage Winters was a bad idea. It was too depressing.

Instead, against my better judgment, I imagined kissing Gage Winters. That lower lip, full and soft. The way he looked at me, the heat in his blue eyes.

When he'd pulled me against him, my nipples had gone tight, and warmth had gathered in my belly and between my legs. I hadn't felt desire for a man since my wedding night. Years had passed, and my body had been dry and disinterested. Sex was something other people enjoyed. Not me.

All I had to do was think about kissing Gage, and my body came to life.

That couldn't be good. I was not going to sleep with my employer's cousin. I wasn't.

I wasn't going to kiss him. I wasn't going to flirt. I was going to be completely professional and appropriate. Just like I always was.

That didn't mean I couldn't daydream about it. Rolling over and wrapping my arms around my pillow, I smiled to myself in the dark. I wasn't going to kiss Gage Winters, but knowing that I wanted to, that my body could still feel desire for a man—that was a relief on a level so deep I couldn't fully process it. I just let the knowledge slide through me.

I wanted to kiss Gage Winters. And in my dreams, I would.

CHAPTER FOUR
GAGE

I slept late the next morning. I'd fallen asleep with the scent of Sophie in my nose, sweet and sultry and out of reach. Just being near her was soothing. She had an inner calm, a strength about her, beneath the gentle exterior. When I was with her, something deep inside me relaxed, even as other parts of me came to life. The sound of her voice eased my mind, but being near her woke my body.

I was starting to love that shapeless, bulky, cotton robe. It showed absolutely nothing, but when I'd pulled her against me, and those soft breasts had pillowed against my chest, it had taken every ounce of restraint I possessed to content myself with stroking my fingers down her arm. She probably knew I'd wanted to kiss her. Any other woman and I might have.

I wasn't sure if I held back because I was afraid to scare her off, or because I didn't want to take advantage of a woman who was essentially an employee in my home. I hadn't hired her, Aiden had. Still, it was a fine and fuzzy line, one I was sure Sophie was acutely aware of. I'd meant what I said. She was safe in Winters House. Safe with me.

I wanted to kiss her. I wanted to strip off that robe and get my hands all over the soft curves beneath. The flush in her cheeks when I'd pulled her to me, the way her breath caught in her chest—I wanted that. I wanted more. I just had to figure out how to swing it.

It felt good to have a project aside from getting my life back in order. I couldn't remember the last time I'd been this interested in a woman. In getting laid, sure. Who wasn't interested in getting laid? This wasn't so simple. I didn't just want to fuck Sophie and leave her. For one thing, we were living in the same house. A one night stand was essentially impossible. And, not to knock anonymous sex, because anonymous sex could be great, but Sophie was more than that.

Just the sound of her voice was enough to calm some-thing inside me I couldn't reach myself. I wanted her in bed, no question, but almost as much as that, I simply wanted to be with her.

When had I ever wanted conversation with a woman almost as much as I wanted to fuck her?

The last thing I needed was one more problem to solve, but the challenge of Sophie felt less like a burden and more like a puzzle. I could be patient, but I would figure her out.

I already knew she was skittish about men after her marriage. It was probably for the best that she hadn't wanted to talk about it. I needed some time to get used to the idea that she'd been married to a man who had, at the least, left her so tied up in knots she couldn't sleep.

How he'd done that... I'd find out from her eventually. I wasn't going to push. There wasn't any doubt in my mind that he'd hurt her, one way or another. There'd been such relief in her eyes when she told me he was dead, it had been a punch to the gut. I'd take my time with Sophie, give her the space she needed, but she'd decide she wanted me as much as I wanted her. I refused to doubt that.

I took a quick shower and jogged down the stairs. With her exceptional radar, Mrs. W met me in the front hall, a regretful expression on her face as she informed me that I'd missed breakfast, and Abel, the cook, was out at the market.

I started to shrug and reassure her I could wait until lunch when she said she'd just served tea and a snack in the living room for Sophie and Aunt Amelia.

I shot Mrs. W a grin that had her smiling back before I turned to the open double doors of the formal living room. Voices came from inside, Sophie's and Amelia's. No one else.

A quick check over my shoulder told me that Mrs. W had disappeared, leaving me alone in the front hall. A furtive glance into the room revealed Sophie and Amelia at the far end, side-by-side on a couch by the fireplace.

Sophie's lap was covered with some kind of white netting. A stack of ribbons lay over one knee. Wedding stuff. Amelia sipped tea from the tray on the table in front of them. They hadn't spotted me or heard my conversation with Mrs. W. Probably because they were bickering good-naturedly over the tea tray. I leaned against the wall beside the open door and eavesdropped.

"Hand me another cookie from the tray, would you?" Amelia asked.

"No more cookies. We'll see what we're having for lunch. Depending on how it will affect your blood sugar, maybe you can have another cookie then."

A suspicious silence, then I thought I caught the sound of skin striking skin. In an indignant voice, Amelia said, "Did you just smack my hand?"

In a calm, low tone, Sophie said, "I told you, no more cookies."

"You can't spank me like I'm a toddler."

"Then don't act like one," Sophie said, a thread of amusement weaving through her words. "Why don't you let me talk to Abel about trying some of the low-sugar dessert recipes I found?"

"Low sugar is like low fat. Might as well not have it at all," Amelia grumbled. I wouldn't argue with that sentiment. I tended to agree.

It sounded like Sophie did as well because she sighed and said, "I know it stinks. But this is reality, Amelia, and you have to deal with it."

"I don't know why Charlie had to hire such a sensible nurse," Amelia grumbled again, but I could hear the affection in her voice. To my surprise, Sophie giggled and said, "Probably because the family was afraid you'd burn the house down. I shudder to think what you would've gotten up to if you had a nurse who was as much of a troublemaker as you are."

"Well, Charlie always was a clever girl," Amelia admitted, making Sophie giggle again. I wished I could see her face when she laughed like that. It made her smooth, low voice sound like a mountain stream, clean and light, like joy made real. I almost stepped into the room, but her giggles faded and I stayed where I was to hear more.

Amelia went on, "She's extra clever since she has you helping out with the wedding. Doesn't she know you're my nurse, not her wedding slave?"

"You could help too," Sophie said.

"I'd love to, but you know, my arthritis." I pictured Amelia holding her age-spotted hands in the air as evidence.

Just like with the cookie, Sophie didn't let her get away with anything.

"You don't have arthritis, Amelia Winters. And Charlie isn't the only Winters who's clever. I've never had a patient who kept me on my toes as much as you."

"Hey, I'm not just a patient. I'm your friend."

"And it's a good thing we *are* friends," Sophie said with mock seriousness. "If I didn't like you so much I might have already smothered you in your sleep."

This time, Amelia was the one who dissolved into giggles. I loved hearing that almost as much as Sophie's laugh. Amelia had always been a prankster, the one dependably fun adult in a sea of proper grown-ups. The last fifteen years had been as hard on her as it had on the rest of us, but for different reasons. While we'd been dealing with losing our parents, she'd watched as a terminal illness has slowly taken the love of her life. By the end, we'd worried we'd lose Amelia, too. It was good to have her home and happy once again.

The heavy front door of Winters House swung open, and Charlie stepped inside as if conjured by Sophie and Amelia's conversation. Dressed in worn jeans and a faded gray T-shirt, her auburn hair a mess of waves and curls that suited her to perfection, she started across the hall to the living room, a smile spreading across her face as she spotted me. I held up a finger to my lips and met her before she got to the living room doors, turning her down the hall to the library.

"Why were you hovering outside the living room?" she asked, giving me a sideways glance.

Without shame, I said, "I was eavesdropping. Are you here to do wedding stuff with Amelia and Sophie?"

"Just for an hour or so. Sophie offered to help. She is an

absolute angel. I don't know what Lucas and I were thinking trying to throw a wedding together in six weeks," she said, tucking a curl behind her ear.

"How complicated can it be?" I asked. "It's a hundred people, and you're getting married at the house."

Charlie elbowed me in the ribs and made an annoyed sound in the back of her throat. "Shows what you know. I got a wedding planner to help, but there's just so much to do. I'm kind of wishing we'd decided to elope."

"Not unless you take the rest of us with you," I warned.

"Yeah, I know. It just seemed like this would be so much simpler when we decided on a Christmas wedding. I didn't realize how many details were involved."

"Too late now," I teased, leading her into the library and shutting the doors behind us.

"What's up?" Charlie asked, setting down her tote bag stuffed full of fabric samples, magazine clippings, and notebooks.

"I need a favor," I said, not sure what Charlie's response would be.

Charlie and I had always gotten along well, but she'd been ten years old when I left home. We were never tight the way she was with Aiden.

Typical of Charlie's determination and open heart, she shoved her hands in her back pockets and said, "Anything."

My family was grateful I was home and alive. I wasn't above using that to my advantage. I sat in one of the leather armchairs, propped my ankle on my knee, and leaned forward. Charlie took a seat in the chair opposite me, curling her legs beneath her.

"I want to go back to work," I said. Charlie's eyes flared with surprise, but she said nothing. I went on, "Aiden's not ready to have me at Winters, Inc. He won't talk to me about coming back. He won't talk to me about anything."

The last part was hard to admit. Aiden and I had always been closer than cousins. Closer than most brothers. I owed him. I knew it. But I couldn't start paying him back if he wouldn't even talk to me.

Charlie's eyes were guarded as she said, "Do you want me to talk to him?"

I shook my head. "No, Charlie, but thanks. Aiden and I have to work this out ourselves."

"Then what do you want me to do?"

"I know you're not working at the company anymore," I said. "But you still know almost everything about Winters Inc. A hell of a lot more than I do after being gone over a decade. I have a lot of catching up to do. I know you're busy, with the wedding and with the house you and Lucas just bought, but if you could find some time here and there to get me up to speed, I'd appreciate it."

Charlie's words were careful when she spoke. "You know all of my information is six months out of date."

"It's a lot more accurate than mine," I countered. "I'm headed out today to get a new phone, laptop, everything I need to get back into normal life. I've kept up with the company on a superficial level, but if I'm going back to work, I need a much deeper grasp of the company's holdings, plans for expansion, everything. I can do a lot of the research on my own, but I need your help, Charlie."

Charlie leaned forward and braced her elbows on her knees. Her ocean blue eyes were intent when they met mine. "You need to give Aiden time," she said.

"I know," I started to say, but Charlie cut me off.

"This isn't a guilt trip, honestly. I was too young when my parents died to judge anyone else. But Aiden was so

45

alone after you left. He needed you. All this time he understood why you were gone, but he's missed you so much, and then we thought you were dead—"

Charlie blinked and swallowed hard. On and off over the years, I'd felt guilty for leaving, but never as much as I did just then. I was a selfish fucking asshole who'd abandoned my family. I sighed.

"I don't know how to make it up to him," I said. "To all of you. But I'm home now, and I'm not leaving again."

"Not leaving would be a start," Charlie agreed. "I'm just trying to say be patient with Aiden. He wants you here. And I know he wants you back at Winters Inc. He does. He just needs time."

"We've got time. And I don't expect him to hand me one of the executive suites. I'm not looking for your old job. I'm not remotely qualified at the moment. I got a degree in economics while I was in the Army and I started my MBA, but then my schedule got... unreliable and I had to put the MBA on hold. I wasn't thinking about coming home back then, so it didn't seem like a big deal. I'm going to look into transferring into a program here, but I haven't walked through the doors of Winters Inc. in over a decade."

I suddenly felt like I was in a job interview. Charlie studied me thoughtfully. For a minute, I thought she was going to turn me down.

I would've understood if she had. Aiden was pissed at me, and Charlie adored Aiden. She loved all of us, but Aiden had practically raised her. Then, surprising me, she leaned back in the armchair and grinned.

"Did anyone ever tell you why I left Winters Inc.?" she asked. I realized no one had.

"No. I guess I just assumed you were tired of the corporate life and wanted something new," I said.

An explosive laugh burst from Charlie. She wrapped her arms around her stomach and bent forward, her shoulders shaking with the force of her mirth. When she had her breath back, she said, "Oh, hell no. I was working eighty hour weeks. I had zero life. A lot like Aiden, actually. He kept telling me to slow down, stop working so much. But there was so much to do, and I didn't want to leave him alone with the company."

"I know, I'm sorry," I started to say, guilt a heavy weight in my gut when Charlie laughed again and waved her hand in the air, dismissing my apology.

"Not the point," she said. "So one day he calls me into his office, sits me down, and fires me. Fucking fires me. Complete with security escorting me from the fucking building."

A giggle escaped, and Charlie wiped away a tear. I stared at her, dumbfounded.

"He can't fire you," I protested. "You have an equal share of stock in the company. And you worked your ass off. You could've gone to the board and—"

"I know, but I wasn't going to go to war with Aiden over my job. The bitch of it was I never liked working for Winters Inc. I only did it because I thought I should, because I thought it was what Aiden wanted. And Aiden fired me because he thought it was what was best for me. Bossy asshole."

"That was why you stole his whiskey," I said, putting the pieces together. Charlie grinned again.

"So totally worth it," she said. "And that was when I met Lucas, so it all worked out, but I haven't forgotten Aiden turning my life upside down because he thought he knew what was best for me. I owe him one."

"So you'll help me?"

"I'll help you," Charlie agreed.

"I know you're busy. With the wedding and everything, if you want to wait until after the holidays we can do that." I didn't want to wait. I wanted to start taking my life back right away. To my relief, Charlie shook her head.

"A lot of what you have to do, you'll do on your own, anyway. Just off the top of my head, I can think of piles of research you need to get through. You can review what I give you and then we'll go over it together. By the time I'm done with you, Aiden won't be able to put you off anymore. He needs you back at the company, even if he doesn't want to admit it. This time, I know what's good for him, and he's going to suck it up whether he likes it or not."

I got up from the armchair. Charlie stood with me, and I pulled her into my arms, kissing the top of her head. "Thanks, sweetheart," I said. Her arms wrapped around me and squeezed tight.

"We all missed you so much, Gage. I know things are crazy right now, with the weddings and the holidays and Aiden being an ass, but we're so glad you're home."

"Me too," I said, speaking the truest words that had ever passed between my lips. Not a day had gone by that I didn't miss my family, miss Winters House. Wrapping my arm around Charlie's shoulder, I turned us to the door of the library. My stomach growled, and I hoped there was enough of whatever was on the tea tray Mrs. W had brought Sophie and Amelia to tide me over until lunch.

An idea occurred to me, a fucking brilliant idea, and I said, "Give me a job. Wedding stuff," I clarified. "I'm not doing anything else right now, other than whatever home-work you have for me, so let me help with the wedding."

Charlie stopped dead in the doorway of the library and stared at me, her blue eyes wide, brimming with amusement and relief. "You want to help with the wedding? Even Lucas doesn't want to help with the wedding."

"Doesn't Lucas have a new job? And you guys bought a new flip house? Sounds like he's got his hands full."

Charlie slipped her arm through mine, and we started toward the living room again. "He does. He seriously does. And he's not a wedding stuff kinda guy. Not that you are either, but if you're willing to help, I'll take it. The wedding planner squeezed us in last-minute after I begged and she doesn't have time to manage everything the way she normally does. I've got lists coming out my ears. I don't know why coordinating a renovation feels like fun, and throwing together a wedding is making me crazy, but it is. We probably should've waited, but we just wanted to be married."

"Consider me at your disposal then," I said, as we walked into the living room. Helping Charlie with her wedding would ease some of my guilt at asking her for her time when she was slammed with her own commitments.

That it would give me an excuse to be near Sophie was just a bonus.

CHAPTER FIVE

GAGE

We strolled into the living room, arm in arm, to find a small plate of sandwiches and a fresh pot of hot water on the tea tray.

Amelia looked up to see us and her face brightened. "The battle-ax said you were coming to raid our tea tray."

Charlie and I sat on the couch opposite the one where Sophie and Amelia had set up camp, the tea tray on a coffee table between us. The gas fireplace had warmed that end of the room with a cozy glow. Winters House was filled with light, even on a gray December day, but the heat of the fireplace was welcome.

I helped myself to one of the small sandwiches. Charlie fixed two cups of tea, one for her and one for me, saying to Sophie and Amelia, "Gage said he would help with the wedding stuff."

"Did he?" Amelia asked, raising an eyebrow at me.

I grinned at her, but mostly I was trying not to stare at Sophie. She sat beside Amelia, her lap covered by a towel on top of which she had a stack of white netting, a pile of pink ribbons and a bowl of what looked like birdseed. She was filling the squares of netting with the birdseed and tying them into neat little bundles.

I had no clue what they were for, and I was pretty sure I didn't want to know. My plan was to do what I was told and take every opportunity to get closer to Sophie while I was at it.

I'd never seen her during the day. In her neatly-buttoned camp shirt, her silvery blonde hair pulled back into a tight braid, she shouldn't have looked tempting. I'll admit to the tiniest flash of disappointment that she wasn't wearing a nurse's uniform. Not that I really would've expected her to.

No one who worked in the house wore a uniform. Not these days. I had childhood memories of the head house-keeper in a starched black dress covered with a white apron, the day maids in similar outfits of gray and white, gardeners wearing dark green shirts and khaki pants. When my uncle Hugh had taken over the house, he cut back on the staff. I remembered him telling my dad that times had changed and a full staff no longer made sense.

So, no Sophie in a nurse's uniform. Probably for the best. I was having a hard enough time resisting her as it was, despite the bulky, shapeless robe she wore at night and the boxy, short-sleeve, button-down camp shirt she had on right now. As far as I could tell, she wasn't wearing much makeup, if any. She didn't need it. Her green eyes were fringed with thick, pale lashes, her cheeks and lips a rosy pink.

I was staring at her lips when the sound of someone saying my name cut into my distraction. I blinked and looked up to see Amelia watching me with a knowing gaze.

To cover, I grabbed another small sandwich and said, "Yeah?"

"I asked you what you thought," Amelia said, and I sensed a trap in her words.

Cautious, I said, "About what?"

"I want Charlie to set Sophie up," Amelia said, her brown eyes sparkling with mischief. Normally, I found Amelia's antics entertaining, but just then I wanted to shake her and send her to her room.

Trying to act casual, I said, "Set her up with who?"

Charlie was watching me with curious eyes. Sophie's cheeks had flushed a deep pink, and her gaze was fixed on the ball of netting-wrapped birdseed in her lap.

"No one in particular," Charlie said. "Sophie says she doesn't want me to set her up with anyone, and I think we should respect her wishes." She sent Amelia a hard look we all knew Amelia would ignore.

Proving us right, Amelia said, "Sophie's been moldering around this old heap long enough with only an old lady and Aiden for company. She's been a widow for two years. If she doesn't get back out there, she'll end up all alone."

I noticed that Sophie had no trouble standing up to Amelia on the subject of cookies, but was oddly silent as Amelia tried to organize her life.

Charlie cut in with, "When Sophie decides she wants to date, *if* she wants me to fix her up, I will." Slanting Sophie a grin she said, "Lucas has some definite prospects on his new team. Smart *and* hot. Really, when you decide you want to date, you let me know."

Sophie's cheeks just flamed hotter. She retied the same bow for the third time, her fingers shaking a little. As Amelia urged Charlie to call Lucas now, I leaned forward and said to Sophie, "Do you want them to leave you alone?"

IVY LAYNE

I wasn't prepared for the sheer relief that washed through me at Sophie's quick nod. My gut had twisted into a tight knot at the idea of Charlie setting Sophie up with one of Lucas's hacker commandos.

I knew who Lucas was, and I knew the type he'd have on his team. Charlie wasn't far off. They'd be smart as hell and in killer shape. I didn't want a single one of them anywhere near Sophie.

Sophie was mine. And no one, not even me, was going to push her into anything she wasn't ready for.

Sitting back, I waited for Amelia and Charlie to stop bickering before I cut in and said, "Drop it."

Charlie immediately turned her attention to the tote bag of wedding stuff at her side. Amelia glared at me mutinously. "It's none of your business," she said.

"It's none of yours either," I shot back. "Meddle with someone else's life. You've got a whole family here to irritate. Leave Sophie alone."

"Fine," Amelia conceded. Looking at Sophie, she said, "I just don't want you to be lonely. You're stuck with me all the time, and you never go out."

The blush in her cheeks had faded some when Sophie looked up at Amelia and said, "I'm not lonely. This is the least lonely I've been in years. I promise. And I like being stuck with you all the time. Being with you is fun, even when I'm worried you're going to get me fired with one of your pranks."

At that, Charlie laughed. "Amelia's pranks aren't going to get you fired, Sophie. We might kick *her* out, but we'll keep you."

Amelia harrumphed. "And that's why you're my second favorite great-niece."

"I'm your favorite, and you know it," Charlie said,

54

unfolding a binder on her lap and scanning down a list. "At least until Annalise comes home, then you'll love best whichever one of us is causing the most trouble."

"You're both my favorite great-nieces," Amelia said with an affectionate smile at Charlie.

"We're your only great-nieces," Charlie interrupted, wryly.

"But after stealing Aiden's whiskey, you're my favorite. For now," Amelia finished.

Charlie cleared her throat and started going through her wedding list. I tried to focus on what needed to be done, but my eyes kept wandering to the curve of Sophie's lower lip, wondering what she would taste like and if she'd let me kiss her.

By the time Charlie was done with the wedding meeting, I had a to-do list and a hard on.

I managed to escape the living room while the three women talked about Charlie's dress, saying something about running errands. I loved Charlie, but I didn't care about her wedding dress, and I had to get moving. I needed a phone, computer, tablet, and a new wardrobe. It was a lot to tackle in one day, but I wasn't a fan of shopping. Better to knock it all out at once.

Before I left, I made a few of the phone calls on Charlie's list and set up meetings with a photographer and two musicians. Charlie had narrowed down the choices and said she trusted me to make the final decisions. After that, it was quick work to get the electronics I needed, and much longer to restock my wardrobe. I was having enough trouble convincing Aiden to let me through the doors of Winters, Inc. A closet full of cargo pants and faded t-shirts would not help my case.

My brother Vance had directed me to a store in Buckhead that didn't exist when I last lived in Atlanta. They carried everything from jeans to the highest quality suits, did custom tailoring on-site, and were happy to serve me a beer while a helpful sales assistant showed me my options.

Not long after I'd been handed my beer, Vance showed up, strolling in with his blonde hair tied back with a twist of metal he'd probably picked up from the floor of his studio. As always, Vance drew the eye. Female—and a few male—heads turned as he tracked me down in the back of the store. He threw himself into the arm chair next to mine, sent the saleswoman a wink when she offered him a beer, and said, "So, how weird is it to be home?"

I shook my head in response. Weird didn't begin to cover it. I wasn't going to try to explain, sitting in public, so I just said, "It's going to take a while to settle in."

"Doesn't help with all this crazy shit going on," Vance said. "Why Tate and Charlie decided to get married in the same week is beyond me."

"I got the feeling the rush to the altar wasn't so much Charlie as Lucas," I said. Not that Charlie was resisting. She was head over heels for Lucas Jackson. I'd only met him once, the night I got home, but from the way he looked at her, I'd say he was just as crazy about Charlie.

"He waited six months to put a ring on her finger," Vance grumbled, "but as soon as she said yes, BOOM—wedding."

"It's not like you waited much longer to marry Maggie," I said.

Vance's blue eyes warmed, and a secret smile played across his mouth. "I had to lock that woman down before she got a better offer," he said.

"Yeah, more likely you wanted to marry her before you had a chance to fuck it up again."

"That too," Vance agreed, easily. "You doing anything after this?"

"No plans, why?"

"Come over for lunch," Vance said. "I told Maggie I'd pick something up. Ella—she helps us with Rosie—is working all day today and she's taking Rosie to the park, so we can have an actual uninterrupted adult meal." Vance gave me a sidelong look. "You're probably used to those."

I thought about the last six months, spent mostly locked in a tiny cage with a dirt floor. Uninterrupted, yes. Meals, not as many as I was used to. My captors had been a lot better with the torture than they had been about feeding me.

I didn't say anything about that to Vance. This wasn't the place, and I wasn't sure I wanted to talk about it with my little brother anyway. I didn't want to talk about it with anyone. Instead, I said, "Lunch would be great."

Vance stuck around until I was done, offering his opinion when he thought it was needed. It would have annoyed me, but Vance always had better taste in clothes than I did, especially after I'd spent more than a decade in some form of uniform.

I loaded the back of the car I'd borrowed from Aiden with my purchases and followed Vance to the restaurant where he picked up his take-out order, then on to the home he shared with Maggie in Buckhead, not far from Winters House.

Magnolia Henry had inherited the Henry family house from her grandmother, and it looked like she'd taken good care of it. It was smaller in scale than Winters House. Most homes were, even in Buckhead.

The white house sat in the center of several sprawling acres, and despite the gray winter skies, it looked warm and welcoming. Vance led me in the front door, pausing to kick off his shoes and nudge a brightly colored plastic train out of the way before leading me back to the kitchen.

CHAPTER SIX
GAGE

Maggie emerged from the hallway at the front of the house. I didn't know her well. I knew *of* her, but she was younger than me and had gone to school in England, her path not crossing with the Winters family until Vance had hired her a few years before.

If you'd asked me what kind of woman Vance would marry, I never would've picked Maggie. Before her, Vance went for easy and flashy. In all things. His life had been about partying, working, and fucking, in that order. He'd had a drinking problem, one we'd been at a loss to deal with until he dragged himself to rehab and turned his life around.

Lucky he had, because, a year after he got sober, the infant daughter he didn't know he'd fathered was dropped on his doorstep. If you'd told me that was coming, I would have sworn Vance wasn't father material, but he fell in love with his daughter at first sight. He'd confessed on one of my short visits home that he'd been after Maggie for years, but it took the combination of sobriety and baby Rosalie to turn her head in his direction.

Maggie wasn't flashy, and she definitely wasn't a party girl. She was smart, with a warm, open heart and the kind of timeless beauty that said she would be just as gorgeous at seventy as she was in her twenties.

"Vance, you brought Gage home," she said as she padded into the kitchen in bare feet, at odds with the neatly tailored suit she wore. She gave me a quick hug and kiss on the cheek before abandoning me to slide into her husband's arms. Vance buried his face in Maggie's red hair, one hand sneaking up to deftly pull out the pins securing her elegant twist.

"How was the meeting?" he murmured.

Maggie kissed the side of his neck before she pulled away and plucked her hairpins from his hand. "I didn't like their numbers," she said. "We can talk about it later. I'm going to run upstairs and change."

I watched Maggie leave, grinning when Vance said, "Hey, stop checking out my wife's ass."

"Your wife has a great ass. It would be rude not to appreciate it."

Vance grinned back at me. Together, we unpacked the take-out containers and set the table. I'd missed this. Missed my family. Once, we'd all been so close. The rest of them had held onto that closeness, but both Annalise and I had run away. Annalise had her reasons, and hers were better than mine. A lot better.

I was done with running, and I was glad to have my family back. Watching Vance with Maggie, it was a relief to know my brother had found love after so many years of misery. He looked younger than when he'd been drinking, fit and tan, vibrantly alive. Happy.

I didn't leave Vance and Maggie's until late afternoon. After I unpacked my things, I hit the gym to get in a workout before dinner. Aiden was absent for the meal, again. I pretended we didn't miss him. We didn't, really.

Dinner with Sophie and Amelia was like watching a play. Amelia was the comic relief, Sophie the straight-man. They kept me laughing until dessert was served. The scowl on Amelia's face at the sight of the bowl of chopped fruit in front of her was no joke.

She ate the fruit, but she and Sophie bickered over it the entire time, Sophie reminding her she'd had too many cookies earlier in the day and Amelia insisting she didn't care. I'd already realized Sophie cared about Amelia, treated her more as a friend than a patient, but that only made her more resolved to safeguard Amelia's health.

Amelia could be demanding, insistent, and never shied away from drama, but she was no match for Sophie's steady, resolute, nature. Sophie absorbed Amelia's outbursts, listened patiently to her complaints, and quietly refused to change her mind. When Amelia grumbled, Sophie commiserated.

My family was made up of strong-willed women, most of whom never shied away from confrontation. In her own way, Sophie fit right in. She was quieter than the Winters women, but watching her over the past few days I'd learned that beneath that calm exterior, Sophie hid a will of steel.

After dinner, Sophie and Amelia took over the family room to watch a few episodes of a TV series they both liked. I spent a few hours unpacking my haul from the electronics store, setting up my new laptop, programming numbers into my phone, and syncing my tablet with both. I sent Charlie my new email address and number. She promised to share both with the rest of the family and to send me my first homework assignment by morning.

I spent the rest of the evening reading back articles on

Winters Inc., trying to catch up on anything I'd missed. There was a lot. Between my sporadic Internet access and the sheer scope of Winters Inc. interests, I hadn't been able to keep up with everything in the years I'd been away.

I read until my eyes burned and the rest of the house had long since gone to sleep. I'd heard Aiden come in, his heavy tread on the stairs, pausing at the top before heading to his own suite. I wondered if he thought about popping his head in my sitting room when he'd seen a light beneath the door.

I knew he needed space. Knew that for everyone else, my homecoming might be enough, but not with Aiden. Never with Aiden. What I'd done to Aiden had cut too deep for that.

We'd had plans, Aiden and I.

Growing up, it was understood that the two of us would take over at the company for our fathers. Unlike the rest of our cousins and siblings, Aiden and I had wanted the company. We both loved it, had loved hanging out with our fathers, even as young children.

After my dad died, I'd tag along with Aiden and Uncle Hugh. Some of my best memories of my dad were there along with a lot of my memories of Uncle Hugh. The company wasn't just a company. Not to me. When Hugh and Olivia died, Aiden had clung to Winters Inc., shouldering the burden of the company without complaint and had expected me to do the same.

Fuck, *I'd* expected me to do the same.

And then I hadn't. I'd woken up the morning after the funeral and been smothered by the weight of grief and guilt and loss. At the thought of taking my rightful place at the company, nausea had turned my stomach. I couldn't do it. I didn't deserve to fill my father's shoes.

I'd been too young to save him and my mother. I didn't have that excuse for Uncle Hugh and Aunt Olivia. I'd been home. I'd been right in this fucking house while they were dying and I hadn't saved them. I didn't deserve my legacy. The idea of walking through the doors of Winters Inc., of claiming my position as the heir along with Aiden, of pretending that I deserved the honor the way that he did, made me sick.

I couldn't live that lie. So I'd run. Aiden had left to go back to college – to finish the semester and then move home. When he'd returned to Winters House, I hadn't been there.

It was the worst betrayal either of us could've imagined. He might never forgive me. I wasn't sure I deserved forgiveness. I couldn't forgive myself. That didn't mean I was going to give up.

I'd almost died in that cell a world away from home and family. Life was precious, and I'd spent enough time being careless with my own. All those hours with nothing more than the rats and my own thoughts for company had forced me to see things clearly.

My penance had become self-indulgence. I'd run away and joined the Army to punish myself for failing to save Olivia and Hugh. Then, once I'd been gone too long, it got harder and harder to come home. To face Aiden.

The rest of them forgave me easily enough. For everything. Never asked why I wouldn't come home. Never demanded to know why I hadn't saved Olivia and Hugh. I don't know that it occurred to them. They were younger and in shock.

Aiden had thought about it. I'd seen the understanding in his eyes, the accusation. He'd lost his parents, and I hadn't saved them. I'll never forget the raw agony in his voice when he asked, "Where were you? Why didn't you help them?"

I didn't have an answer.

Not one that would satisfy him. It sure as hell didn't satisfy me.

The past weighed on me. It weighed on all of us. But that was life. You can't escape where you come from; you can only chart your course for the future. I couldn't fix the past. I couldn't bring our dead back to life. And I wasn't going to let Aiden hold a grudge forever.

After another hour of reading, I closed the laptop and forced myself to go to bed. I already knew I wouldn't sleep well, but I had to try. My mind drifted off after only a few minutes in bed, drawn into dreams that twisted into nightmares.

I'd only been out for an hour when I woke, heart pounding, every nerve firing in a remembered pain so real I looked down and expected to see blood staining my sheets.

I was whole and un-injured.

Laying back against the sheets, I tried to calm my ragged heartbeat and steady my breath. The torture had been worse in the beginning. The first two months they had me, my captors had vacillated between punishing me just for being an American soldier and using me for leverage.

At first, they'd attempted to trade me, but my mission had been so far off the books the military refused to acknowledge that I'd even been taken. Not officially. Officially I was still back on base.

That was part of the deal, and I had no resentment over it. I'd just been relieved I'd managed to get my team clear before I'd gone down. Once they realized they couldn't trade me, they'd been determined to coerce me into making one of those videos. They wanted to broadcast an American soldier renouncing his government. That wasn't going to happen. Didn't stop them from trying.

I'd always had a high pain tolerance, but I fucking hated being shocked. When we were teenagers Aiden and I had gotten our hands on a game, intended for adults, that was little more than a rubber ball with metal sensors embedded on the outside. The game was simple: toss the ball back and forth. If you dropped the ball, you lost. The catch was in the metal sensors that delivered electric shocks at random intervals.

Aiden mastered that thing like a pro. Even the strongest jolt didn't faze him. He got endless amusement out of the way I'd drop the ball at anything other than the mildest shock. The crawling, prickling sensation of electricity, the pain that wasn't pain, short-circuited something deep in my brain, something visceral.

I hated it. Fucking hated it. My captors could bring out the knives, and I wouldn't flinch, but that fucking car battery with the wires attached made me crazy. The nightmares were bad enough, but when they were about that fucking car battery...

I rolled out of bed and headed straight for the shower, needing to wash off the cold sweat. The house was cool in the winter night, but not cold. Still, I was covered in goosebumps, the sweat slicking my body stinking of fear. I'd had enough of these fucking nightmares.

Turning on the steaming water and stepping beneath the spray, I considered again if it was time to think about talking to someone. Was I willing to risk word getting out? And if it did, what would that do to my chances of getting back in through the door of Winters Inc.? If it became common knowledge that I was seeing a psychiatrist, Aiden might use that as an excuse to shut me out.

I'd think about it later. Pulling on a T-shirt and a pair of cargo pants, I left my suite and jogged silently down the stairs. I wasn't going for a drink, and I didn't want a book. Remembering that sad bowl of sliced fruit at dinner, I knew exactly what I wanted.

Looked like I wasn't the only one thinking about a midnight raid on the kitchen. The lights were on when I got there. At the sound of my feet on the hardwood floor, Sophie jumped and let out a tiny shriek. She whirled, the refrigerator door swinging shut behind her, and clutched her hands to her chest, her green eyes wide.

The warmth that flooded my chest at the sight of her took me by surprise. I thought I was coming to the kitchen for food, but once I saw Sophie, wrapped in that bulky white robe, her silvery blonde hair spilling over her shoulders, I knew what I really wanted was her.

Chapter Seven

Sophie

almost had a heart attack when I turned around and saw Gage standing there. I still wasn't used to running into someone else in my nightly wanderings. Plus, he'd caught me raiding the fridge. That would've been fine if this were my house, but it wasn't. I knew better.

I was an employee. I wasn't family. I shouldn't be raiding the fridge after midnight, looking for something sweet. Especially after lecturing Amelia on eating too many cookies. I was such a hypocrite. But I wasn't a diabetic and, secretly, I completely agreed with Amelia. Fruit was great, but it wasn't dessert.

Mrs. W had texted that there was leftover chocolate cake hidden in the vegetable drawer of the fridge where Amelia was sure not to look. I wasn't going to pass that up, even if the chocolate might keep me awake. It's not like I was sleeping anyway. I'd tried.

I'd washed my face, drank a cup of my normal sleepy-time tea and had dutifully gotten into bed. Nothing. I lay there staring at the ceiling for two hours before giving up, pulling on my robe, and coming in search of the mythical chocolate cake.

Standing in the doorway of the kitchen, Gage grinned at my shriek, and I felt my cheeks turning pink. If I could get through one day without embarrassing myself in front of this man, I could die happy. So far, it hadn't happened.

It didn't help that just the sight of him made me blush. It wasn't my fault. Gage Winters was hot. His face was beautiful, those blue eyes, sharp cheekbones, and full lower lip. But his body... Every inch of him was chiseled, the muscles of his biceps straining the sleeves of his T-shirt and his forearms—I'd never gotten distracted by a man's fore-arms before. I couldn't remember the last time I'd been distracted by a man at all, and then definitely not by his forearms.

I could stare at Gage all day.

"Hungry?" he asked, his eyes scanning me from head to toe, something in them making my blush hotter.

"Huh?" Why was he staring at me like that? His expression was almost predatory, but I didn't feel threatened. The way he was looking at me was... It was like he wanted me. But that didn't make sense. I wasn't Gage Winters's type. I couldn't be. Not in a million years.

"You're standing in front of an open refrigerator," he clarified, "so I assumed you were hungry."

"Oh," I said, stupidly. "Not hungry, exactly." I opened the vegetable drawer and spotted the cake plate nestled among stalks of broccoli and a bunch of asparagus. I lifted it out and showed it to Gage. His eyes widened in appreciation, and he grinned.

"I take it Amelia doesn't know about the cake?" he asked.

I shook my head.

"How do *you* know about the cake?" he probed, pacing closer. I resisted the urge to back up. Instead, I carefully placed the cake on the kitchen island between us.

"Mrs. W told me," I said, opening the drawer to retrieve two forks.

"She told you about chocolate cake, and she didn't tell me?" Gage took one of the forks and dug into the generous slice of cake. "I can't believe it. I'm her favorite."

Without thinking, I said, "I know. But I think she felt like she owed me one after the bugs in the lamp incident." I took my own forkful of cake, smaller than Gage's, and lifted it to my lips. Bittersweet chocolate melted across my tongue and I closed my eyes in pleasure. Gage made a low sound in his throat, and my eyes flew open. He was staring at me again with that same look.

Predatory. Possessive. Hungry.

I watched him lift a forkful of cake to his own mouth, my eyes riveted as his lips opened and his straight, white teeth pulled the cake from the fork. When his tongue flicked out to catch a stray crumb, a shiver went down my spine, and heat bloomed between my legs.

This was bad. I should have left. I should have put down the fork and gone back to my room. I had no business staring at Gage's mouth. Even if I put aside the fact that I worked for his family, that I was, in a way, his employee, Gage Winters was the last man I should look at to break my dry spell. For so many reasons.

I should have put down the fork and gone back to my room and made a list of all the reasons I should stop staring at Gage's mouth.

I didn't. I watched him take another bite of cake, and the heat between my legs grew. So stupid. I was so stupid. Stupid, and helpless beneath his blue gaze.

I dug my fork into the cake for another bite. I wasn't paying attention, and I ended up with mostly frosting. I licked it off the tines of the fork and Gage made another low sound in his throat. Risking a quick look at his face, and I saw his eyes narrowed on me.

I stood there, frozen in place. My first instinct was to run, a gut response to the tension in his muscles, the heated intent in his eyes. I stayed where I was. If I ran, he would chase me.

Gage Winters was the predator, and I was the prey.

But that wasn't why I didn't run. I wasn't afraid of Gage. I probably should've been. He was twice my size, and I was alone with him. Not only was he a lot stronger than me, the night we'd met he'd proven he wasn't quite stable.

I wasn't afraid of Gage. I was afraid of myself.

Gage moved, breaking the stillness between us and digging his fork into the slice of cake. I didn't expect him to bring it to my mouth, the cold metal of the fork urging my lips open. The chocolate melted on my tongue, sweet and rich.

Gage set the fork on the island with a click of metal on marble. Lifting a hand, his fingers slid along my chin, his thumb brushing my lower lip.

I swayed into him, the heat of his skin a magnet. He dropped his head and whispered, "You have chocolate on your mouth."

Then he kissed me.

All thought of running dissolved as his lips slid over mine, light as a whisper. I made a sound somewhere between a whimper and a moan, and Gage's arm wrapped around my waist, pulling me flush to his hard, tall body.

My lips parted, and Gage was there, kissing me harder,

his tongue running along my lower lip. He tasted of chocolate and man.

I fell into the kiss, goosebumps covering my skin as his fingers tightened on the back of my head, tilting my face to his. He lifted me, setting me on the counter and moving between my legs, one strong hand on the small of my back, pulling me against him.

With me on the island, the difference in our heights wasn't a problem. Gage's hands went to my waist, jerking on the belt of my robe and pulling it free, pushing back the thick fabric to bare my nightgown-covered body.

My nightgown wasn't anything special. Plain white cotton trimmed in lace, it covered me from my collarbone to my knees. It was pretty and feminine, but the furthest thing from seductive.

Gage didn't seem to care.

The cotton was so thin, the heat of his hands felt like we were skin to skin. I was barely thinking, all of my attention captured by his mouth moving on mine, the utter possession in his kiss. If I *had* been thinking I would've expected him to go straight for my breasts. The few men who'd gotten this far with me had done exactly that.

I should've known Gage would be different.

One hand slid up my body, moving over the side of my breast to my shoulder and sliding up my neck, sending shivers over every inch of skin he touched before his hands buried themselves in my hair and he pulled my lips to his, kissing me deeper.

His other arm wrapped around my waist, pulling me to him, pressing my body to his until there was no space between us, my breasts flattened to his hard chest, his hips forcing my legs open, the hard length of his cock pressing into me. Only a few layers of fabric separated that cock from my heat. His cargo shorts, my underwear. Not much.

I didn't care. I didn't care about anything but Gage touching me. Kissing me. He was heat and strength, surrounding me, taking me over. I wrapped my legs around his narrow hips, holding him tight, rolling my hips into his. His chest rumbled with a groan as he lay me back on the island.

Tearing his mouth from mine, he dropped his face into the crook of my neck, his breath hot against my skin. He was holding back, restraining himself so fiercely his muscles shook in barely perceptible tremors. I rolled my head back on the cold marble of the island, pressing my breasts up into him.

I didn't know what I was doing. I wasn't thinking. Gage had kissed me, and at the touch of his lips, something inside me had broken open, something feral and needy. After so many years of emptiness, my body had woken up, and it wanted.

Gage's mouth closed over the side of my neck, sucking and tasting my skin, his tongue tracing my frantically beating pulse. At the touch of his long fingers on the side of my breast, I went wild, squirming against him, shuddering when his fingers closed over my nipple and squeezed. A bolt of pleasure streaked between my legs, and I gasped his name. "Gage."

His mouth moved to my ear, and he breathed, "Sophie. Fuck. Sophie."

A thump sounded down the hall, followed by a tumbling noise as if someone had knocked over a stack of books. We both went still, breath caught in our lungs, hearts pounding frantically. Ice washed through me as I realized where I was, spread out over the island in the kitchen of

Winters House, Gage Winters between my spread legs, his hand on my breast, his mouth on my neck.

What the hell was I thinking? I was going to lose my job. And Gage – Gage hadn't struck me as the kind of man who took advantage of a woman working for him, but here I was.

He hadn't exactly taken advantage though, had he?

At that thought I shoved him back and scrambled off the island, yanking my robe shut and tying the belt in a tight knot. I couldn't meet his eyes.

"Excuse me," I said, moving to sidle past him and escape the kitchen.

Gage's hand shot out and closed around my wrist. I jumped in surprise. I didn't mean to. Some reactions are too ingrained to outgrow and, for me, being grabbed by a strong hand is one of them. I went still under his grip, then carefully twisted my wrist in his hand, trying to free myself without struggling. Struggling only made it worse.

Gage's fingers held me securely, but his grip wasn't tight. Wasn't painful. Voice so low I could barely make out his words, he said, "Wait. I heard something. You heard it too, didn't you? I don't want you to walk out there by yourself."

Gage's demeanor had shifted, and I'd been so panicked from his hold on my wrist, I'd missed it. A minute ago, leaning over me on the island, he'd been shaking with tension. Now he was the same, but it wasn't passion firing his nerves.

I looked up into his eyes and realized he was on high alert, every one of his senses focused on the sound we'd heard down the hall.

"Maybe it was Aiden," I whispered. I knew it wasn't Amelia. She slept like a rock and after months of working for her, she'd never woken a second earlier than she had to. But, for that matter, I'd never known Aiden to be awake in the middle of the night either. I was up often enough; I would've noticed.

Agreeing with my inner thoughts, Gage said, "No, it's not Aiden. I would've heard him on the stairs, and Aiden never wakes up in the middle of the night."

"You think someone's in the house? The alarm is on. Isn't it?" My gaze swept the kitchen, settling on the lighted panel by the door to the laundry room. Red lights glowed, indicating that the alarm was set and operating normally.

Gage's hand tightened on my wrist, and I winced. Immediately, his fingers fell open, and he released me. His blue eyes met mine, focused and intent but somehow haunted. Something lurked there, dark and afraid. Until that moment, it hadn't occurred to me to be afraid. But I remembered someone had broken into this house once before, and when they had, two people had been murdered.

"I need to go check it out," Gage said. "I don't want to leave you in here. Too many entrances. It's not secure. I want you to follow me down the hall. Stay right behind me, okay?"

I nodded. I wasn't completely sure there was someone else in the house. The alarm was on, and I'd heard something, but maybe I'd misunderstood. Maybe it was the air compressor kicking on, or the refrigerator in the garage. It was a big house, and old.

Odd sounds weren't unusual, and at night things like that always seemed amplified. What you might ignore during the day grew to a threat in the dark. That didn't mean there actually *was* a threat.

I felt a little calmer after talking myself down, but that didn't mean I didn't follow Gage closely out of the kitchen.

He guided my hand to his belt loop, silently threading two fingers through the strip of canvas. I shuffled down the hall behind him, pausing as we reached the doors to the dining room.

Gage stopped, scanning the moonlit room. A moment later he nodded to himself, and we moved on, through the entry hall, stopping again at the doors to the living room. Gage did another quick scan before we moved on.

The library and Aiden's office were at the end of the hallway, facing one another, the wine room in between. Gage pressed me to the wall outside the library, crowding me with his big body. Shielding me, I realized.

"It was here," he said, "the library or the office. I need to check them out."

"I can help," I said, inanely. I wanted to help, but honestly, what did I think I was going to do? I was a nurse. Unless there was someone standing in the middle of the room holding a sign that said *I'm the intruder*, I wasn't going to be much use.

Gage must've agreed because he said, "No. I don't have time to take you to your room and clear it."

Making a decision, he led me to the wine room in the back of the short hall between the library and Aiden's office. Gage swung the door open, tucked me behind his big frame, and quickly determined the room was empty. Flipping on the light, he led me in, saying, "Lock it behind me. Don't open the door until I come back."

"Be careful," I said.

Gage gave a short nod and pulled the door closed. I flipped the bolt and settled in to wait.

CHAPTER EIGHT

SOPHIE

T he wine room was less a room and more an oversized walk-in closet. The proportions were cozy, the design intimate. Racks of wine bottles lined the sides and back walls from floor-to-ceiling, the bottles secured behind glass, a discrete digital display showing the temperature.

In the center of the small room was an island with a small sink, dishwasher, racks of wineglasses, and drawers that probably contained all sorts of wine-related tools I wasn't familiar with. I wasn't a big wine drinker. I wasn't a big drinker at all. My husband had loved wine and had expected me to enjoy it with him. Reason enough to avoid the stuff now.

With the door securely shut, I couldn't hear a thing from outside the wine room. The more I turned it over in my head, the less I was sure we heard anything. Maybe it was my own guilty conscience.

Gage had kissed me. And worse, I'd kissed him back.

I needed to get my head together. I was not going to mess up my life like this. The last thing I needed was a man.

My brain thoroughly agreed, but my body—still humming from the feel of Gage between my legs, his mouth on mine, his calloused fingers exploring me—my body disagreed.

I'd never felt anything like that before. Never. I'd kissed a few boys in high school, hadn't dated much in college or nursing school. I'd been too busy, too worried about losing my scholarship and trying to finish as quickly as I could to bother with something as trivial as a social life.

Then I'd met my husband on my first job, and that had been the end. Anthony had been my first lover, and never once had he inspired the reaction Gage did. Not even close. I'd thought kisses like Gage's belonged in the movies.

A quick knock sounded on the door to the wine room, followed by, "It's Gage."

I unlocked the door and opened it. "Did you find anything?"

Gage shook his head. "No one's there. Everything's fine. I'll walk you to your room."

I tried not to wonder if Gage was going to kiss me again. I doubted it. As we crossed from the back corner of the house, where the library was, to my bedroom in the front, Gage kept his arm securely around my waist. His eyes scanned the space around us with each step.

When we reached my door, Gage followed me in. For a second my heart leaped in hope before I ruthlessly reminded myself there was nothing to hope for. If Gage thought he was here to pick up where we left off in the kitchen, he was mistaken.

We shouldn't have kissed, and it wasn't going any further than that. When he led me to the bed and pushed me down to sit, my mind and my body went to war, my brain insisting that I set him straight and my body ready to lay back and let him do anything he wanted.

I cursed myself for a fool. Gage left me sitting on the side of the bed and methodically searched my room. Here I was, trying to talk myself out of sleeping with him when Gage was only here to make sure I was safe.

He was quick but thorough—checking my closet, my bathroom, behind the curtains at the window seat, even beneath my bed.

"Lock your door," he said abruptly when he was finished.

"You sure everything's okay?" I asked from my seat on the edge of the bed.

In answer, he said, "I'm not going to let anything happen to you, Sophie. Lock your door."

Then he was gone.

Slowly, I stood and went to the door, turning the lock. I wasn't sure if I was locking Gage out, or myself inside.

I didn't fall asleep until dawn. I wasn't afraid of the sound we'd thought we heard. By the time I'd locked the door of my bedroom, I'd convinced myself it had been nothing more than the overreaction of a guilty conscience.

No, I couldn't sleep because I couldn't stop thinking about kissing Gage. Every nerve in my body was awake, alive. Needy. I'd never felt this before. Maybe a little in those long ago high school fumblings with boys I could barely remember. Had I felt this with Anthony?

If I had, the memory was lost, the pleasure of desire burned away by everything that had come later. I wracked my brain for memories of those first dates with Anthony, but of all the emotions that rose to the surface, none of them was desire.

I'd been awed by Anthony. He was older than I was, successful, wealthy, and he'd wanted *me*. He'd taken me out to elegant restaurants, opened the door for me, treated me with respect and care. I'd been too young, too inexperienced, to understand. To see beneath his good manners to the monster lurking within.

Of all the things I'd felt with Anthony, I'd never desired him. Not like this. Not with every cell in my body, with a need that drove me so mindless I forgot where I was, who I was, and only wanted more.

More of Gage. More of his hot mouth on my skin, his hands on my body. I was alive. For the first time in my life, every part of me was alive. Awake, and ripe, and ready.

Even before Anthony, I'd felt as if my body were sleeping. I liked the idea of romance, of flowers and dates and kisses, but no one had really gotten to me. I'd never had a real crush, the kind that keeps you up at night, has you craning your neck to see if he's walked in the room, straining your ear for the sound of his voice. I thought there was something wrong with me, that I was lacking some essential element of being female. Of being human.

After I married Anthony, I was convinced it was true. I felt desiccated, dried out like an autumn leaf. He'd told me I was beautiful, called me his perfect girl, but he didn't want me. Not like that. Not with his body. In another marriage, it would've been a tragedy. By the time I fully realized what was missing, I was grateful.

Our wedding night had been chaste. As chaste as you can get while still having sex. I'd expected romance. Wasn't I supposed to? He hadn't been cruel; he'd been indifferent. I'd waited for him in our bedroom in a silky black negligee I'd shyly bought for the occasion.

Anthony's eyes had tightened at the sight of it, and he'd gently helped me into my robe before leading me to the bed. He lay me down on the side, pulling my hips to the edge of the mattress and gone to his knees between my legs. A moment later he touched me there. I remember jumping in surprise and his amused chuckle.

Then pressure and a tearing pain, Anthony moving over me with quick hard thrusts. He'd stiffened, emptying himself into me. For one brief second, we were frozen—me in confusion and Anthony in release—before he'd withdrawn from my body, tucked himself away, and stood. He hadn't said anything, just nodded and left.

The next day all of my nightgowns had been replaced with thick, white flannel that covered me from my neck to my toes. They were ugly and sexless, the kind of thing I imagined a grandmother might wear if she had terrible taste and was freezing cold.

Anthony came to my bed once a month. A doctor showed up a few weeks after our wedding to insert a birth control implant in my upper arm. They were supposed to last several years, but Anthony had the implant replaced every year, like clockwork, just in case. Anthony didn't want children yet. It never occurred to him to ask what I might want. The moment he decided to marry me, my wishes became irrelevant.

Irrelevant to him. I still had plenty of wishes, for all the good they did me.

It didn't take long to realize that Anthony didn't want a wife. He wanted a possession. He alternately praised me, punished me, or forgot about me entirely, depending on how I fit into his plans.

One night, he might inform me we were having guests and expect me to play hostess. He'd praise my cooking, and kiss my cheek and give the perfect impression of a loving couple. The next night he might pull me from my bed in the dark and come at me with closed fists, his eyes cold and empty.

I rarely knew why. Anthony was completely self-contained. Nothing ever showed through the mask he presented to the world. There were no cracks, no signs of what was coming. At dinner, he might thank me for ironing his shirts so perfectly and hours later beat me unconscious. I knew his job was stressful, though I didn't entirely understand what he did, and by the time we'd been married a month I knew better than to ask.

Obedience was survival. I never knew what set Anthony off, but I knew he expected me to obey his every order. I thought if I did as I was told, I might be able to save myself.

I tried. There was no escape. I thought about it constantly. Anthony played the part of a loving husband, but he knew what he wanted, and he was clever. We lived miles from anywhere, buried in the country. When we gave small dinner parties, Anthony's friends would tease us, commenting on a sophisticated young couple like us choosing such a rural setting. Anthony always pulled me close and said that we liked the privacy.

His property was bounded by a tall fence, patrolled by well-trained dogs, and there was always, always a guard. They never spoke to me. The first time I tried to leave, the taxi had been politely turned away by the guard, and I'd been told to go back inside. I hadn't yet understood that I wasn't just Anthony's wife, I was his prisoner. Anthony had punished me without a word, pulling me from my bed in the dark, the only sounds in the room his fists striking my body and my gasping promises never to leave.

I'd tried again when I worked up the courage. That time I made it as far as the fence before I was found and returned to the house. Anthony punished me that night with a white-hot rage I'd never seen before. I'd been sure he would kill me as he struck me over and over, kicking me when I fell to the floor. At the end, he dragged me up, his arm around my neck, and choked me until my vision went black and I passed out.

It was the only time he left a mark on my face. My eyes were swollen shut when I woke the next morning, my body so bruised I could barely move. Anthony had been there at my side, holding my hand. He spooned broth through my torn lips and, for the first and last time in our marriage, he explained why he wanted me. Why he couldn't let me go.

"It grows in me," he'd said, as calmly as if we were discussing the weather. "The darkness builds up, every day. Telling me to do things. Bad things. The darkness wants blood. You're the only one who makes it go away. It likes you. So sweet and pure. If I give you to the darkness for a while, it leaves me alone."

That was when I understood. Really understood. Anthony wasn't cruel. He wasn't mean. He was completely insane. He was a monster, hiding behind the mask of a normal man.

Only once did I work up the courage to ask what he'd done about the darkness before he found me. Once was enough.

Anthony had shaken his head sadly and trailed a fingertip down my cheek, saying, "Sweet Sophie. If I told you, it would give you bad dreams. The darkness needs blood. It's happy with just a little of yours. Anyone else, and it needs so much more."

I never asked again. I didn't want to know. Maybe I should have been glad that his beatings spared some other person a more horrible fate. I wasn't. I didn't want to sacrifice myself for the good of some stranger. I just wanted to be free.

Freedom was a dream. A fantasy. I ordered my clothes from catalogs, my groceries from a list I gave to the guard. Every few months a stylist came to trim my hair, working in silence while the guard watched us both.

Once Anthony brought me home after our wedding, I never left that house until he died, three years later.

Two years had passed since the day the kind police officer had informed me of Anthony's death. I'd gone through the motions, half-paralyzed by the tentative hope that I might have been granted a second chance at life. I sold our house and quietly moved away.

For the first year, I'd focused on getting my nursing license current and finding a job. After so much time away from the world, I found that I preferred working in private homes rather than the hectic environment of the hospital or clinic.

I thought about going to therapy. I knew I should. But, something inside me revolted at sharing the humiliating details of my marriage.

I knew it wasn't my fault.

I understood that having the bad judgment to marry a man like Anthony didn't mean that I'd asked for what had come after. He'd been so charming when we'd met, he completely swept me off my feet. I'd been too young and inexperienced to see the truth. And I hadn't deserved anything that had happened. I knew that.

Knowing it wasn't my fault didn't mean I trusted my own judgment. And even if I did, my best judgment told me Gage Winters was the last man I should be thinking about.

So what if he set my body on fire? So what if this was the first time I'd ever felt real lust for a man?

Was it worth risking my job?

And even if I didn't care about my job, which I did,

Gage was not a safe bet. He was clearly suffering from post-traumatic stress and had admitted himself that he wasn't entirely stable.

With my history, the last thing I needed was to get wrapped up in some guy who couldn't control himself. Too much risk. Too much danger. Too much everything. I owed myself more than that. I had to be smart, and kissing Gage Winters was not smart.

CHAPTER NINE

SOPHIE

My alarm woke me only minutes after I finally fell asleep. I dragged myself from bed feeling hollow and fuzzy. A hot shower didn't do much to help. I covered the circles beneath my eyes with makeup, knowing Amelia would spot the camouflage and scowl at me.

Having never suffered insomnia a day in her life, Amelia was of the firm conviction that all I needed to do was close my eyes and simply fall asleep. As if I hadn't tried that a million times. I braided my wet hair and pinned it into a bun. Buttoning a carefully ironed camp shirt and tucking it into my jeans, I wished for a uniform, for something that would clearly divide me from the rest of the household and remind everyone that I didn't really belong here.

Gage wasn't at breakfast, but surprisingly, Aiden was. He was usually out of the house by the time Amelia and I went in to eat. When I entered the room, he said, "Sophie, I'll be leaving town on business for a few days. I'd like to have a short meeting in my office before I go. After breakfast."

"Of course. Just let me know when you're ready."

He rose from the table, folding his newspaper to take it with him. Sending Amelia an affectionate smile, he said, "No rush. Enjoy your breakfast and when you're done stop by my office." To Amelia, he said, "Behave yourself while I'm gone."

Amelia smiled a Cheshire grin and winked at me. It was pretty much a guarantee that Amelia would not behave herself while Aiden was gone, but then Amelia never placed a high priority on behaving herself at any time.

I did my best to keep her under control, for her own health if not the sanity of everyone else living here, but secretly I loved her irrepressible sense of mischief. I envied it.

I was a lot of things. Responsible. Dutiful. Loyal. I was not mischievous, and I noticed that people who were, people like Amelia, always seem to be having more fun. Fun had never been a big priority in my life, but maybe it should be. Maybe I was doing this all wrong.

A quick glance around the palatial dining room reminded me that it was all well and good for people like Amelia Winters to be lighthearted and mischievous. She had a family fortune to pay her bills. I'd been responsible because I'd needed to get scholarships if I wanted to go to college for nursing school and after that, I had to work hard to keep them.

I couldn't afford to lose my job because I thought every day should be more about fun than hard work. I adored Amelia Winters. I truly, honestly did. But she and I were playing from a different set of rules, and I couldn't forget that.

We finished breakfast, and I settled Amelia in front of the fireplace in the library before crossing the short hall to Aiden's office. He looked up from his desk with a quick smile and gestured to the chair in front of him, saying, "Sophie, take a seat."

I did and waited. "One second," he said, looking back at the paper in front of him, making a few small notes and quickly scanning the words, his dark eyes flashing back and forth rapidly before he signed at the bottom and neatly placed the paper to the side.

Aiden Winters wasn't the type of man to make you sit and wait as a power-play. That was one of the many things I liked about working for the Winters family. They were wealthy, and powerful, beyond my conception of it, really. But they weren't all caught up in their egos, didn't feel the need to prove anything to anyone.

In the six months I'd known him, Aiden had been honest, forthright, and fair. Yet again, I reminded myself that I did not want to lose this job. I felt a trickle of fear that somehow Aiden knew what had happened in the kitchen the night before and had called me in here to fire me.

But, no. If Aiden were going to fire me, he wouldn't have smiled at me and told me to take my time at breakfast. I'd seen Aiden unhappy before. He didn't lose his temper, didn't rage and throw things. No, when Aiden Winters was angry he went icy cold.

I tried to relax. Finally, he looked up with another smile and said, "Sorry to ask you in here and make you wait. I wanted to finish going through those documents while they were fresh in my mind."

"It's no problem. Amelia's settled in the library, and we don't have any plans this morning."

Aiden rose from behind his desk and crossed the room

to close the door to his office. When it was securely shut, he turned and went back to his seat behind his desk. "Amelia has ears like a hawk," he said in explanation.

I couldn't help laughing. "When she notices you closed the door, she may go get a water glass to hold up against it," I said.

Aiden grinned in response, and I couldn't help grinning back. Aiden was so often serious, almost grave. He carried so much on his shoulders and didn't smile as much as he should. When he did, he was almost painfully handsome.

Not my type. His beauty was refined, elegant, austere. After Anthony, that style of male good looks would never spark my interest, but I could appreciate the view all the same. Especially knowing that Aiden was no Anthony. He was a good man who loved his family.

"We'd better talk fast before she gets back here with that water glass," he said. "I just wanted to check in with you that everything is good. Her occasional pranks aside, Amelia's well?"

I laughed again. "As much as they can be inconvenient, I'd say her occasional pranks are one of the signs that Amelia is doing very well. As you've probably noticed, she's still resistant to her adjusted diet, but she's been sticking to it for the most part, and we've been able to keep her blood sugar under control with diet, which is very important at this stage. We've been doing exercises every day, a combination of yoga and walking and floor exercises to enhance her flexibility. We haven't been able to use the pool now that the weather has changed, but overall I've been pleased with her progress. She has excellent mobility for her age."

"That's good to hear. I'm very glad you're with us, Sophie. I knew when Amelia moved in that I wouldn't be home as much as I'd like, but work has been even more hectic in the last few months than I'd expected. It's reassuring to know that she's not only looked after, she has a friend."

My cheeks heated at his praise. Truthfully, I said, "Amelia is easy to like."

A laugh exploded out of Aiden, surprising both of us, I think. After he got his mirth under control, under his breath, he said, "Tell that to Mrs. W."

I shrugged a shoulder and shook my head. "Mrs. W is a special case."

"I haven't missed the way you run interference between them, and it's appreciated. They're both very important to us. Amelia, obviously, is family. So is Mrs. W, and I know that all of us were concerned there'd be fireworks with those two in the same house no matter how big this place is. You've done an admirable job keeping the peace."

"It helps that Mrs. W has her cottage. If she lived in the house itself I think that would be too much temptation for Amelia," I admitted. In a low voice, in case Amelia was listening at the door, I asked, "Do you know why they dislike each other so much? Neither of them will tell me."

Aiden shook his head, more in resignation than denial. In an equally low voice, he said, "It's an old story, and I'm giving you this secondhand so I don't know how accurate it is, but you know Amelia left home years ago and moved to the West Coast to be with Janice, her partner?"

I did know. It was common knowledge, and Amelia spoke often of Janice, who had died a few years before after a very long battle with cancer. Janice had been the love of her life, and though Amelia played it down, I could only imagine the uproar when, decades ago, one of the premier debutantes in Atlanta society had run off to California with another woman.

Her family hadn't cut her off financially, but the older generation had made it clear she wasn't welcome home. It was obvious that none of their children agreed because the Winters family I knew openly adored their aunt Amelia.

"We've talked about it, quite a bit," I said, in answer to Aiden's question. "Is that why Mrs. W doesn't like her?" I asked carefully. I adored Helen Williamson but I wasn't sure how that adoration would hold up if she disliked Amelia for being gay. Aiden gave a sharp shake to his head, dispelling my worry.

"No. No, she doesn't. We've talked about it, so I know that's not it. But, based on a conversation I overheard between my mother and Mrs. W years ago, I got the impression that Amelia overheard comments Mrs. W made about her and completely misinterpreted them. My mother tried to run interference and explain, and Amelia accused her of sticking up for Mrs. W.

"Which she was, but she was doing it truthfully. Mrs. W would never admit it, but she'll never like Amelia. She likes order, and proper behavior, which makes her perfect to keep all of us in line, but will always set her against Amelia, who lives to cause trouble."

"Those two are polar opposites," I agreed. "I think I get along with them both because I appreciate order and proper behavior, but I like a little mischief. Amelia keeps me from being too serious."

"Me too," Aiden agreed, sending me a wink. We smiled at each other, in friendly harmony, when the door swung open. I turned around, expecting Amelia. My smile froze when I saw Gage scowling down at me, his arms crossed over his broad chest.

His eyes flicked from Aiden to me and back again. His scowl deepened, the lines around his mouth hard, his eyebrows dark and drawn together. His skin looked a little pale, and he had circles under his eyes. I knew without asking that he hadn't slept since I'd seen him last.

I glanced to Aiden and saw that his smile was gone, his face frozen. Expressionless. Raising one eyebrow, he said to Gage, "Can I help you with something?"

His tone was so chilly, instinctively I wrapped my arms around my chest. Something was very wrong between Aiden and Gage. It wasn't my business. It couldn't have been any *less* my business. This wasn't my family. But Amelia and Charlie both told stories of Aiden and Gage as children, how close they'd been. Closer than cousins. Closer than most brothers. They weren't close now.

Ignoring Aiden, Gage said to me, "Did you tell him? About last night?" My heart froze in terror. Of all my worries about that stolen kiss, it had never occurred to me that Gage would be the one to rat us out. My heart restarted in my chest when he said, "The sound we heard?"

I bit my lip, clawing back my composure, and finally said, "Oh, no, I hadn't mentioned it."

Gage's eyes studied me for a long moment before he said to Aiden, "If you and Sophie are done, I need to talk to you."

"I think we're finished here," Aiden said. I stood, and before I could flee the room, he said, "Sophie, I'll be out of town for the rest of the week, but if you need anything you have my numbers."

Nodding to both of them, I said a quick, "Thanks, have a good trip," before I made my escape from the cold tension between the two men.

CHAPTER TEN
GAGE

"You and Sophie shouldn't be alone in here with the door shut," I said, ignoring the look of surprise on Aiden's face.

It wasn't what I'd planned to say. I wasn't there to talk about Sophie. But they'd looked far too cozy behind that closed door, smiling at each other as if they shared an inside joke.

I didn't want Aiden alone in a room with Sophie, laughing with her, and sharing jokes with her. Aiden was all wrong for Sophie. He was too cold, too controlled.

"I was having a private meeting with an employee," Aiden said, dryly. "You should know that I would never engage in inappropriate behavior with a woman who worked for me, especially one who works in this house."

I knew what he was getting at. What he was implying. I wasn't taking the bait. Just in case I'd missed his point, Aiden went on, "Please tell me you're not bothering Sophie."

I didn't answer. Anything I said would either be a lie or start a fight. Aiden's eyes narrowed on me, his expression icy.

"Sophie is a valuable member of our staff. Aunt Amelia considers her a friend. We are not going to do anything to jeopardize her position in this household. Do you understand?"

"So she's just an employee? Then what were you two laughing about in here?" I asked, knowing I sounded both jealous and a little unhinged.

I couldn't help myself.

Impulse control had been just one of my problems since I'd gotten home. Normally, I could match Aiden's icy stare with one of my own. Not now, and not when it was about Sophie. The memory of their shared laughter grated on my nerves.

"Our conversation is none of your business," Aiden said, flatly. "Now, what did you need to see me about?"

I wasn't ready to drop the topic of Sophie.

"If you're going to have meetings with Sophie, you should do it with the door open," I insisted, knowing I sounded ridiculous.

Aiden visibly gritted his teeth. "There is nothing going on between me and Sophie. She is an employee, and I was getting an update on Amelia which necessitated a closed-door because Amelia is nosy. Everyone in this house knows that, and the only one who thinks it's suspicious or inappropriate is you. Which makes me wonder exactly what's going on between you and Sophie."

My hands dropped to my sides, my fingers curling into fists. I couldn't bring myself to lie, not to Aiden, but I wasn't going to reveal any information that might compromise Sophie. I settled for saying, "Sophie hasn't done anything wrong."

"I never thought she had. Stay away from her, Gage. We can't afford to lose her. Amelia would never forgive you."

Sitting back, he flipped his pen over in his fingers. In a low voice, he said, "I haven't looked into the details, but my understanding is that she had a very bad marriage before her husband died. According to Amelia, she hasn't dated since. The last thing she needs is to get involved with a man she can't depend on. Leave her alone."

Between the mention of Sophie's bad marriage, the direct order to stay away from her, and the very thinly veiled accusation that I couldn't be depended on, I was ready to launch myself across Aiden's desk and start swinging my tightly clenched fists.

Impulse control.

I wanted to hit him so badly I could feel the impact of his cheekbones on my knuckles. Feel the crash as I took him from his oversized desk chair to the floor.

I don't think I ever wanted to hit someone in my entire life as much as I wanted to hit Aiden right then.

It took every ounce of willpower I had to stay where I was, my fisted hands at my sides, my jaw tight. I didn't like hearing that Sophie had suffered through a bad marriage. I really didn't like Aiden ordering me around. But the worst, the hardest to swallow, was Aiden implying that I was undependable. Because he was fucking right.

I wasn't myself. It had nothing to do with Sophie. I knew I shouldn't have kissed her in the kitchen, but I wouldn't take that back for a million dollars.

One kiss.

It couldn't have lasted more than a few minutes. I could still taste her in my mouth, feel her sweetly curved body under my hands. I could've kissed her for hours.

But Aiden was right; I *was* undependable. I didn't know if he was referring to my running out on the family twelve years before, or the fact that I'd come home a fucked up mess, but either way he had a point.

And it burned even more that he was right about her being an employee in our home. She didn't work for me. I hadn't hired her. But I was a Winters, and we signed her paycheck.

This had never been a house where a woman at work felt vulnerable. Never.

My grandfather, my father, my mother, Uncle Hugh, Aunt Olivia—all of them had made it clear that our staff was to be respected and treated as professionals at all times. There was no chasing after the maids when I was a teenage boy, no matter how pretty they might be.

I didn't want to walk away from Sophie. Since I'd come home, she was the only person who made me feel like me. Ironic that the one human being in this house who made me feel at home was one who technically didn't belong here.

It killed me to admit that Aiden was right. Sophie deserved better. I wasn't saying I wouldn't pursue her, but now was not the time. I had to get my shit together. There was always the chance that once I was back to normal, this insane attraction would fade. Maybe something in my subconscious was just grasping at Sophie because she felt safe.

Maybe. But I didn't think so. I wasn't myself, I knew that. But the way I was drawn to Sophie, it was more than a reaction to stress. I closed my eyes, remembering the scent of her skin, sultry and sweet. The sound of her laugh, joyful and clear.

Sophie was mine. I could give her space. I could wait until I was in better shape to pursue her, but she was mine.

Opening my eyes, I sent Aiden a level look as I took a

seat opposite him and said "I'm not going to bother Sophie. But I'd better not find out you are behind my back."

"Is this what you wanted to talk to me about?" Aiden asked in a dismissive tone.

"No. I couldn't sleep last night, and I went to the kitchen. Sophie was up, and we were talking. We heard a noise, sounded like someone knocking something over. Were you awake?"

Aiden sat up straighter, dropping the pretense of disinterest. "No. I went to sleep around eleven and didn't wake up until five thirty. What time was this?"

"It was three twenty-seven when we heard the noise. I made sure Sophie was secure and then went to take a look around."

"Did you find anything?" Aiden asked.

"Nothing conclusive. A stack of books was out of place in the library. So was a lamp, but nothing was broken. There was no sign of forced entry. But we did hear something fall over. If there was no one else in the house, we should have seen what it was. Instead, everything looked normal."

"You're saying that someone was in the house and they put back whatever it was they knocked over?" Aiden asked.

"That would be my guess. But the alarm was on. It was armed when we heard the sound, and it never turned off. If you were in bed, Sophie and I were in the kitchen, and Amelia was asleep... It's possible it could have been Abel. Does the alarm for the house include his garage apartment?"

"It does. Theoretically, he could've been in the house. I'll check with him this morning. If it wasn't Abel, I'll ask Cooper to come out and go over the system again."

"When was the last time Sinclair Security reviewed the system?" I asked.

Sinclair Security was the best private security company in the country, and it was run by the current generation of Sinclairs, who happened to be our closest friends. Convenient when it came to things like having one of the best alarm systems known to man installed at Winters House. Since the death of our parents, no one at Winters House took security lightly. At my question, Aiden looked uncomfortable, and my nose for trouble went on high alert.

"What?" I demanded. Aiden shifted in his seat and shuffled the papers on his desk, not meeting my eyes.

"We've had a little trouble this year. We were under the impression it had been resolved but—"

"What kind of trouble?"

Aiden's explanation turned my blood to ice in my veins. It seemed that one of our parents' old friends had gone completely insane and had been leaving crime scene photographs of our parents' murders for the family to find. First Jacob, with a picture of my parents' murder. Then Vance, with the doctored version of the same photograph. Finally, she went to Charlie, where they caught her trying to leave another photograph.

The culprit, Marissa Archer, had been a crony of our parents' and our uncle William. She'd also, apparently, gone stark raving mad, ranting on Charlie's front porch about how only she knew the truth and it wasn't over, he was still out there. We all assumed she was talking about the murders, but shortly after she'd been shut away in a mental health facility, she'd stopped talking completely.

Aiden said they were keeping a close eye on her, but since she'd fallen silent, there'd been nothing. It's not like she was a reliable witness, anyway.

"Were any of you planning to tell me about this?" I asked.

"There didn't seem to be much point in bothering you with it," Aiden said, evenly. "You weren't here, and you weren't planning on coming home. It wasn't your problem."

"Of course it's my problem," I burst out. "This is my fucking family."

Aiden raised one cool eyebrow at me as if to ask—*Is it?*

"How sure are we that Marissa Archer was working alone?" I asked, ignoring Aiden's taunt.

He shrugged one shoulder. "We're not sure of anything. Nothing has happened since she's been locked up, but that isn't proof."

"Is there any chance this is related to the papers Charlie found? Have you had any luck finding out what happened to the baby?"

I couldn't call the missing child my brother. Not yet. Not until we knew what had happened to him. I'd had a lot of shocks when I'd come home, but finding out that my mother had borne a child before she married my father and given him up for adoption was the biggest.

Charlie had found the records, carefully hidden for years until a leak in the roof caused old boxes to be repacked and shuffled around, bringing the buried paperwork into the light. I hadn't gotten my head around the idea that there was another one of us out there somewhere.

We knew so little about what had happened. I guessed my father knew because the papers had been among others he would've seen. But we had no idea who had fathered the child or why she'd given him up. We didn't know anything, including where he was or what had happened to him.

Aiden shook his head. "The Sinclairs have been looking into it, but it's starting to look suspicious. Every time they follow a lead, it falls apart or doubles back on itself. Almost like someone—"

"Like someone left a false trail?"

"Exactly. Cooper and Evers both agree it feels like it has their father's fingerprints all over it."

I dropped my head in frustration. "Shit," I said. "If Maxwell Sinclair hid the baby, we're screwed."

"They're all on it," Aiden said. "Cooper, Evers, Knox, even Axel. They're taking it personally, not that they weren't before. They're going to find him. It's just a matter of time."

"Is it possible we're stirring things up by looking into it?" I asked.

"Anything's possible," Aiden said.

"We have to keep looking," I said, stating the obvious. We'd lost enough family as it was. If there was another one of us out there, we had to track him down.

"Agreed. I'm leaving this morning for a business trip," Aiden said, changing the subject. "I won't be back until Sunday evening. I'm sure you won't need anything, but if anything happens, call Cooper."

I stared at him, his words leaving me speechless. If anything happened, he wanted me to call Cooper Sinclair and not him. Hard not to see that as a slap across the face. But worse, he was leaving? The next day was the anniversary of his parents' murder, and he was leaving?

"You're leaving on a business trip? Through the weekend?" I couldn't quite bring myself to call him out, but Aiden knew what I was getting at.

He turned away, not meeting my eyes, and went back to straightening the papers on his desk. "Is that a problem?" he asked, in his iciest voice.

"No, fine. Whatever." What was I supposed to say?

Yes, it's a big fucking problem. It's the first year I've been home on the anniversary since they died and you're fucking taking off.

Was this betrayal and abandonment the way Aiden had felt when I left? I should be over it by now. Thirteen years had passed since my aunt and uncle had died. More than enough time to process everything—their deaths, the part I'd played. I'd thought I was past it. Being home, surrounded by memories of my parents and Aiden's, I knew I wasn't even close.

I wasn't going to argue with Aiden about his travel plans. Instead, I decided to take a shot at mending the rift between us.

"Are we ever going to talk about it?" I asked, trying to keep my voice level, though I couldn't help the thread of challenge that wound through my words.

Aiden's eyes flashed with anger, and maybe something else, maybe hurt, before he said, "There's nothing to talk about, Gage. You left. Now you're home."

I resisted the urge to be a smart-ass and said, "If there's nothing to talk about then why do you keep shutting me out? I know I shouldn't have left. I know I walked out on all of you, and it was a shitty thing to do."

Looking carefully past my shoulder, at me but not meeting my eyes, Aiden said, "Water under the bridge. It's been a long time. No need to talk about it now."

"I think we do. We used to be friends, Aiden. Now you'll barely look at me."

Aiden picked up a pen and drew a stack of papers in front of him. He couldn't have been more clear about wanting me to leave if he'd walked me to the door himself.

I knew how to take a hint, but I was also good at ignoring them when I wanted to. I stayed where I was, sitting in the chair across from his desk, and stared him down.

Finally, he said, "I don't know what you want from me, Gage. We're not kids anymore. You left. My parents were dead, the kids were crying themselves to sleep at night, no one knew what the fuck was going on, and you just disappeared. Fine, I get it. I got it back then. You felt too guilty to stay, and you had to get out of this house. I understand. But it doesn't change the fact that you've been gone over a decade. Coming home for a few days here and there doesn't make up for that, and you can't just move back in and think it's all going to go back to how it was."

Aiden always knew how to hit where it hurt. He was right. About everything. After the night Uncle Hugh and Aunt Olivia were murdered, I'd been steeped in guilt, drowning in it. I couldn't face my family. I couldn't face myself.

I'd left to escape. To spare them the sight of me, the reminder that I'd let them die. I wondered if it would be better if I were gone. My stomach turned over, my breakfast curdling in a wave of nausea. I didn't want to leave again. I wanted to be here, in Winters House. I wanted my family back.

I stood. Talking to Aiden wasn't getting me anywhere. He wasn't ready to give me a chance, and I couldn't force him to. Maybe we'd be better off if we just avoided each other for a while.

"I'll let you get back to work then," I said. I thought Aiden was going to ignore my retreat, but he looked up and met my eyes, his own deadly serious.

"I meant what I said. Stay away from Sophie."

I gave him a sharp nod, turned on my heel, and left, closing the door behind me.

A lot of things about being back in this house reminded me of the days when Aiden and I had been tighter than brothers, but nothing so much as the overwhelming desire to slam my fist into his face.

Most of the time, we'd gotten along in an almost scary synchronicity, knowing what the other was thinking before he had to speak. That didn't mean we didn't fight. We fought over big stuff, over stupid shit. When we were seven, and when we were seventeen, Aiden and I had been responsible for our share of bloodied noses and bruised knuckles.

I missed the relief of solving our disagreements with our fists. These days, our problems couldn't be solved with something as straightforward as a fistfight.

Aiden still blamed me for his parents' deaths, and I couldn't do a thing about it. Worse, I was starting to think that he was interested in Sophie, which, in a way, was a much bigger problem. Hugh and Olivia's murders were in the past. Sophie was here, and now.

Aiden had talked a big game about staying away from a woman working in our home, but the way he'd said it... I couldn't stop wondering. Hearing them laugh together. Seeing the smile on his face freeze as I opened the door to his office. Aiden wasn't a big smiler. It could've been inno-cent. I was sure it was on Sophie's part.

But Aiden... Was Aiden warning me away from Sophie so he could have his own shot with her?

She wasn't exactly his type, with her practical clothes and neatly braided hair. Aiden went for glamour. But Sophie, Sophie was naturally beautiful. She didn't need a ton of makeup and a couture wardrobe to highlight her assets.

I didn't want to think about what a bombshell she would

be if she bothered with all of that. I could barely keep my hands off her as it was. If she was irresistible in a floor length nightgown and thick cotton robe, I couldn't imagine how I would stay away if she started flashing cleavage and left her hair down.

My mind raced over the problem of Aiden and Sophie. She'd been living here six months. Maybe Aiden had seen her dressed up and realized she *was* his kind of woman. Maybe he was taking his time in his courtship.

I knew he hadn't kissed her. I couldn't believe he'd touched Sophie the way I had. She'd responded like a woman who hadn't been kissed in years. If Aiden had managed to get his mouth on Sophie, he wouldn't have let her go.

If we hadn't heard that sound in the library, I wouldn't have either. I'd almost fucked her right there in the kitchen, so drawn in by the feel of her in my arms, her mouth under mine, that I hadn't cared where we were.

I needed to see her again. I thought about hunting down Sophie and Aunt Amelia, and just as quickly rejected the idea. Amelia had sharp eyes, and I didn't want her to see my interest in Sophie. She'd either get in my way, if she disapproved, or, possibly worse, try to help.

I didn't need Amelia's help with Sophie. I needed to get my shit together. As pissed as I was after that conversation with Aiden, he'd had a point. I wasn't dependable.

I wanted to be.

I had been, for years. Any one of the guys on my team would've beaten the shit out of my cousin for calling me undependable.

I understood why my family might see me that way, but I'd spent the last thirteen years in the Army defining the concept of dependable. I always followed through, always completed the mission, and I never left one of my guys behind. Fuck, the insurgents who'd grabbed me in the desert, miles from our base, only got me because I was buying time for my team to finish the mission and get clear.

When you went to the heart of it, Aiden was wrong. I was dependable. I was loyal. And I would fight for the people I loved. But in another way, he was right. I didn't have a job. I still wasn't sleeping. I was plagued by nightmares. Loud noises set my heart racing and left me fighting the urge to dive for cover. I was too quick to anger, and I couldn't control my emotions.

Gage Winters was dependable and steadfast. But some time during my six months of captivity, I'd lost touch with that Gage Winters, and I hadn't quite found my way back. Sophie deserved better.

Not Aiden. He couldn't have her. He was too stiff and formal for Sophie. I didn't see her wanting life as a society wife. She'd want a home and children and affection. I didn't know if I was the man to give her that. But I knew I wanted to find out.

CHAPTER ELEVEN

SOPHIE

I should've stayed in bed. The night before, I'd been smart. Instead of roaming Winters House when I couldn't sleep and risking a run-in with Gage, I'd curled up in the window seat in my bedroom and stared out into the dark night.

Things had gotten out of control with Gage in the kitchen. I couldn't afford to let it happen again. Just the memory of his mouth on mine, the feel of his hands on my skin, and I was wet. No man had ever had this effect on me. One minute I was admiring his eyes, or the stretch of his shirt over his shoulders, and the next I was dizzy with lust, willing to risk everything for just one more minute with him. Stupid.

I knew better. I loved my job. Getting involved with Gage was a complication that could drive me from the only home I'd had in years. I'd decided to do the only responsible, mature thing—I was avoiding him.

I hadn't seen him since he'd interrupted my meeting with Aiden. He hadn't come to lunch or dinner for two days, staying closeted in his room. I knew I shouldn't, but I couldn't help worrying about him.

A somber mood hung over the house, infecting everyone. Amelia, Mrs. W—even Abel seemed subdued. When I asked Mrs. W about it, she explained that it was the anniversary of Hugh and Olivia Winters murder.

When Charlie still lived in the house, she'd told me, Aiden would come up with a business trip that required both of them to leave town until the anniversary had passed. Even when the children had still been young, Mrs. W said Aiden had emptied the house every year rather than face the memory of the night his parents had been killed. She said she wasn't surprised he'd left again this year, only that he hadn't taken Gage with him.

Pouring myself a cup of tea, I'd said, "They don't seem to get along very well."

Mrs. W rarely gossiped about the Winters family. She was loyal to the core and loved them like they were her own, so I was surprised when she said, with a shake of her head, "Those boys. They were tight as ticks when they were young. But after Gage left and Aiden had so much on his shoulders..." She trailed off. Briskly assembling a snack plate for Aunt Amelia, she went on, "They'll work it out. They just need some time. But I don't like Gage on his own. Not tonight."

She slanted me a look I couldn't read. No one in the house knew that Gage and I had met in the middle of the night more than once. As far as everyone else was concerned, we were strangers, sharing a few meals at the dinner table and no more.

But the way Mrs. W looked at me, the suggestion I thought I saw in her eyes—did she know? Sometimes it seemed like Mrs. W knew everything that happened in Winters House. Maybe she did.

I couldn't get her words out of my mind. I'd managed to fall asleep when I tucked myself into bed, but I'd woken not long after midnight from a nightmare of grasping hands and swinging fists.

Like most of my bad dreams, this one took place in the dark. My memories of Anthony belonged in the dark. Still half asleep, fighting my way out of the dream, I rolled over and flicked on the light. One day, I would sleep through the night, but it wouldn't be tonight.

I got out of bed and pulled on my robe. For the first time in ages, I wished I had something a little more feminine. The waffle-weave white cotton was clean and crisp, attractive in its own way. Attractive, but not at all feminine. Not sexy. When did I start worrying about being sexy?

Since Anthony, I'd done my best to downplay my more attractive features and focus on my skills over my looks. Not that I was a raving beauty or anything, but between the almost platinum shade of my hair and a curvy figure men seem to like, I drew attention.

I'd never be a supermodel or a movie star, but since I'd hit adolescence, my looks had attracted men. I'd always been a little too shy to make the most of it, and after Anthony, I had no interest in any kind of attention, especially attention based on the way I looked. That could only get me in trouble.

I definitely shouldn't wish I had a different nightgown. I looked down at the thin white cotton trimmed in lace and shook my head. I dressed like someone's maiden aunt. After years in the thick flannel chin-to-toes nightwear Anthony gave me, the light, thin cotton felt like freedom.

I wasn't ready for anything more skin bearing. This

nightgown was sleeveless, and that was enough to make me feel daring and exposed. I tried not to remember the negligée I'd chosen for my wedding night. I hadn't worn anything like it since.

I'd thought about it, mostly wondering if I should replace my white cotton with silk and satin—reclaim some of what Anthony had stolen from me. In theory, it was a great idea, but when I looked at those filmy negligées in the department store, I shuddered with memory. White cotton would have to do.

I paced my room for a few minutes, caught in an argument with myself. I wanted a cup of tea. Hiding in my room when I couldn't sleep only made it worse, gave me a sense of being trapped, of hiding, that I hated.

I didn't want to risk running into Gage. Avoiding him seemed like the most sensible move, but I was worried after talking to Mrs. W. He was having enough trouble adjusting to being home. I knew there was no way he was asleep that night of all nights, the anniversary of his aunt and uncle's death.

I was leaving my room before I'd consciously made the decision. Heading down the hall, I saw the flicker of fire-light in the library and thought about making tea. Two cups, one for each of us.

In the dark, I could sneak by the library without being seen. Winters House was built on a large square, the court-yard in the center. My room and Amelia's were on the front right corner, closest to the driveway and inner gate. The library and Aiden's office were in the back right, the kitchen opposite in the back left. Most of the rooms opened right into the hallway, but the doors to the library, Aiden's office, and the wine room were tucked into a separate small hall-way, shielding both rooms from anyone passing by.

I could easily sneak past the library without being caught. There was no reason to poke my head in before I went to make tea.

I was through the doorway before I decided I wasn't going in. I didn't have time to be annoyed at my indecisiveness or the way I kept acting against my best interests. The moment my eyes fell on him, Gage commanded all of my attention.

He was sprawled on the leather couch, his feet propped on the coffee table, a crystal decanter of whiskey beside them, a half-full cut crystal glass in his hand. I'd never seen Gage drink before. Not like this.

His eyes were glazed, his limbs loose. When he caught sight of me the side of his mouth curled in a sardonic smile. The clarity of his speech took me by surprise. Based on the way he looked, I would've expected him to be slurring his words.

Instead, each word was perfectly clear when he said, "Sophie. My angel come to rescue me in the dark."

His voice was a growl. Shivers skated down my skin, prickling my nerves from the back of my neck to the bottom of my feet, waking every part of my body.

I didn't move from my spot just inside the doorway, my eyes locked on his. When he kept speaking, I swayed forward just a little, mesmerized by the low rumble of his voice.

"The first time I saw you I thought you were an angel. That hair, those eyes, the white robe. I figured it was the end. Coming home was a dream, and you were here to take me with you. Then I heard your voice, and I knew you were no angel. No angel could have a voice like yours. So sweet."

"Are you drunk?" I asked, and wished I'd kept my mouth shut when he threw back the rest of the whiskey in his glass. He refilled it, his movements precise and controlled. The brown liquor poured cleanly into the crystal glass, the stopper sliding easily into the decanter without a clink.

His hands were steady, and the way he was speaking clear enough, but the glaze in his blue eyes and the things he was saying... Gage Winters was not sober.

In answer to my question, he shook his head. "Not yet, Angel. But I'm working on it. Come keep me company."

I stayed where I was. Shoving my hands in the pockets of my robe, I held my arms tight to my side and said, "I don't think that's a very good idea. I shouldn't have let you... We shouldn't have... In the kitchen the other day, I—"

My mouth snapped shut, and I fell silent.

Gage took a sip of his whiskey, studying me with hooded eyes. I tried to look away, but I couldn't stop staring at his face. I'd rarely seen him so relaxed. Even knowing it was the alcohol easing his tension, Gage became even more magnetic when he wasn't wound tight. If it hadn't been for the sadness in his eyes, I might've thought it was a good thing.

But the sadness was there, clinging to him, weighing him down. And he was only relaxed because he was drinking. I knew he avoided alcohol for exactly this reason.

"Do you want me to apologize for kissing you?" he asked, his eyes fixed on my mouth. Before I could answer, he said, "Because I'm not going to. Kissing you might be the best decision I've made in the last thirteen years, and I'm not apologizing for it."

"I don't want an apology," I said, honestly. "I just don't think we should do it again."

"We'll have to agree to disagree on that, Angel. Come have a drink with me. It'll help you sleep."

I took another step into the library before I drew short. His voice was wrapping itself around me, cajoling and tempting. How could something so soothing feel so dangerous?

I tried to tell myself to turn around and go back to my room. I didn't listen. I didn't want to go back to my lonely room and stare at the ceiling until the sun rose. I wanted to be here, with Gage. I wanted—I cut that thought off before I could finish it. I wasn't in a position to want anything with Gage.

For so long I'd had a single focus in life. First, it was to get through college and nursing school so I could get a job and support myself. Then it was surviving marriage to Anthony. Then I was free, and my life was all about finding work and moving forward.

Until the day Gage came home to Winters House. From the moment we'd met my focus had split. A part of me still thought my job and my future should be my most important priority. That part of me was practical. Sensible. Before Gage, I'd never wanted anything more than security.

Now there was a new Sophie. The Sophie that had kissed Gage in the kitchen. The Sophie who wanted to curl up next to him on that couch, take a long sip of his whiskey, and kiss him again. That Sophie didn't give a crap about her job or security. That Sophie was tired of sleepless nights and bad dreams and feeling like she was dead inside.

The new Sophie wanted to be alive.

She wanted to dream.

She wanted to want.

I hovered there, one step into the room, my arms crossed tightly over my chest, and watched Gage lift the glass to his lips. He took a slow, long sip of the whiskey. Sensible

Sophie yelled at me as my feet carried me across the room. I ignored her.

Gage's eyes flared as I moved to the opposite side of the couch and sat, tucking my feet beneath me and leaning against the arm. With Gage sprawled against the opposite arm, a good three feet separated us.

Leaning forward, he filled a second glass with a small splash of whiskey and handed it to me. I took it, thrilling more than I should have when his fingers stroked the back of my hand before withdrawing.

I took a sip of the whiskey and coughed. I didn't like whiskey. The sour fire of it burned my throat. I didn't really like alcohol in general, but if I was going to stay up half the night drinking, whiskey would never be my first choice.

I wasn't here for the whiskey. I was here for Gage.

CHAPTER TWELVE

SOPHIE

Deciding not to play games, I said, "Mrs. W told me why Aiden left. Told me what today is. I'm sorry."

Gage's eyes dropped to the whiskey in his hand. He swirled the glass and took a sip. "This is the first year I've been home on the anniversary since it happened."

"Was it easier? Being away?" I asked.

"I would've told you no. But now that I'm here? Yeah, being away was easier. I found them right here, you know." He gestured to the Persian rug with his whiskey glass. "Right there on the rug."

"You were home?" I asked.

I don't know why I thought no one was home when Hugh and Olivia Winters were murdered. I didn't know much about the crime. I hadn't lived in the area when it had happened, and it felt creepy to spy on my new employers by reading all the media coverage.

A simple web search had uncovered pages of headlines, click bait and trashy. I hadn't read a single one. Seeing the haunted guilt in Gage's blue eyes, I was glad I hadn't.

"I was home," he said in a distant voice. "I was here the whole time, and I didn't save them. Just walked in and found them laying on the floor. Exactly the same way my parents died. Almost the same position on the rug. Same room. Different house."

I didn't know what to say. I didn't know a lot about the Winters' tragic history, but I did know Gage's parents had died when he was a child, in their own home a quarter-mile away. And I'd known those deaths had been called a murder/suicide by the police, just like Hugh and Olivia Winters' murders had been.

The headlines I'd seen had fed on that angle, but Gage hadn't said, "I didn't stop them." He'd said, "I didn't save them."

I turned the problem over in my mind, wanting to ask what he meant and afraid to make it all worse. Had they been murdered and he'd been home? It suddenly occurred to me how narrowly the teenage Gage might have escaped being killed himself.

I watched him drain half the whiskey in his glass, tipping his head back as it ran down his throat and staring at the ceiling, shrouded in the darkness of the room. The flickering light of the fire gilded his skin, turning his tan to gold and setting flames into his blue eyes.

He was almost impossibly beautiful in his own rugged way. When my eyes caught on the curve of his lower lip, I looked away and took my own long sip of whiskey, fighting back the urge to cough and choke as it burned its way to my stomach.

I expected Gage to say something else about his aunt and uncle, the anniversary, but his next words almost sent me fleeing the room.

"You were married," he said, flatly. "What happened with your husband?"

I took another sip of the whiskey to cover my reluctance to answer. I never talked about my marriage. With anyone. I'd only told Amelia a little.

His dark rumble of a voice carefully gentle, Gage said, "It was that bad?"

"I don't talk about it," I admitted. "And I don't want to talk about it now."

"Fair enough," Gage said. "I don't want to talk either."

In a fluid movement, too graceful for a man who'd been drinking whiskey all night, Gage surged forward and pulled the half empty crystal glass from my hand. Before I could move out of reach, he closed his hand around my arm and tugged me forward.

It happened so fast, I lost my balance and fell into him. I started to struggle, to fight my way free when his arms closed around me and he pulled me into his side, pressing my head to his chest.

"Settle down, Angel. I'm not going to do anything you don't want me to. I swear. I'll never hurt you. I just want to hold on to you for a few minutes. Just let me hold onto you."

I went still in his arms, confused. The second the fight went out of me, Gage settled me into his side, smoothing my robe down over my legs and wrapping his arm around my back.

His heart beat under my ear. His solid body was warm against mine, smelling of whiskey and man.

I felt his breath against the top of my head, his lips in my hair as he murmured, "I just want to hold onto you for a little while."

The tight knot in my chest unfurled, and I melted into him, letting my legs twine with his and laying my arm across his chest. Bit by bit I relaxed, my body molding to his, my eyes sliding shut.

I don't know how long we lay there. A while. Long enough for me to get comfortable. So comfortable I never realized I'd shifted the arm I had across his chest and was exploring his body in lazy strokes, my fingers sliding over his shoulders, tracing his collarbone, dipping into the ridges of muscle at his abdomen.

I was lost in my own head, warm and safe, my hands on Gage as if he were mine, as if I had license to do whatever I wanted with him.

Gradually, I realized that his breath had shortened. His heart beat had sped up. My hand stilled on the side of his neck, and his voice rumbled against my palm when he said, "Don't stop. I won't do anything if you don't want me to. Just don't stop."

I didn't know what to do. I didn't want to stop. I wanted to keep touching him. I wanted to dive my fingers under his shirt and feel the heat of his skin on mine. I wanted more of Gage, and I didn't want to worry about the consequences.

So many wants and all of them were foolish. I knew I should get up and leave. I didn't move.

I lay there, completely still, my hand curled around the side of Gage's neck, silently arguing with myself. I might have been there forever if Gage hadn't slid his fingers around my chin and urged my head up, his eyes searching for mine.

I shifted over him, maybe trying to get off the couch, away from temptation, but as I moved my body over Gage's his hands closed on my hips, holding me on top of him.

I was slow to react. I lay there, straddling Gage Winters, thinking that this was the exact opposite of what I'd intended. I was supposed to be climbing over him, off the couch, and scurrying out the door. Away from temptation. Away from trouble.

Gage's fingers sank into my hips, but I could have moved easily enough if I'd really wanted to. I didn't want to move. I knew what I wanted.

Ignoring all my doubts, I leaned down and touched my lips to his.

Gage froze beneath me, his muscles tight with tension as I brushed my lips against his. Sinking my fingers into his thick hair, I did it again, slower, flicking out my tongue to taste the full lower lip that always drew my eye. I couldn't resist sucking it into my mouth, opening him to me, fitting my lips against his and tasting him.

My tongue touched his and Gage came back to life, his hips rolling beneath mine, his erection hard against my heat. His need was unleashed in his kiss, his mouth taking control, taking everything it wanted. I fell into the kiss, forgetting that just moments before I'd been ready to flee the room.

Yanking at the voluminous fabric of my robe and night-gown, Gage went for the bare skin beneath, stroking his hands from my knees to my hips and up my sides. My breath caught in my throat as his big, rough hands closed over my breasts.

Gage broke our kiss, his head falling back as he groaned, "Fuck, Sophie."

My lips met his again, and his kiss was hungry. Demanding. When one hand traced down my spine to dip between my legs, I settled back into him, my knees spreading wider, my hips tilting up.

I was wanton, as hungry, as needy, as he was. He plucked at my nipple, sending shocks of sharp, sweet plea-sure through me. One thick finger delved into the heat between my legs, carefully, patiently opening my body to him. I panted into his mouth, overcome with sensation, too much and not enough.

A second finger joined the first, and I let out a low cry, tearing my mouth from his and dropping my forehead against his neck, panting and rocking back into his hand, undone by the pleasure.

Two fingers pumped deep in my pussy, a hard callous thumb pressed into my clit, and I let out a keening wail, gasping for breath. I think I called his name.

My cheeks were wet with tears or perspiration. I didn't know. I didn't know anything. Just Gage's hand between my legs, his fingers teasing my nipple, his strong, solid body supporting my weight as I shuddered and wept through a wave of pleasure, unlike anything I'd ever known before.

Afterward, I was shaking, tiny shocks of bliss echoing through my body, a heavenly ache pulsing between my legs. I was aware of Gage withdrawing his fingers, smoothing down my nightgown and robe as he arranged my legs beside his. I couldn't help but notice the long, thick bar of his erection straining the front of his pants.

I wanted to touch him, to see what he felt like in my hand, to make him feel the way he'd made me feel. So good. So alive.

I reached for him, and Gage's hand closed over mine, leading it to his chest. I propped myself up on one elbow and looked down at him in confusion.

"Don't you want me to?"

Not releasing my hand from his, he sat up a little and kissed me gently, skating his lips along my jaw and nipping my earlobe.

"Angel, you have no idea how much I want you to."

"I want to touch you," I said, ignoring the blush I could feel in my cheeks.

"I want you to, but not yet. Not tonight."

"Why?" I asked, searching his eyes, trying to understand.

"You gave me a gift, Sophie. You trusted me to make you feel good." Seeming to change the subject, he said, "I love the sound of your voice when you talk. So low and sweet, it soothes all the jagged parts inside me. Did you know that? But the sounds you make when you come—. Fuck, Angel, I could listen to that for the rest of my life. It almost makes me feel whole again."

"Then why—"

"We're not ready for that. I'm a fucked up mess, Sophie. You deserve better. And if you let me get inside that sweet angel's body of yours, I'm not going to be able to let you go. Do you understand?"

"You're protecting me? From you?"

"I promised I'd keep you safe," he said, in answer.

Gage sat up, bringing me with him, and stood, pulling me to my feet. My legs were shockingly wobbly. I realized he planned to walk me to my room. I knew he was going to leave me there, alone.

If I were alone, he'd be alone, too.

"Are you going to sleep tonight?" I asked. Gage scanned the library, his eyes bleak. He shrugged. That meant 'no.' Pulling my hand from his, I said, "I'm not leaving you. We can play cards. Watch a movie. Something. But I'm not leaving you."

"Angel," he started.

I planted my hands on my hips, keeping my eyes on his. I wasn't very big, and I wasn't loud, but I was stubborn as hell. Gage's tight shoulders dropped in resignation.

"Fine."

We stood there for a full minute, in silence, watching each other. Gage seemed to come to a decision because he took my hand and led me back to the couch. Turning on a speaker in the book shelves I hadn't noticed, he put music on low. Big band. The old stuff.

Gage spread out on the long couch and pulled me into his arms, tucking me securely between his big body and the back of the couch. My head on his chest, his fingers combed through my hair as the flames of the fire flickered across the room, and the lively tones of the music drifted to our ears.

"My uncle Hugh and aunt Olivia loved this music. I used to walk in on them dancing together."

He fell silent, his fingers tugging gently through my hair, lulling me to sleep. Letting out a long breath, he relaxed beneath me. I stretched my arm over his chest, my hand on his side as if I could hold him to me. As if I could keep him safe from the demons in his memories. I couldn't change his past. I couldn't heal his wounds. All I could do was hold him close to my heart and hope it was enough.

CHAPTER THIRTEEN
SOPHIE

My head pounded in fatigue the next morning. I'd dozed on the couch with Gage for a few hours, drifting between talking and sleeping. Long before dawn lit the sky, Gage had helped me to my feet, clicked off the fire and the music, and walked me to my room. He left me at the door, pressing a tender, lingering kiss to my mouth, saying only, "Thank you, Angel."

I'd crawled into my bed and tried to go back to sleep, but sleep refused to come. I couldn't stop thinking about Gage. I tried not to compare him to Anthony, but it was impossible. For one thing, they were the only two men who'd ever really touched me, sexually.

If you added up every single episode of sexual contact in my marriage with Anthony, the total wouldn't come close to that explosive encounter on the couch with Gage. I thought I'd understood what an orgasm was, thought I'd given them to myself, alone in my bed in the dark of night.

I'd had no clue. That kind of pleasure... It was distracting and seductive.

Gage was nothing like Anthony. They had surface

things in common. Anthony had been wealthy. So was Gage, though on a different level. They were both physically fit and attractive, though again in different ways. Anthony had been refined. Elegant. More like Aiden, actually.

There was a rough earthiness to Gage that I found reassuring. Maybe it was because Anthony and Aiden, men with that type of refined elegance, reminded me of my father. My cool, restrained father who had had only enough warmth in his heart for one woman, my mother. When she'd died, he'd buried himself in his job.

He'd told me not to marry Anthony, and when I hadn't listened, he cut me off. I'd managed to call him twice during my marriage, hoping he might offer a lifeline, but he'd told me calmly that I'd made my bed and I'd have to sleep in it. Literally. I hadn't seen him in five years.

I didn't think I could be attracted to a man who reminded me of my father or Anthony. I trusted Aiden as an employer, and I could appreciate his good looks, but they didn't do anything for me.

There was something about Gage I couldn't shake off. He was raw and honest and purely himself.

His control the night before had been intense. Not like Anthony. Another superficial thing they had in common that was completely different under the surface. Anthony had lived for control. Everything about him was a way to control others. The charming façade he presented to the world. The way he locked down every emotion except those he wanted to show.

When the ugly parts bubbled to the surface in a fit of violent rage, he'd still had enough control to save it all for me. And the moment he'd released enough of that rage through his fists or his belt or his kicking feet, the façade snapped back into place. Anthony used self-control as a shield and a weapon.

Even in his worst attacks on me, he'd been in control. He never left a bruise I couldn't cover with clothing. He never broke a bone. He bruised my kidneys once or twice badly enough that there'd been blood in my urine, but otherwise, I had no lasting damage.

If he'd injured me, I might have had to get medical attention, and that would reveal the truth of our marriage. Worse yet, a broken bone or internal bleeding would've required that I go to the hospital and Anthony refused to allow me to leave the property. More of his obsession with control. Sometimes I thought he'd married me so he could exert his will over another human being in every possible way.

After Anthony, I should've hated being near a man with that same iron control. But Gage didn't use control as a weapon; it was a part of his strength. He used it to protect the people around him.

The night before, dazed with pleasure and shaking in his arms, I would've given him anything he asked.

Never mind that he was right, I wasn't ready. I wasn't sure how I felt about Gage making that decision for me, but I'd felt the steely heat of his erection. If I hadn't touched him, I never would've known how much he wanted me. I wouldn't have understood what it took for him to hold back, to give me so much pleasure and take none in return.

Anthony had used his control to bring me a nightmare of pain. Gage used control to keep me safe. Even from himself.

"You need another cup of coffee," Amelia said from across the table. I sent her a weak smile, and she said, "You didn't sleep well again, did you?"

"No, not really." I didn't volunteer the exact nature of my *not sleeping*. Amelia was endlessly nosy and interfering. I didn't want to think about what she might do if she'd found out I'd spent the night with Gage. The possibilities were horrifying.

"Are you sure you don't want to try that tea again?" she asked.

I shuddered. I couldn't help it; the memory of the tea was *that* awful. I took a sip of coffee just to wash the thought of it away.

"I'll make a deal with you, Amelia," I said. "I'll drink another cup of that tea right after you drink two of them."

"Why two?"

"Because you have more than enough grit to force yourself to drink one cup of that stuff, but two cups is an entirely different story. You'd never make it through two cups. No human being would voluntarily drink two cups of that tea."

"That bad, huh?" Amelia winked at me, and I scowled back. "I'll find something else. Something that doesn't taste so terrible."

"It's okay. I'm used to it by now," I said.

Getting up from the table, I went to the buffet on the sideboard and took a few more pieces of bacon and another serving of eggs. With Aiden still out of town, there were only three of us eating regular meals at Winters House, but that didn't stop Abel from putting out a full spread every morning.

"You shouldn't be used to it," Amelia said. "You're a nurse; you know a good night's sleep is important. Going day after day without sleeping is terrible. It's inhuman."

"You only think so because you're part sloth," I said, dryly. Sometimes I thought she was. I envied Amelia her close relationship with sleep. She went to bed early and slept until eight in the morning, sometimes getting as much as ten hours a night.

It wasn't unknown for her to doze off in the middle of the afternoon. She wasn't fatigued, she just loved to sleep. Normally, as people age, their need for sleep lessened, and Amelia had admitted she could get by on a lot less. She just didn't want to.

Some nights, when I was laying in bed staring at the ceiling, I thought I would've killed to be able to sleep like that.

"Maybe you need to find a therapist and talk about your nightmares," she said, quietly. "Or exercise. Exercise is supposed to be great for helping you sleep."

"Unfortunately, I have an allergy to exercise," I said with a straight face. "Every time I do it I start sweating and get short of breath. It's terrible. I have to sit down until it goes away."

Amelia rolled her eyes at me. "We should walk more," she said, decisively. "We've been staying in too much since the weather turned cold. We should put on our jackets and go back to our regular walk in the Gardens."

I didn't mind walking. Walking wasn't real exercise. Not the way we did it. In warmer weather, Amelia and I had gone to the Botanical Gardens a few times a week. The paths were wide and paved, perfect for Amelia, who could walk for hours but wasn't up for the grade changes and unstable terrain of hiking. Both the Botanical Gardens and Piedmont Park where they were located, were scenic and interesting.

"We could do that," I agreed. Amelia looked out the windows of the dining room to the gray drizzle outside.

"Not today," she said. "When is the weather supposed to clear up?"

I pulled my phone from my pocket and opened the weather app. "Partly cloudy with some sun in the afternoon tomorrow," I said.

"We'll go tomorrow then. Today we might as well finish those birdseed things for Charlie's wedding."

I raised an eyebrow at Amelia. "Don't you mean *I* should finish the birdseed things? I don't remember you helping."

Amelia shrugged one shoulder and grinned at me, digging her fork into her scrambled eggs. "I helped organize the ribbons," she offered before scooping eggs into her mouth.

Amelia's irrepressible sense of mischief was one of the many things I loved about working for her. She really didn't need a nurse, and by taking this job, I knew I was letting my skills atrophy. The little real nursing I did was isolated to monitoring her blood sugar, her blood pressure, and overseeing her diet.

But I was happy here, and I couldn't deny Aiden paid me well, especially considering room and board were included in the deal. When I decided to leave Winters House, I'd have more than enough saved to cover any retraining I needed.

I got the second cup of coffee Amelia had recommended and waited for her to finish her breakfast. She tried to talk me into letting her have a muffin, I reminded her muffins were just cake with no frosting, she glared at me, and I laughed.

We went through some version of the same conversation every morning, and it always made me smile.

I headed for the living room, where I'd left my box of materials for Charlie's birdseed favors. Amelia didn't follow me in. Continuing down the hall, she said over her shoulder, "I want the library today. The living room looks cold."

It wasn't cold, and it had a fireplace, but I knew what she meant. The living room was a bright, light-filled space, with high ceilings, pale walls and tall windows. In contrast, the library was paneled in dark wood, with heavy curtains and a bigger fireplace. The couch and armchairs all had blankets folded over the arms.

The living room was formal. Every room in Winters House was formal, but the living room always made me feel like I should change into a cocktail dress. The library invited me to stay, to curl up with a book and settle in.

It had been one of my favorite rooms in the heat of summer, the dark paneling and thick drapes giving off the feel of a cave, cool and dry—so unlike the heavy humidity that blanketed Atlanta that time of year.

I'd expected to find the room too cold once winter came, but it was the opposite. The dark paneling and thick drapes made it cozy, and the bigger fire threw off warmth that turned the room into a haven.

I smiled to myself as I walked through the door, holding the big box in my arms, and stopped short at the sight of Gage occupying one of the oversize armchairs, working on a laptop, a stack of papers and a mug on the side table to his left.

"Oh," I said, stupidly. "We're interrupting. We can go somewhere else."

"Nonsense," said Amelia, settling in on the end of the couch closest to the fireplace, exactly where I'd sat the night before. "We won't bother Gage."

A flush settled into my cheeks, and I looked at Gage. He was watching Amelia, a small smile playing over his lips. At the sight of that smile, my cheeks warmed another degree.

"You won't bother me," Gage said.

I walked past him, not quite meeting his eyes, and said under my breath, "Liar."

He smiled but said nothing. I sat down in the middle of the couch, setting my box beside me on the opposite end from Amelia, where Gage had been sprawled out the night before. This put me right next to Amelia, and about as far as I could get from Gage unless I somehow talked Amelia into giving up her spot close to the fire.

I wasn't ready to be around him yet. Everything had changed between us the night before. Not just physically, though that would've been enough. He'd had his fingers inside me. I remembered the way I'd straddled his body, pushed myself back on those fingers and ridden his hand to orgasm.

My cheeks burned at the memory. I'd never done anything like that before. I'd felt lush and eager. Open. Willing to do anything if it meant he'd keep touching me.

Sitting there in the library beside Amelia, carefully pouring birdseed into squares of white tulle and securing them with pretty ribbons, wearing my neatly pressed camp shirt, jeans, and white Converse sneakers, I was my normal, buttoned-up self.

Why did my normal, buttoned-up self feel like a pair of shoes that were too small? There was safety in being proper and well behaved. At least, I wanted to think there was. Having orgasms with Gage on the couch was not safe. It was definitely not proper and well behaved.

I was not going to think about it while I was sitting next to Amelia. I tried to change my train of thought, suddenly worried that Amelia was secretly psychic and would figure out what was going through my head. If she looked closely, she'd see the flush in my cheeks.

I needed to get myself together and forget that Gage was sitting on the other side of the room. He appeared to be ignoring us, focused on whatever he was doing on the laptop. Every once in a while he would pick up some of the papers of the stack beside him and shuffle through them, find something he was looking for, nod to himself and return the papers to the end table. I lost myself in wondering what he was working on, jumping a little when Amelia interrupted my thoughts.

"Tear off a piece of paper from this. About an inch square," Amelia said, handing me a notepad.

I tied off the ribbon on my bundled birdseed and set it aside in the box with the others before taking the notepad and doing as she asked. I tried to return both the pad and the square of paper, but she plucked the paper from my fingers and gestured for me to keep the pad.

"That's perfect, thank you," she said. I looked at her lap to see a single drinking straw balanced on her knees. Amelia's blue eyes sparkled as she crushed the square of paper into a ball, popped it into her mouth to get it wet, and then picked up the straw.

Oh, no.

CHAPTER FOURTEEN
SOPHIE

"Amelia Winters, you put that down right now," I hissed.

"Put what down?" she asked, sounding so innocent I almost wanted to believe her despite the straw she held in her hand and the spitball she was carefully plugging into one end.

"What? Are you in second grade? This is a low point, even for you," I said, exasperated. What was I supposed to do with a seventy-eight-year-old woman who thought spitballs were funny?

"You've vetoed everything I've come up with in the past week," Amelia said, annoyed. She turned the straw in her fingers making sure the spitball filled the end, not leaving any gaps for air to escape.

"You know why I vetoed them," I whispered. I didn't want Gage to hear our conversation since he'd been the reason I shot down Amelia's pranks. Remembering what he'd said the night we met, I refused to let her tape an airhorn to Aiden's desk chair. Ditto for attaching one to the back of the door. Random air horns going off in the house were the last thing Gage needed.

I'd also refused to sprinkle sprout seeds in Aiden's keyboard, on the grounds it would likely get me fired, and had said I absolutely would not put a square of bullion in Mrs. W's shower head so she'd end up bathing in chicken soup. That was just mean. And gross.

"You're no fun," Amelia said, lifting the straw.

"I know," I said. I wasn't fun. I'd never been the fun type. If you wanted someone to help you with your homework or show up on time to get you at the airport, that was me. I was reliable and loyal, and honest, and I worked hard. But I'd never been particularly fun.

I wasn't sure I knew *how* to be fun. As that depressing thought drifted through my mind, Amelia put the straw to her mouth and blew. Her spitball struck directly between my eyes. Of course, Amelia would have excellent aim with spitballs.

The spitball fell to my lap where I retrieved it and dropped it on the coffee table. I didn't bother to pretend to be annoyed. I wasn't mad; I was resigned. Anyway, I adored Amelia, spitballs and all.

"If you apologize for that, I'll tear more pieces of paper for you. But only if you promise not to aim them at me."

"Deal. And I'm sorry," Amelia said, sounding genuinely contrite. I knew her too well.

"No you're not, but I appreciate the effort."

I set aside my birdseed project and quickly tore a sheet of notepaper into a stack of one-inch squares. Handing them to Amelia, I scooted toward the other end of the couch, picking up my box of birdseed supplies and placing it between us.

When she got caught, I wanted plausible deniability.

Of all the things Amelia had proposed in the last week, spitballs were the most harmless. If I didn't let her get this out of her system, she'd stop asking for my help, and then who knew what she'd get up to? I couldn't forget the story I'd heard about a prank involving a candle, a set of curtains, and a fire in the living room.

I was just going to sit on the other side of the couch, work on my wedding project, and pretend I didn't see anything else in the room.

I had to stifle a giggle when a spitball hit Gage's shoulder, and he looked up, his gaze flicking around the room to spot whatever had interrupted his focus. Amelia was the picture of innocence, pretending to read a magazine, using the pages to hide her straw and squares of paper.

Watching her from the corner of my eye, I had to admire her methods. Amelia was sneaky. If I hadn't already known what she was doing, I never would've noticed her hand going so often to her mouth and would've thought she was straightening her glasses, or tucking her hair behind her ear.

She was a master of deception, which was a little scary. But I already knew that. After six months she was still finding new places in her room to hide cookies.

A wet paper missile winged Gage's ear, and he looked up again, his eyes going from me to Amelia, then back to me. One dark brow lifted in question. I gave a quick shake of my head and forced my attention back to my lap and the bundle of birdseed I was tying closed.

I did my best to look innocent, but I already knew Gage didn't buy it. I was a terrible liar, and he'd been trained to read people.

Amelia waited a few minutes before her next attack, probably hoping Gage's attention would be drawn back into his work. She should have known better. Her next spit-ball was aimed right at his face, but it never reached its target.

So fast I thought I'd imagined it, Gage's hand whipped up and plucked the spitball from the air. Picking it out of his palm, he held it between his thumb and forefinger, examining it, before looking at Amelia and saying, "What are you eight? A spitball?"

"I think I should try that on Aiden," Amelia said. "You two have no sense of humor."

"And Aiden does?" Gage asked, incredulous. I had to agree with his question. I'd never seen any evidence Aiden had a sense of humor.

"Aiden has a magnificent sense of humor," Amelia said, "and you know it. Besides, he lets me get away with anything."

"Seventy-eight and still a brat," Gage said, shaking his head.

"You know you love me," Amelia said, smiling fondly at her great-nephew.

"I do," Gage agreed, "but I'm trying to get some work done here."

"If you want to work, use the office," Amelia said. "The library is for relaxing."

"The office is Aiden's. I can go work at my desk upstairs," he offered.

"What are you doing, anyway?" Amelia asked.

Finally. I wanted to know, but I wasn't going to ask. Not only was it none of my business, asking Gage what he was doing might make Amelia wonder why I cared.

"I'm trying to get up to speed on the company," he said. "I've been gone a long time. If I want to go back to work, I have a lot to learn."

"Aiden's coming around then?" Amelia asked, sounding satisfied.

Gage's eyes darkened, and he shook his head. "No. Aiden's being an ass. Charlie agreed to help me."

Amelia worried her lower lip in her teeth. "I'll talk to him. You children have lost too much to be at odds with each other, and he's held a grudge long enough."

"No," Gage interrupted. "We'll work it out in our own time. I don't want you to talk to him. That'll just make it worse."

"Stubborn," Amelia said. I agreed.

Aiden and Gage were both stubborn, though I had to admit I didn't really understand what was wrong between them in the first place. *Not my business*, I reminded myself.

Amelia spoke up again, "I won't talk to Aiden if you put that work away for a little while and play cards with us."

Gage closed his laptop. "Fine," he said.

Amelia popped up from her spot on the couch, saying, "I'll go get us a snack tray."

"We just had breakfast," I protested. At least Mrs. W or Abel would make sure whatever was on the snack tray was allowed on Amelia's diet.

Gage arranged his papers, stacked them on the laptop and set his work on a table near the door. Turning around, he gave me a long look, his eyes scanning me from head to toe, bringing the blush back to my cheeks.

Amelia would be back any second. It was bad enough that there was something going on between Gage and myself. If Amelia found out—I didn't want to think about it.

Gage crossed his arms over his chest and said laughingly, "Spitballs? You can't control her at all, can you?"

Relief speared through me. Eventually, we would have to face what had happened the night before, and two days before that in the kitchen. But not now. Not in the middle of the day when Amelia would come strolling through the door any second.

I shrugged. "It's not my job to control her," I clarified. "My job is to keep her healthy and keep her company. And sometimes keeping her company involves spitballs. At least today, it did. Believe me, if you knew some of the ideas I managed to stop..." I shook my head.

Amelia strode in, interrupting me. "Sophie is no fun," she said, sending me an affectionate smile to soften her criticism.

Gage raised one eyebrow at her. "Sophie is an angel for putting up with you," he said.

"That's true," Amelia agreed. "Aside from just being with my family again, Sophie has been the best part of moving home."

My heart ached at her words. Amelia was a handful, no question, but I loved her. Knowing she felt the same way warmed my heart.

This was why I hadn't moved on to a job more suited to my skills. Amelia was the closest thing to family I'd had in a long time. I wanted to savor it for as long as it lasted. My heart brimming with affection, I watched as Amelia crossed the room and made herself comfortable in an armchair, neatly arranging things so Gage and I would have to sit together on the couch.

Affection turned to exasperation. At the twinkle in her light blue eyes as she observed Gage and I standing awkwardly beside the coffee table, I realized Amelia hadn't missed a thing.

"I'll get the cards," I said, resigned. I couldn't make a fuss about sitting next to Gage or Amelia would call me on it. I retrieved a pack of cards from a drawer in one of the end tables and turned back to the couch to find Gage sitting almost in the middle. If we were going to play cards on the coffee table, I'd have to sit right next to him.

Both of them had expressions of innocence, which was enough to tell me that they were up to something. I had the unmistakable sense of being maneuvered by masters.

I still hadn't figured out what I wanted to do about Gage, so I resolved to ignore the situation for the rest of the day. That proved both easy and impossible.

Easy because Gage and Amelia made it so, picking a card game and dealing the cards, keeping everything light-hearted and friendly. We had fun until lunch, laughing and joking, and trying to catch Amelia cheating. Gage almost always spotted it.

I never did, mostly because I was impossibly distracted by Gage sitting beside me. Every time his hand grazed my arm, I had to fight a shiver. When he tangled his right foot with my left, I started in surprise, only to see the glint in his eye and realize that he was teasing me. I tried to pretend I was unaffected by his presence, but I don't think I pulled it off.

After lunch, Gage disappeared into his suite with his papers and laptop. It was still too cold and drizzly to go outside, so I drove Amelia to Phipps Plaza where we window shopped for a few hours. Well, I window shopped. Amelia actually bought things.

It would've been a completely normal day, if it hadn't been for the presence of Gage, woven through the hours like bright spots. The flash of his smile, a touch of the back of my hand. It was a little scary how much I wanted to see him, the way my heart jumped in my chest when his eyes met mine.

My protests to myself were growing weaker. Getting involved with Gage Winters was inappropriate and foolish.

Every time I looked in his eyes, I was less sure I cared. Something was happening between us, and I wanted to see where it would go.

Yet again, I fell asleep with relative ease and woke gasping for breath, tangled in my sheets, my heart racing as if I were being chased. Which I had been, in my dreams.

Lost in the dark and running from Anthony. That had never happened in real life. In real life, I'd been too scared to run. His anger was explosive when I did nothing to earn it. The few times I'd tried to leave him... I'd learned my lesson.

The thought of actually running in Anthony's presence brought a sense of dread. *He's dead*, I reminded myself. *He's dead*, and it was just another bad dream.

I got out of bed and straightened the covers, erasing the evidence of my troubled sleep. My hair had come loose from its braid, and I ran my fingers through it, thought about putting it back up, and then decided I needed tea more than anything.

The house was dark and silent when I left my room. No light flickered from the library fire. I was alone. I tried not to be disappointed. If Gage was in his room, it might mean he was sleeping, and that was good. I didn't want him to be up all night, even if it meant I'd be with him. Neither of us had gotten much rest the night before.

There was no reason to feel let down. We hadn't made any arrangement to meet. That was a step I wasn't ready to take.

My mind on Gage, and on a cup of tea, and whether I wanted a snack to go with the tea, I didn't see the shadow move in the hall between Aiden's office and the library until I was almost on top of it.

I turned in greeting, a smile curving my lips, only to see the shadowy figure stop short in shock. I barely had time to register that whoever it was, they were too short to be Gage or Aiden and not broad enough to be Abel.

The intruder lunged across the space separating us. I opened my mouth to scream, and everything went dark.

Chapter Fifteen

Gage

I needed to sleep. I'd barely slept the night before, though laying on the couch in the library, Sophie in my arms—the sweet and sultry scent of her, the silk of her skin under my hands—had been light years from the punishing insomnia I was used to.

I could've lain with her like that forever, her legs tangled with mine, her body relaxed and languid. She'd drifted in and out of sleep, her fingers stroking my chest, her breath warm through my shirt as she dozed and woke and we whispered about everything and nothing.

If I could have that back, maybe I wouldn't notice that I was awake. I tried to go to sleep. I did. After dinner, I'd hit the gym in the basement for two hours, trying to wear myself out.

It didn't work. I lay in bed for an hour, staring at the ceiling, before giving up and going to my desk. If I couldn't sleep, I'd get some work done.

I'd rather hunt Sophie down and talk myself into her bed. I wasn't doing that. Sophie hadn't told me much about her marriage, but from Aiden's comment and small things she'd said here and there, I had the feeling she'd had enough of pressure and coercion to last a lifetime.

I wanted her.

After spending the morning with her and Amelia, listening to her laugh and her dry sense of humor, I knew this was more than lust.

I wanted more than her body. I wanted everything that was Sophie to be mine. If I pushed her into something she wasn't sure she wanted, I'd never get close.

I could be patient. Sophie was worth it.

I worked at my desk for hours, watching midnight come and go, hearing Aiden come home. The beep of the alarm being deactivated and then turned back on, the thuds of his feet on the stairs.

He sounded tired. I thought about leaning into the hall, saying something. Anything. Asking him if he wanted to share a beer. How his trip had gone.

I stayed where I was. Aiden was another one who just needed time. My cousin could be a stubborn fuck. No one knew that as well as I did.

I was just as stubborn. Eventually, he would give in and stop being such an asshole. Nothing was more important to Aiden than family. He wouldn't be able to hold out against me forever.

I was studying a spreadsheet and the accompanying report when I heard a sound that had every hair on my body standing straight up.

A scream. Muffled, then cut off, but definitely a scream.

I was on my feet before the sound died out. I grabbed my 9mm and was through the door a second later, gun in hand, my mind calmly sifting through scenarios as I ran down the stairs.

It had been a woman's scream. The only two women in

the house were Sophie and Amelia. Mrs. W slept in her cottage, a few hundred yards from the main house. I would've heard her deactivate the alarm if she'd come in.

Amelia slept like a rock, and it was unlikely she'd be out of bed. If she'd screamed in her room, I wouldn't have heard it in my suite, so odds were the scream came from Sophie.

I ignored the chill in my gut at the thought that something had happened to Sophie. Fear and hesitation wouldn't help. I had to stay focused until I found her.

I didn't have to look far.

Sophie's crumpled body lay outside the door of the wine room, right between the library and Aiden's office, her silvery hair spilling across the dark hardwood floor, her white robe glowing in the moonlight streaming in from the hall windows.

I wanted to go straight to her, but I didn't have time. I flicked on the light and gave her a quick, searching glance. No blood.

Her eyes fluttered open, and she whispered, "Gage?"

"Don't move, Angel. Stay right there for me, okay?"

She blinked again, a look of confusion on her face. She was conscious, which was good, but it was clear she wasn't sure what had happened. I'd deal with that later.

"Don't move," I ordered, again. I couldn't take care of Sophie until I was sure she was safe. As quickly as I could, I checked the library, wine room and office.

Empty.

I jogged down the hall and checked Charlie's unoccupied suite, then Sophie's room. Both were empty. I carefully swung open the door to Amelia's room to find her fast asleep and undisturbed.

Whoever had hurt Sophie, they were probably long gone, and I wasn't willing to leave her for another second.

I'd verified there was no immediate threat. Now, Sophie was my priority.

Kneeling beside her I was relieved to see her chest rise and fall in deep even breaths.

"What happened?" she asked, in a whisper.

"I don't know yet," I said, running my hands over her body, making sure she didn't have any broken bones or hidden bleeding. She winced when my fingers slid over the rising knot on the back of her head, but otherwise, she seemed unharmed.

I flicked on the safety and shoved my gun in my belt. Scooping Sophie into my arms, I rose and strode down the hall to the stairs.

"Gage, what are you doing?"

"Taking you to Aiden. Do you remember what happened?"

Her eyes squinted up at me as if she were thinking. Speaking slowly, she said, "Someone was in the house. I came down the hall, and there was somebody there. I knew it wasn't you or Aiden or Abel. Too short. And then –" She trailed off and blinked. "Did you find anyone?"

"No," I said, striding up the stairs with her held securely to my chest. I wanted to run, but I wasn't going to bounce her head around any more than I had to. "Did you get a good look at him?"

"It was dark, and it all went so fast. I saw him; I'm pretty sure it was a man. He wasn't as tall as you, but he was tall. Then I realized there was a stranger in the house and... He must've hit me."

"It's okay," I reassured her. "As soon as I make sure you're safe with Aiden, I'm going to search the house."

"Should we call the police?" she asked, eyebrows pulled together from the pain in her head.

"No. I'll talk to Aiden, but we don't want to call the police over something like this. Word would get out, and we'd have the media parked at the end of the drive for weeks. Not worth it."

I reached Aiden's door and kicked it a few times with one foot, giving him a little warning before we interrupted his sleep. Balancing Sophie's weight on one arm, I turned the handle and shoved the door open.

Aiden was stumbling through the bedroom door into the sitting room, dressed in a pair of boxers and nothing else. Before he could talk, I said, "Go get dressed. Someone was in the house, and they hit Sophie. I need you to watch her while I do a search."

Aiden's eyes widened in shock, but he'd already turned back into his room to grab clothes. A minute later he reappeared, wearing his discarded dress shirt over a pair of athletic shorts. Staring at Sophie, still cradled in my arms, he said, "Is she alright?"

I settled her onto the couch in Aiden's sitting room. "Looks like just a bump on the head, and I don't think there was any loss of consciousness, but I'll check her out more thoroughly after I search the house. He's probably long gone."

Aiden looked to the door of his suite, at the discreetly placed alarm panel beside it. All the lights were red, indicating the alarm was set. "The alarm is still on," Aiden said, looking from me to Sophie, and back to the red lights glowing on the wall.

"I know." I pulled my gun from the small of my back and started out the suite, saying over my shoulder, "Lock the door behind me. I won't be long."

That was optimistic. Winters House covered four floors and was over seventeen thousand square feet. I couldn't search the whole thing by myself. At least not quickly.

I didn't bother with the second level or the attics. The only way to get up there was the main staircase. I'd been between Sophie and that staircase after she screamed, and no one had passed me in the dark.

Winters House was built in a square around the central courtyard, but the front side was bisected by the driveway and gate at the front of the house, creating dead ends out of both Sophie's hallway and the mirror hallway on the other side of the house where Jacob and Annalise's suites were. If the intruder had hit Sophie outside the door of the library and Aiden's office, there was only one place he could've gone without my seeing him.

The basement.

CHAPTER SIXTEEN
GAGE

I strode down the hall to the library, turning on lights as I went. I had a feeling the intruder was long gone, but I wasn't going to give him any convenient shadows to hide in.

The library appeared undisturbed, neatly straightened since our card game, the pillows fluffed, the blankets carefully folded. Not a thing was out of place and the door in the far corner, carefully concealed to look like part of the wood paneling, was securely shut.

Standing before the door, I examined it for any evidence of tampering. The staircase from the library to the hall outside the theater room below wasn't a secret, per se. It was on the plans of the house and most of our close friends and frequent visitors knew it was there. On the opposite side of the house, a similar discrete door and staircase connected the laundry room to the hall by the kitchen storage room.

Those two staircases were the only ways to enter the lower level, though the staircase on the kitchen side of the house was used more often. It was wider, better lit, and easier to access.

This door, in the library, was built into the paneling, nearly invisible if you didn't already know it was there. My great-grandfather had liked the idea of a secret passageway. It was impossible to open unless you knew the trick. Unfortunately, a lot of people knew the trick.

Crossing the room to the fireplace, I slid my fingers into a groove under the marble mantelpiece and pushed. A quiet click sounded. Behind me, the door to the staircase swung open. The lights in the library illuminated the first few feet of the secret passage.

I paused for a moment in the doorway, listening. Nothing. I flipped the light switch beside the door and started into the passage. Brass sconces with flickering bulbs lined the curved stairwell, giving it the look of a dungeon staircase in an old school horror flick.

Normally, I thought it was cool. Hunting an intruder in my house, I was annoyed by the way the steep, curving stairs cut off my sight lines and slowed my descent.

I knew how to move in complete silence. With every step, my ears strained for a hint that the intruder was still in the house.

Nothing.

If this guy was smart, he'd taken off the second Sophie had screamed. He was getting in and out of Winters House without setting off the alarm so he couldn't be stupid.

I reached the bottom of the staircase and stepped into the hallway that ran the length of the basement of Winters House. Empty. The doors to the theater room, immediately to my left, were closed, just as I'd left them the day before.

Further down the hall, the double doors to the gym were open, also as I'd left them. As it always was, the door to the storage room was shut. I jogged up the stairs at that end of the hall to check the laundry room. Empty and undisturbed.

I wanted to get back to Sophie. I needed to make sure she was all right. I was almost positive she was. She hadn't been unconscious, and the hit probably hadn't been hard enough to give her a concussion, but I needed to see for myself.

I didn't like leaving her alone with Aiden.

It wasn't jealousy.

It wasn't.

Aiden couldn't protect her like I could. He didn't have my training. He could handle a weapon. We all could. I knew he regularly used the Sinclair's range to keep his skills sharp, but occasional target shooting wasn't the same as over a decade in special forces. Someone had hurt Sophie, and I needed to make sure she was safe.

Me, not Aiden.

First, I had to search the basement. Logically, this was the only place the intruder could have gone after he hit Sophie.

Methodically, I searched the kitchen storage room, marveling at the sheer amount of stuff Mrs. W had packed away to decorate, feed, and maintain Winters House. There were shelves of canned goods, extra kitchen equipment, and stacks of linens, neatly folded and wrapped in clear plastic. Two entire shelves of vases for flower arrangements.

I'd grown up in this house, but I'd spent more than a third of my life living in army barracks and in conditions that made the barracks look like Winters House. No wonder I was having trouble adjusting to being home.

No one hid in the storage room. Ditto for the gym and the theater room. Frustrated, I made my way back upstairs, turning off lights as I went. I did a second check of all the rooms on the first floor and found nothing. Amelia still slept soundly, and the other rooms remained dark and empty just as they'd been the first time I checked.

Fuck.

Frustrated, I went to the kitchen to grab a bag of frozen peas from the freezer before jogging back up the stairs. I entered Aiden's suite without knocking. He sat in a chair beside the couch, talking quietly to Sophie. They looked way too cozy together.

"Did you find anything?" Sophie asked.

"Nothing." Ignoring Aiden, I crossed the room and crouched beside her. "How's your head?"

Sophie tried to force a smile, but the lines bracketing her mouth and the furrow between her eyebrows told me she was afraid and in pain.

"Aiden gave me some ibuprofen," she said weakly.

Sliding my hand behind her neck, I lifted her head carefully, placing the bag of frozen peas behind it. "Any blurry vision, nausea, loss of consciousness?"

"No, I'm okay," Sophie said.

I flicked my eyes to Aiden for confirmation. He gave me a short nod. It was likely she didn't have a concussion, but that knot on the back of her head was going to hurt like hell. Rising from my crouch, I nudged Sophie deeper into the cushions and sat on the edge of the couch, taking her hand in mine.

I couldn't forget the sight of her, crumpled on the floor, the look of confusion in her eyes as she stared up at me. The thought that she'd been hurt in my house, under my protection, was intolerable.

Aiden watched us with an inscrutable expression.

Abruptly, I lost my patience.

"What did Cooper say about the alarm? This has to be the same person we heard in the library a few days ago. When the hell is Cooper getting out here to check the system?"

It wasn't like the Sinclairs to put us off. Our fathers had been best friends, and they were like family. Usually, if any of us had a problem, we shot straight to the top of their list.

Aiden's eyes fixed on my hand holding Sophie's, my thumb stroking her knuckles gently. Without looking at me, he said, "I didn't call him."

I exploded off the couch, dropping Sophie's hand. "What the fuck do you mean you didn't call him? I told you there was someone in the house. I told you I heard something."

It took everything I had not to throw a punch at Aiden's smug face. He sat there, arms crossed over his chest, and watched me with an appraising look as if he were waiting for something.

Probably for me to lose it—to start screaming, or jump him, or do something equally unhinged. I wanted to. God damn, I really wanted to. Adrenaline surged through my body, lighting my nerves on fire, demanding I act.

Aiden would've deserved every punishment I could mete out.

"Gage," Sophie said, the low, smooth, sweet tones of her voice calming me, soothing me just enough to remind me of all the reasons I didn't want to beat the shit out of my cousin.

Well, not *didn't want to*. More like shouldn't. The first of which was it would probably scare the crap out of Sophie. She'd been through enough for one night.

Curling my hands into fists, I did my best to get myself under control. I hated this. This volatility wasn't me. I didn't

155

have a temper. I was analytical and contained. Ice cold under pressure.

Tremors shook my muscles—adrenaline overload with nowhere to go. I paced to the closed door of Aiden's suite and stood there, my back to Aiden and Sophie. I took a deep breath. Then another.

When I thought I could carry on a conversation with Aiden—without killing him—I turned back and said, "Explain yourself. I told you we heard someone in the house. You said you would call Cooper and get the alarm checked. Then you left town. You left us unprotected."

Aiden had the grace to look ashamed, if only for a second. Sitting forward, he braced his elbows on his knees and leaned close to Sophie. My fist itched to put a few more feet between them.

"Sophie, I'm very sorry if anything I did or didn't do contributed to you getting hurt. I should've called Cooper."

"I'm okay," Sophie said.

But what the hell else was she going to say? I knew her well enough by now to know Sophie wouldn't complain. She definitely wouldn't accuse her employer of almost getting her killed.

I reclaimed my place on the couch, crowding Sophie further back into the cushions and taking her hand in mine again. The touch of her skin grounded me, reminding me what was important.

This bullshit tension between Aiden and myself was not the point. My unreasonable jealousy whenever Aiden got close to Sophie was not the point.

The bump on her head and the intruder in our home – they were the priority.

"Why didn't you call Cooper?" I asked, slowly and evenly.

Aiden gave me a long, measuring look before he said, "You've been erratic since you got home."

"You thought I made it up?" I asked in disbelief. "I was standing right there when Sophie said she heard the sound, too. Was she making it up?"

She squeezed my hand, and I knew she didn't want me dragging her into the argument. I gave her a squeeze back and said, "All you had to do was call Cooper."

"You both said nothing had been disturbed," Aiden said, finally looking a little uncomfortable. "This is a big house, and it's old. It makes noises at night."

I gritted my teeth, fighting off the rage flooding me, threatening to send me off balance. Aiden had called me erratic. He wasn't wrong but damned if I was going to prove him right. Especially not in front of Sophie.

As calmly as I could manage, I said, "I grew up here. I know the house makes sounds. All houses make sounds. That's not what we heard."

"It didn't sound like you heard much of anything," Aiden shot back. "Not enough to justify a complete overhaul of the security system."

"Someone was in this house," I said, slowly, as if explaining algebra to a toddler. "Someone bypassed our alarm system and got in this house. They hit Sophie over the head. Do you have any idea what could've happened to her? Think about it for a second. Unless you think *I* hit her?"

I threw that last part out more in frustration than anything else. I wasn't expecting Aiden's pause.

Son of a bitch.

I hadn't been myself since I got home. That was true. But I'd never hit a woman in my life, and I sure as hell wasn't going to start with Sophie.

Sophie made a sound of distress in the back of her throat and started to sit up. My hand shot out and pressed her shoulder back. I stroked a thumb across her cheekbone and murmured, "Keep your head still, Angel. It'll hurt less if you let those peas stay where they are."

In a strained voice, she said, "It wasn't Gage. Gage would never hurt me, but it wasn't him. I couldn't see much, but he was shorter than both of you and thinner than Abel."

Our cook was a few inches shy of six feet and built like the proverbial brick shit house. Abel made ample use of the basement gym, and it showed.

Finally, Aiden said, "I'm sorry. I should've called Cooper. I take it you didn't find a sign of anyone."

"No. Nothing." Looking down at Sophie, I said to her, "I'm taking you back to bed. I don't think that bump is bad enough for a trip to the hospital, but you need to rest."

"I thought you weren't supposed to sleep after you get hit in the head, in case you have a concussion," Aiden said.

"That's an old wives tale," I said. Carefully, I lifted Sophie from the couch, leaving the bag of peas. I'd get a new one from the kitchen after I got her to her room. "Call Cooper now. Have him send a guy over to watch the house for the rest of the night. I'm staying with Sophie."

"You don't have to—" she started to say.

I silenced her with a kiss to the top of her head and said, "I'm not leaving you alone right now. Deal with it."

I had Sophie settled in bed a few minutes later, a dish towel wrapped ice pack under her head.

"I'm not going to be able to sleep," she said, worrying her lower lip between her teeth. I toed off my shoes and stretched out beside her, taking her hand in mine and wrapping both of our arms around her waist.

"That's okay. Just rest."

She drifted off a few minutes later in the middle of a story about the time Aiden, Jacob, Vance, and I had tricked Holden and Tate into the secret staircase and locked them in. We'd all gotten grounded, but it had been worth it.

Apparently, the story was less entertaining in the retelling. When Sophie relaxed, her eyes slid shut and she was out.

Not long after, I heard the beep of the alarm system deactivating, the familiar creak of the front door swinging open, and low voices. I thought about going out there, briefing whoever Cooper had sent over.

I didn't move. The situation was simple, and Aiden was more than equipped to explain it. I wasn't leaving Sophie's side until morning.

CHAPTER SEVENTEEN
SOPHIE

T ran through the dark halls of Winters House, fleeing the nightmare that stalked me. The walls extended before me, wreathed in shadows, stretching longer and longer as I ran. In the distance, firelight glowed in the library.

If I could get to the library, I would be safe.

I don't know why I was so certain of that, but I knew it to my soul. Feet pounded behind me, hands reaching. I ran faster, my legs wobbling with fatigue, lungs burning. The longer I ran, the further the hall stretched, the firelight drifting away.

In the distance, I saw Gage. I cried out, calling his name. My voice was sucked into the vacuum of air around me, silent a moment after it left my mouth.

Fingers grazed the back of my shoulder, hooking in the collar of my robe. I screamed again, twisting free and running faster. Harder. For a second, it seemed like I was making progress. I passed a window in the hall, then another, moonlight spilling over the fountain in the courtyard.

How many windows were between my room and the library? Two? Three? In this fun house mirror of a hallway, it looked like a hundred.

The hand closed over my wrist, wrenching me back, spinning me on my heel and throwing me off balance. I landed hard, my head bouncing off the wood floor, screaming in terror as Anthony loomed above me.

I knew that carefully blank expression. The icy look in his eyes. I'd seen it before, far too many times. I rolled to the side and scrambled to my knees, ready to launch my body forward like a sprinter at the starting line.

Muscles coiled, I propelled myself away, that flicker of firelight and Gage's shadow my goal, my finish line. If I could just get to the end of the hall I'd be safe.

With a burst of exhilarated relief, I flew forward, only to feel the belt of my robe cut hard into my stomach as a hand yanked me back. I fell face first and rolled to face Anthony. As he had been so many nights before, he was silent, his fury channeled through his fists. And, as I *never* had before, instead of laying there, mute and terrified, I screamed. I screamed out my rage and my pain and my fear.

Arms flailing, legs kicking, I fought with everything I had. I was done being his victim. He was dead, I was free, and I wasn't going back. Anthony would have to kill me first.

His blows never landed. I felt my hands striking flesh, fingers closing around my wrists, but there was no pain. He wasn't hitting me. Why wasn't he hitting me?

A voice echoed in my ear, rough and insistent. Calming. "Sophie. Sophie, Angel, wake up. It's okay."

"No! Let me go. Let me go."

Heavy weight settled over my legs, pinning me down.

Strong fingers held my wrists together, pressing them down into my chest. An arm wrapped around my back, rolling me into a long, hard body. Lips grazed my ear, and a familiar voice said, "Sophie, I've got you. I've got you. You're safe. Wake up. You can wake up now."

Finally, I did. I opened my eyes to find myself wrapped in a cocoon of Gage, his leg over mine, his arm around me, holding me close.

I looked up at him, words crowding my mind. "What are you doing here?" I asked, settling for the least confusing and humiliating question.

Releasing my wrists, Gage lifted a hand to smooth damp strands of hair back off my face. "I couldn't sleep. I was checking the house, and I heard you scream." He stroked gentle fingers over my cheek. "Are your nightmares usually that bad?"

I looked away. Of all the people I'd known in my life, Gage was the only one who would understand. He had his own demons, memories that haunted him and stole his sleep. He knew what it was like to wake in the middle of the night, heart pounding, filled with terror.

But Gage had been a soldier. He'd earned his demons because he was brave and because he put himself at risk to protect the innocent, to do what he thought was right. All I'd done was marry the wrong man and then find myself unable to leave him. Not exactly heroic stuff.

The callused pad of his thumb smoothed over my cheekbone, wiping away a tear. Gage said, "You don't have to talk about it, but I want to know if you want to tell me."

Unable to meet his eyes, I pressed my forehead to his chest. When I finally worked up the nerve to speak, it was in halting whispers.

"He used to hit me. I never knew when. Or why. He would just be there, so angry, and start hitting me until he was done. He said he had a darkness inside him and the only way to hold it back was to give it to me."

I heard what I'd said, and a sob choked my throat. It was pathetic. I was pathetic. How could I have married him? How had I not seen what he was?

Knowing Gage was probably wondering why I'd stayed with Anthony, I tried to explain, "I wanted to get away. I tried. He wasn't like that when I married him. He was sweet and attentive. Charming. Then we were married, and he wanted me to quit my job at the hospital. It was important to him, so I did. Then he wanted us to move. He bought a house without asking me, far out in the country on so much land. There was nowhere to walk to. I didn't have a car. And he had security. A guard. He said it was for my protection."

"Why did you need protection living out in the country?"

"Anthony said it was his job. That he needed the peace and quiet to relax, but he wanted to be sure I had protection when he was away."

"What kind of job did he have that he thought his wife needed protection?" Gage asked.

"He was an accountant," I said quietly. Gage was silent. I knew it didn't add up. The luxury cars, the huge house in the country, the 24/7 security. "I didn't see how weird it all was until we were married. Before that, he was very careful to only show me what he wanted me to see. And when I tried to leave, the guards always brought me back."

"Did they hurt you?" Gage asked in a careful, measured tone. His muscles had gone tight, his heart beating faster in his chest, thudding beneath my cheek. He didn't like what I was telling him. Neither did I.

"No. Never. They didn't even speak to me. I think Anthony forbade it. They just brought me back and told Anthony. After the second time, I stopped trying. Anthony was so angry. I realized he wouldn't take me to the hospital and—"

I couldn't say it. I couldn't tell Gage that I'd been afraid my husband would kill me in a fit of rage and I'd end up buried in the woods behind our house, my body forgotten and abandoned in the cold dirt.

"How did he die?" Gage asked.

"A car accident." Car accidents weren't usually considered good luck, but in my case, it had been a gift. Freedom. A second chance.

"Did he—" Gage cleared his throat. "Did he—"

Gage couldn't get the word out, but I knew what he was asking. Slowly, I said, "No. No, Gage. He barely touched me. I think he had other women for that. He didn't want children. At first, I thought maybe there was something wrong with me, and later I was just glad. Looking back, I think he just didn't see me that way. I was there to take care of him. To cook for him, to belong to him. To hold back his darkness. But he didn't want me for sex."

"How often do you have nightmares like this?" Gage asked, his voice gruff.

"This bad? Once a week, maybe twice. Less often than I used to."

"Did you ever see anyone after your marriage? A therapist or counselor?"

"No," I whispered. "I should, but I don't want to talk about it."

"You're talking to me," he said quietly.

A tear slid down my cheek, and I whispered, so quietly it was little more than a breath, "I'm ashamed."

"No, Angel, you don't have anything to be ashamed of. No one is going to judge you. It's been two years, and you still can't sleep. You can't go on like this. You need to talk to someone."

He combed his fingers through my hair, smoothing it away from my face and down my back. He did it again, his fingers rubbing my scalp, petting me. I wanted to purr. The fear from the nightmare was gone. I don't think I'd ever felt that protected, with Gage curled around me, stroking me, soothing me.

Maybe that was why I felt brave enough to flatten my palm against his chest, meet his eyes, and say, "I will if you will."

He stared at me in surprise. Feeling daring, I went on, "You have nightmares too, don't you? Isn't that why you can't sleep?"

Gage nodded, his eyes locked on mine.

"Are yours always the same thing?" I asked. "Mine are. Always some version of Anthony chasing me until he catches me. I run, and I run, but I never get away."

Gage's eyes searched my face, looking for something. He must've found it because he said, his voice barely more than a whisper, "Not always exactly the same. Sometimes it's the explosion when they took me. I can't get my team clear and they all die. Sometimes it's things that happened while they had me. Things they did. Sometimes it's finding my aunt and uncle."

"Have you always had those? The dreams about your aunt and uncle?"

"For a year or two after they died, I'd dream about them.

Those dreams stopped for years. I don't remember dreaming much at all until the last six months. Sometimes I think—" He stopped.

"What? Sometimes you think what?" I prodded, afraid of what he was going to say.

"It's not what you think it's going to be," he said slowly, lost in memory. "They grabbed me after an explosion, an IED, that was supposed to kill most of my team. They weren't after me specifically, they just wanted leverage. Any one of us would've done. My head was all wrapped up in making sure my team got clear, making sense of what was happening in the dust and the noise.

"Then they grabbed me, took me to their base and came at me with threats and ultimatums. And you think that's what it's going to be. The shouting and the pain. But then they throw you in a cell and leave you there. Alone. You think it's going to be all about the torture, but the boredom is almost as bad.

"Sometimes I think that's what knocked something loose in my head. All those long stretches of nothing and then *boom*. I'd be tied to a chair, and there'd be a camera, and they'd be trying to get me to confess to... Whatever they wanted that day. And everything inside me would focus on just not dying, just not talking, and then I'd wake up back in the cell, and I'd wait."

A sob of sheer relief broke free in my chest. *He knew.* Gage knew something I never thought I'd be able to put into words. It wasn't just the pain; it wasn't just the randomness of the attacks. It was the long stretches of isolated boredom in between.

It was the waiting that made you crazy.

I'd had a beautiful house, but in the end, it hadn't been much better than Gage's cell. I'd been alone. No one to talk to. No Internet. No telephone. No friends. Endless days alone interspersed with sudden, terrifying violence. I never in my life thought I'd find another person who understood what that was like, the way it warped your sense of reality.

"Angel, don't cry. Please, don't cry."

His thumb rubbed the tears from my cheek, and I said through hitching breaths, "I'm okay. I'm okay. It's just... *You know*. You know what it was like. The way it gets in your head and –"

His arm tightened around me, and his lips dropped to my forehead, rubbing my skin as he said, "I know, Angel. I know."

I don't know how long we lay there, Gage holding me against him, our legs tangled, my tears soaking his T-shirt as he stroked my cheek and ran his fingers through my hair.

He only spoke once. "I'll go if you go. I'll talk to Cooper. He's got someone on staff. Those guys see some shit in their jobs, and he has a lot of ex-military. He'll have some names for me. He'll probably be able to suggest someone for you. I don't want you to live like this anymore, with these nightmares, remembering what he did to you." Before I could speak, Gage went on, "I don't want to live like this anymore either. I want my life back."

"Okay," I said, winding my arm around his back and stroking my fingers down his spine.

He'd go if I'd go. I'd spent so long living in fear, but I'd been willing to accept a lesser version of it as normal. As safety. But it wasn't normal. As long as Anthony could stalk me in my sleep, I'd never truly feel safe.

I relaxed against Gage, letting him surround me, sinking into the feel of his fingers in my hair, his hard chest beneath my cheek, the muscles of his back under my hand. I don't know when it changed. When those strokes on my skin shifted from soothing to sensual.

I don't remember deciding to reach up and pull his face to mine. I just remember his mouth, gentle at first, then opening, his tongue stroking mine, his body shifting to press me back into the mattress, rising above me.

CHAPTER EIGHTEEN

SOPHIE

He kissed me like that forever. Long, drugging kisses that had my head spinning. Then he was on top of me, settled between my legs, his fingers on the top button of my white nightgown. I tried to sit up, and he raised his head, his blue eyes hot on mine when he said, "Don't move. I don't want you to hurt your head."

"My head doesn't hurt," I lied. I'd gotten so used to the dull ache from the bump on my head I was almost able to ignore it. I'd spent most of the day in bed, despite insisting that I was fine, outvoted by every single person in the household. Hell must have frozen over because even Mrs. W and Amelia had agreed I belonged in bed.

Gage shook his head. "If you think you can lay still, I'm going to undo this button. Then I'm going to undo the next one. And the one after that. But if you're going to move..."

I opened my mouth to argue, then abruptly snapped it shut. What the heck was I fighting about? Did I really want Gage to stop? I knew if I did, he would. All I had to do was tell him I wasn't interested, or I needed time, and he would back off.

In answer, I settled back into the pillows, a smug little smile playing across my lips as Gage slipped free the first tiny, faux pearl button. My nightgown, like my others, was made of sheer white cotton, trimmed in lace. It wasn't sexy, by any means, but it wasn't the virginal white flannel Anthony had made me wear.

It wasn't seductive, but it was pretty. Feminine. This one had a row of buttons from the scooped neck line to below my waist. So many tiny buttons and Gage was undoing them, one by one.

He lay between my legs, propped up on one elbow, his eyes fixed on the inches of skin he was baring, button by button. When he reached the bottom of my rib cage, I was sure he would fold the nightgown back to reveal my breasts, but he didn't.

He traced a finger along the inner swell of one breast, sliding it beneath the cotton to stroke my warm skin. A low hum of appreciation sounded in his throat before he withdrew his hand from the nightgown and went back to the buttons.

He slid down a few inches, putting his face level with my breastbone, and turned a little on his side so he could reach the last of the buttons, just below my belly button. Finally, *finally*, he folded the nightgown back, carefully, precisely, baring my breasts to his hot blue gaze.

"Sophie," he breathed. That was it. Just, *Sophie*. Then, a little louder, his voice gravelly and strained, he said, "If you change your mind just tell me to stop, okay? Just tell me, and I'll stop."

I didn't want him to stop. I couldn't imagine ever wanting him to stop. I wanted him to speed up, not stop. My nipples had drawn into tight beads under his eyes, my breasts swollen and hot, needing his touch. I shifted restlessly beneath him, and his eyes flashed at mine.

I saw a quick, mischievous grin before he murmured, "Don't move and I'll give you what you want."

I tried. I swear, I really tried. But as his hot mouth closed over one nipple and his finger teased the other, I just couldn't. I arched my chest, pressing my breast harder into his hand, rising to the heated suction of his mouth, the flick of his tongue against the tortured peak.

I heard myself gasp and moan. My knees lifted, legs wrapping around his body. I whimpered his name. I may have begged a little. He only switched sides, scraping his teeth against my skin, sending shards of pleasure arcing through my body.

When he lifted his head and said, "I'm taking this off," I was so out of my head I had no idea what he was talking about. He tugged on the cotton pooled around my waist, and I understood. My nightgown. He wanted to take my nightgown off. Hallelujah. It was about time.

"You too," I said, eyeing his T-shirt and pants. I wanted his skin against mine.

"Don't move," he reminded me.

I narrowed my eyes at him. "My head feels fine."

"Humor me," he said. Sliding his hands beneath the nightgown, over my shoulders, he peeled it down my arms, tugging it off beneath me, urging me to raise my hips just a little. Hooking his fingers in my panties, he drew them down along with my nightgown. He eased off the end of the bed, taking the nightgown with him, and I watched with wide eyes as he stripped off his own clothes.

At the sight of his aroused, naked body, my mouth went dry. Gage was beautiful. Strong and tall and imperfectly perfect with scars on his smooth skin and all those gorgeous muscles. My eyes took in his erect cock and skated nervously away. I'd never really seen one, an erection, up close like this. Anthony had been a strictly *in the dark missionary* kind of guy, over and done before I could really pay attention.

Gage's cock was a thing of beauty, long and thick, standing proudly. It was enticing, and a little scary. I hadn't expected it to be so intimidating. My brain said it wasn't going to fit, but my body was more than willing to give it a try.

Then he was back on the bed, but he only came halfway up, stopping with his shoulders pressing my knees wide, his face between my legs. I started to sit up, tried to put my hand there to block him, suddenly embarrassed and awkward. I knew what he wanted to do. At least I thought I did. I'd read about it, but no one had ever—I hadn't really imagined.

Before I could get my thoughts together, Gage's hand closed over mine, and he eased it back, baring my body to him.

"Do you want me to stop?" he asked.

Before I could get my head together enough to answer, he pressed a kiss right there, right on the center of all my need, all my pent up desire. I shuddered with the illicit pleasure. I'd never imagined being kissed there, but now that Gage had, I wanted him to do it again.

He pulled back and rose up above me, his eyes on mine. "I'll stop if you want me to, but I think you should trust me. Can you do that?"

His lips touched mine, and I tasted myself on him. I was done with thinking. Done with being embarrassed or afraid. I nodded. Gage settled back between my legs.

I tried to brace myself for what was coming, but I had

no clue. His tongue traced me, taking his time. He wasn't in a rush, or racing to some end goal, trying to make me come so he could get his.

Gage explored me, tasting, teasing me until I was writhing against the pillows, gasping from the rising tension. When he closed his lips over my clit and sucked, the crash of pleasure took me by surprise, and I cried out, rolling my hips into his mouth. He murmured his approval against me, the rub of his lips drawing out my orgasm.

He pressed his cheek to my thigh, stroking my legs as the tremors in my muscles calmed, and I caught my breath. Just when I was sure he'd move over me, one long finger slid inside, parting my heated flesh, filling me.

I had the fleeting thought that if one finger felt like that, there was no way he would fit. He proved me wrong when a second finger joined the first, smoothly pumping in and out, his fingertips grazing something inside that sent hot shivers up my spine, had me rocking into him, taking his fingers deeper and harder.

I was panting, calling his name, every nerve in my body wound tight with blissful tension when, finally, he withdrew his fingers and rose above me. I watched with desperate, fascinated attention as he picked up a condom from the side of the mattress and rolled it on.

Then he was back, pressing into me, and the stretch of his body inside mine was delicious. Perfect. I arched into him, taking more, wishing he would slam into me and push me over the edge into the orgasm that hovered just out of reach.

Gage thrust in slowly, in gradual pulses that teased more than satisfied. It seemed to take forever before he filled me all the way. He stayed there, motionless, his breath ragged. His mouth came to mine, and he kissed me, more of those long, deep, languid kisses that spun my head in dizzy passion.

His hips moved in the same slow, patient rhythm, drawing in and out, fucking me with iron control. Gage trembled above me, pushed to the edge from holding himself back. For me.

This man, this warrior who could take what he wanted, who could have anything, was claiming my body in slow, dreamy strokes, protecting me, treasuring me even in this.

The pleasure built higher with each stroke. Every time I thought I'd hit the peak and would tumble into bliss, he slowed down and pushed me higher.

I tore my mouth from his and begged. "Please, please, Gage, please. More."

His mouth took mine again, this kiss raw and a little rough as he rode the edge of control. He moved faster, fucking me harder, sliding his hand under my shoulders and bracing me, trying to keep his thrusts from jolting my head.

I wasn't feeling any pain. All I felt was Gage and the wave of pleasure he'd built so high I thought I would lose myself when it broke. And I did. The tension cracked open, and I fell into a bliss so sharp, so sweet it sucked me under, drowning my senses. Drowning me in Gage.

He stiffened between my legs, taking me in short jerky thrusts, drawing out my orgasm. I tightened my legs around him, holding him to me, my mouth pressing kisses anywhere I could reach, his jaw, his neck, his shoulder.

Tension drained from his body, and he rolled to his back, pulling me on top of him, his fingers stroking my hair from my face. When we both had our breath back, Gage slid out from under me and disappeared into the bathroom. I heard the water run and the toilet flush before he reappeared, a washcloth in his hand. Warm, soothing heat between my legs. He was gone again for a minute before he returned, sliding into bed and pulling me into his arms.

"How's your head?" he asked, his voice heavy and languid.

I giggled, the light, happy sound surprising me. I tightened my arm around his chest in a squeeze of reassurance. "All of me feels wonderful," I whispered. I drifted into sleep, holding onto Gage, his heat and strength and kindness, and trying not to think about what we'd just done. How it would change everything.

I couldn't forget what he'd said that night on the couch.

If you let me get inside that sweet angel's body of yours, I'm not going to be able to let you go.

The memory of his words washed through me. The last thing I needed was another man who thought he owned me. Gage wasn't Anthony. I knew that. That didn't mean he was what I needed. I wanted to be sensible. Smart.

But more than that, I just wanted Gage.

Chapter Nineteen
Gage

My sneakers struck the pavement in a familiar cadence that felt so much better on a road than a treadmill. Winters House was a haven, but it was also becoming a trap. Or, it *would* if I didn't push the boundaries of my life. It was too easy to stay home, to bury myself in work. Especially with Sophie there.

With Sophie around, why would I want to leave?

If I wanted my life back, I had to start living it. I couldn't remember the last time I'd gone running in the neighborhood, though when I'd lived here full time I'd done it every day. Buckhead was an urban anomaly: big lots, bigger houses, and winding lanes shaded by old-growth trees.

If someone dropped you in the middle of Buckhead, you'd think you were out in the country and not just north of the heart of Atlanta. Minutes away you'd find busy streets, high-end shopping, office buildings, and freeways, but here in the silence of early morning, I was surrounded by the trees and only the occasional passing car.

I had plans for the day, and they started with a run.

When I got back, I'd hit the weights in the gym before I took a shower. A few hours of work, and then I was taking Sophie to lunch. We were having a family dinner that night to celebrate Annalise's return sometime that afternoon. Before the hordes of Winters descended, I wanted Sophie to myself.

The night before had been beyond anything I'd expected. I won't lie. Since the night we'd met when I grabbed her in the dark, I'd been imagining getting Sophie naked. I'd had my hands on her, and I knew what she was hiding under that bulky robe and her starched camp shirts.

For almost as long, I'd known this was about more than her body. Meeting Sophie had been a one-two punch—I touched her, I heard her voice, and I knew.

Sophie Armstrong was it for me.

Coming back to Winters House should have been it. Should have been the thing that made me feel at home. I'd grown up there. But when I'd walked through the door, I'd only felt out of place. With Sophie, I was home.

Everything about her called to me. Her stubbornness, her kindness. The deft way she handled Amelia—keeping her out of trouble without trying to squash her spirit. Her smile, and the sweet, soothing tones of her voice. It didn't hurt that she was sexy as hell and looked like an angel with all that silvery blonde hair and those green eyes.

By some kind of fucking miracle, she seemed to see something in me that she liked. We hadn't known each other long, but I knew in my gut that Sophie wouldn't have slept with me for sport. The way she kissed me, the way she'd stayed with me that night in the library. Sophie never would've let that happen unless she felt it too.

We had a chance for something if I didn't manage to fuck it up.

I wasn't going to fuck it up.

I grinned, remembering the way she'd gotten me to agree to talk to a shrink. Smart, stubborn, and a little sneaky. I liked it. It didn't hurt that she'd agreed to see one herself. I could deal with my own mess. I'd seen this kind of thing before. I knew what I was dealing with, and I knew it would be a lot easier to handle with help.

I just didn't want to go. Who did? No one. Especially guys like me. We spend our lives training to handle every eventuality. To never give up. To push to the end. Seeing a shrink is like admitting we can't handle it. Fuck that. I can handle anything the enemy can throw at me. I've proven it over and over.

I could handle anything except the nightmares and the insomnia. The volatility and bursts of temper. That shit wasn't me.

It had been just over a month since I'd made my way out of that hidden camp in the desert. Too soon to expect to feel normal again. Fuck, I had no idea *when* I could expect to feel normal again. Another reason seeing a shrink wasn't a bad idea. All the times I'd given that advice to other guys, never thinking I'd have to take it myself.

If not for Sophie, I might've spent who knows how long insisting I could handle it on my own. One look into her green eyes, wet with tears, and I hadn't been able to say no. I could've gotten through my shit on my own. Eventually.

Sophie deserved better. Her husband had been dead for two years, and she was still trapped by fear. She deserved to move on. She deserved to feel whole and strong. Seeing a shrink wasn't a magic pill that would fix everything, but it was a start.

I'd call Cooper first thing and see if he could recommend anyone. I knew he'd have a name for me, and I hoped he'd have one for Sophie as well.

Thirteen years ago I'd walked away from my life. I was ready to take it back. Sophie was my catalyst. She was my reason.

All those long months locked in a cell had given me time to plan. I'd decided I was coming home, decided I was taking back my place in my family and in our company, but it hadn't seemed real.

I'd walked through the doors of Winters House feeling out of place and off balance, as if my goals were a consolation prize. All my dreams felt like something to do because I didn't have anything else. I was alone, alive when I hadn't expected to be, aimless and lost. Until Sophie.

She made me want more. For her, I wanted to be the man I imagined I could be. I wanted to give her everything she should have. A home. Stability.

Love.

Let's not bullshit around. I couldn't help but laugh at myself. Sophie had proven she was more than capable of providing her own home and her own stability. But I could give her love. I just had to convince her she wanted it.

I turned the corner on the loop that would take me back to Winters House and mapped out my strategy to win Sophie. She already had feelings for me, or she wouldn't have let me in her bed. And she liked having me there. No one was that good at faking it.

Sophie had loved the way I touched her, the way I'd fucked her. I wasn't above using sex to win her over. It wouldn't be a hardship for me. Finally getting into Sophie's bed might've been the high point of my life.

Just remembering the way she'd taken me, her gasps and moans, the feel of her heavy, full breasts in my hands, the way her fingers gripped my hair as she rolled her hips into mine.

Time for a new train of thought. Running with an erection is not fun, though that wasn't a problem I'd had before.

I needed to think. I needed a plan. I didn't think getting into Sophie's bed would be the problem. She might even invite me back if she wasn't second-guessing herself this morning. No, the hard part would be bringing our relationship into the open. As far as I knew, other than Aiden's vague warning before he left on his trip, no one had any idea there was something between us.

Knowing Sophie, she'd want to keep it that way. She'd say she worked for my family, which made me off-limits. Except, I was pretty sure Aiden would kick me out of the house before he'd fire Sophie.

If Aiden fired Sophie, Amelia would go ballistic. No one wanted to handle Amelia if she was pissed. I shuddered to imagine the shit she would pull without Sophie to rein her in. Sophie's position in Winters House was safe. I just had to prove it to her.

I tried to catch her at breakfast, but Mrs. W informed me that she and Amelia had left while I was in the shower, planning to eat out and then go for a walk in Piedmont Park and the Botanical Gardens.

After a few not-so-subtle questions I learned they didn't have any plans for the afternoon. I sent Mrs. W a wink and went upstairs to tackle the rest of the homework I'd gotten from Charlie. She'd said she had more when I was done with this batch and was ready to move forward. I was starting to get a picture of the scope of the company's dealings.

I wasn't ready to get back to work, but I would be soon, with Charlie's help. While I was at my desk, I made a few calls, nailing down details on wedding stuff too small for the planner to bother with. I sent Charlie a quick update email and let her know I'd be stopping by later.

When I was done, I touched base with the head of the Sinclair Security team at the house checking the alarm. So far they hadn't been able to find a weak point in the system, but they were going to keep looking until they did. Someone was getting into Winters House without setting off the alarm. No one would be safe until we figured out how they were getting in and stopped them.

I was waiting in the kitchen when Sophie and Amelia returned, their cheeks flushed pink from the cold, Sophie laughing at something Amelia had said. She stopped short when she saw me, the color in her cheeks deepening to red. Her eyes met mine shyly, then flicked away.

To Amelia, I said, "If you two don't have plans, I'd like to borrow Sophie for a few hours."

Amelia gave me a speculative look. "That depends. What did you want to do with her?"

"I thought I would take her out for lunch, then to Annabelle's for a hot chocolate. I have to stop and see Charlie, and I thought Sophie might want to see their new project."

"It's not my day off," Sophie started to say, but Amelia cut her off.

"Don't be silly. When a handsome young man wants to take you out to lunch, you don't spend the afternoon with an old lady."

Sophie rounded on her, sending me a quick glare before saying to Amelia, "I can spend my afternoon how I want. And you are not an old lady."

"Are you saying you don't want to go to lunch with Gage?" Amelia asked, sweetly. This was going better than

I'd hoped. If Amelia was on my side, Sophie didn't have a chance.

Before Sophie could answer, Mrs. W bustled in the kitchen and, seeing Sophie and Amelia, said "You're back. Will you want lunch or did you eat? Abel went to the market, but I can fix you a sandwich—"

"Soup and a sandwich are fine for me," Amelia said. "Sophie and Gage are going out for lunch."

Mrs. W turned and looked from Sophie's face, flushed and annoyed, to mine. She smiled and said, "That's lovely. You two have fun. The rest of the family will be here around five for pre-dinner cocktails, so make sure you're back by then."

"We will be," I promised.

Sophie stepped back and crossed her arms over her chest. "I can make my own decisions, and I never said I was going anywhere. It's not my day off. I shouldn't—"

I stepped in front of her. Looking down, I said quietly, "Sophie, would you please take the afternoon off and come out to lunch with me?"

She let out a breath and stared up at me, worrying her lower lip between her teeth. "Gage, I don't think we should —" she cut off and looked quickly from Amelia to Mrs. W, taking in their unabashed interest in our conversation. "It's not a good idea."

"Why isn't it a good idea?" Amelia interrupted in a strident voice. "Is there something wrong with my nephew?"

Sophie attempted a retreat, but her back hit the kitchen island, and she was stuck. She shook her head, looking at the three of us ranged around her and said, "Of course not. Of course, there's nothing wrong with Gage. But we shouldn't —I can't just leave Amelia and—"

She sent Mrs. W a beseeching look. I braced. Mrs. W

was notorious for her strict adherence to the line between help and family. Amelia might be on my side, but Mrs. W would be on Sophie's.

She shocked the hell out of me when she tilted her head to the side and studied Sophie, then me, and said, "I'll keep Amelia company, Sophie. Go out to lunch with Gage."

We all stared at her in shock. Mrs. W went on, as if nothing were unusual, and said, "Gage, help get Amelia settled in the dining room. I'm going to make her soup and a sandwich, and I'd like a moment alone with Sophie."

CHAPTER TWENTY
GAGE

Without another word, I hooked my arm around Aunt Amelia's shoulders and ushered her out of the room. Sophie looked uncertainly at Mrs. W, still chewing on her lower lip. As soon as we cleared the kitchen, Amelia murmured, "I never thought I'd see the day that old battle-ax and I agreed on something."

"Don't call Mrs. W a battle-ax," I said.

Mrs. W was in her late forties, but she looked a decade younger. She had the posture of a ballerina and the kind of bone structure that told you she'd been beautiful in her twenties and would still be beautiful when she was Amelia's age. Even in her severe dresses, with her dark hair in a tight bun, she was in no way a battle-ax. "I don't understand why the two of you have never gotten along, and I don't want to know. I'm just glad she's on my side."

Amelia let me pull out her chair. When I went to leave, she said, "Sit. Sophie will be in the kitchen for a few minutes, and I want to talk to you."

I sat in a chair beside Amelia's. "Don't you want lunch on a tray in the living room or the library?" I asked. The dining room was huge, with more than enough room for the entire family plus guests. Lunch for one would be lonely at the long table.

Amelia smiled and looked around the room, her dark eyes taking in the polished table with loving warmth. "I have a lot of good memories from this room, Gage. When you get to my age, memory can be company."

I thought of all the meals I'd eaten in that room when my parents had been alive and the whole family packed the table. Later, nightly dinners with Uncle Hugh and Aunt Olivia surrounded by my siblings and cousins. They were all here, the living and the dead, a part of the very fabric of this room, this house.

I'd spent so many years running from my memories, haunted by them. I never stood still long enough to see that Winters House was the one place where my family was always with me, even those that were gone.

"I know what you mean," I said, finally. Amelia reached out to take my hand and squeezed.

"I know you do." She gave my hand another squeeze and held it in hers. "You take care of that girl, Gage. I know you too well to think you're playing with her, but I need to warn you anyway. If you don't treat her right, I'll be very disappointed in you."

After a long silence while I tried to come up with some kind of response, something funny, something that would deflect the seriousness of the conversation, I gave up and just said, "I think I'm falling in love with her."

Amelia gave me a brilliant smile and said, "I already know that. You two think you're so subtle. The looks you were giving each other over cards yesterday, I thought you were going to set the library on fire."

"Don't tell Sophie that," I said. "She'd die of embarrassment."

"I know that, foolish boy. I can keep things to myself when it's important. I know you've got a lot on your plate right now, and I know that you're head over heels in love with the girl. I'm just asking you to be careful with her."

"I will," I promised. Standing, I pressed a kiss to Amelia's wrinkled cheek and left, saying, "I'll tell Mrs. W you're ready for your lunch."

I bumped into Sophie in the hall on my way back to the kitchen. Giving me another of those shy looks, she said, "Just let me change. I'll be right back."

Then she was gone, striding down the hall to her room. Whatever Mrs. W said to her, it must've worked. Leaning in the kitchen doorway, I watched her efficiently assembling Amelia's sandwich as she heated soup in a small pot on the gas stove.

Seeing me, she speared me with a sharp look and said, "Don't make me regret this, Gage."

"I won't, I swear."

"It goes against everything I've always thought appropriate," she said, crisply, "but Sophie has a good head on her shoulders, and she'd never think to take advantage. See that you don't either."

I nodded. I probably should've been offended that everyone was more worried about Sophie's well-being than mine. This was *my* family, not hers. It was just one more reminder that she'd been here, a part of their everyday lives, and I'd been gone.

But, as much as they adored Sophie, I knew that if Amelia and Mrs. W didn't trust me to take care with her, they wouldn't be scheming to get her to go out with me. In a weird, backward way, them pushing me and Sophie together felt like forgiveness.

Mrs. W and Amelia were easy. Aiden, however, would be a problem. I'd deal with him later. For once, his long hours and habit of avoiding me were coming in handy.

Sophie came back down the hall wearing the same jeans she'd had on before, now with a red wool turtleneck sweater. She'd taken her hair down, and it spilled over her shoulders in silvery blond waves. The sweater covered every inch of skin above her waist, but it was snug and did nothing to hide the full swell of her breasts or the curve of her waist.

I stared too long before I caught myself, imagining peeling up the soft red wool and sliding my hands over the creamy skin beneath.

Mrs. W cleared her throat. "We'll be back in a few hours," I said. "Is anyone using the Land Rover?"

"I think Abel took it to the market."

Damn. I needed to get my own car. It hadn't been a priority in the short time that I'd been home. Sophie interrupted, "We can take my truck."

That piece of crap truck in the garage was Sophie's? I'd assumed it was Abel's. Looking down at her I said, "Okay, but I'm driving."

She laughed and bumped her shoulder into my arm. "Are you one of those guys who never lets the woman drive?"

I took her hand in mine and pulled her through the kitchen to the mud room and garage, giving Mrs. W a quick wave as we left. "Is that a problem?" I asked.

I hadn't really thought about it like that, though if I were being honest then *yes,* I was definitely the kind of man who didn't like the woman to drive.

"I don't know," Sophie said. "I guess it depends on what we're driving."

I grabbed the keys to the truck off the hook by the door. She'd already climbed into the passenger seat and was fastening her seatbelt. The truck needed a new paint job. The tires didn't look great either. It was a midsize model, not huge and not a toy, but it still looked too big for Sophie.

"So you don't mind me driving your truck, but if it was something else you might fight me for the keys?" I asked, trying to figure her out.

"I used to have a Volkswagen Beetle. Vintage, not one of the new ones. No way would I have let you drive my girl."

I could absolutely see Sophie driving a vintage VW beetle, and at her comment, I couldn't help but laugh. "Sophie, Angel, there is no way in hell I'd fit into a vintage Beetle."

She let out one of those giggles I loved, and something in my chest squeezed. "If you were driving a Beetle before, what made you buy this?" I asked, turning the key and wincing at the coughing rumble of the engine. It didn't sound very reliable. As I put it in gear and backed out of the garage, I thought it sounded like the transmission was going to fall out any second.

"I didn't buy this; Charlie lent it to me. Lucas bought her a new truck a few days after my Beetle died. I didn't want to spend money on a new car—I barely drive as it is—and Charlie didn't feel like selling this one, so she said I could borrow it."

"Lucas bought her a new truck?" I asked. Charlie was fiercely independent, and I couldn't see her letting any man, even her fiancé, buy her a truck.

"He hated this one when she bought it," Sophie said, "I got the impression they fought about it. A lot. And when he went behind her back and bought her a brand-new one, she decided it wasn't worth fighting over anymore. I kind of think she gave me the truck to prove to Lucas that he couldn't make her sell this one, even if he bought her a replacement."

"That sounds like Charlie," I said looking around the interior of the truck.

The upholstery was faded and torn in places. The stereo looked like it hadn't worked in a decade. I was too smart to say it out loud, but I was with Lucas. This truck was a piece of shit and, if it was up to me, Sophie would never sit in it again.

Later. I'd had enough of a battle getting her to eat lunch with me. Buying her a new car would have to wait.

"What did Mrs. W say to you?" I asked, unable to contain my curiosity.

Sophie slid me a sidelong look and said, "Not much. Just that there were exceptions to every rule and that it was smart to be cautious, but you're a good man and worth the risk."

My throat got unexpectedly tight. That was high praise from Mrs. W. I'd felt mostly like a mess since I'd been home. I was trying to get my bearings, to figure out how I fit into the world I'd left behind so many years ago. It was easy to forget that these people were my family.

They would always have my back, just as I'd have theirs. Even Aiden. Probably, Aiden most of all.

I reached out and took Sophie's hand. "Look, I know this is complicated because you work for Amelia, but I don't want to hide. We can take this slowly, but I don't want to sneak around."

"And what about when it's over? We live in the same house, Gage."

"This is our first date," I said, annoyed. "Do we need to talk about the end already? At least give me a chance to fuck something up before you talk about breaking up with me."

Sophie pulled her hand from mine and gripped her purse, playing with the zipper and avoiding my eyes. "Are we together, then? We haven't really talked about it, and then last night—" She cut off and looked out the window.

"Are you sorry we slept together?" I asked, carefully.

"No," she said. "But I wasn't expecting it, and this is all happening too fast."

"Do you want me to take you home?" I asked, hoping she wouldn't say yes. I'd promised myself I wouldn't push Sophie into anything she didn't want, but at the time I hadn't thought that would include lunch with me.

"No," she said, more quietly this time. "I just didn't expect this, that's all."

"Did you think I was just going to sleep with you and then pretend nothing happened?" I asked. The guilty look she sent me was adorable. Realization dawned. "Or was that your plan with me? You were going to use me for sex and ignore me in the morning?"

I loved it when Sophie blushed, almost as much as when she laughed.

"I wasn't planning to sleep with you," she said, and then in a prim voice, "I wasn't the one who had a condom in his pocket."

"It's a good thing I did, or we'd be having a different conversation this morning," I pointed out. "It's funny, everyone warning me off taking advantage of you, no one thinking to tell you the same."

"I wasn't using you for sex," she protested. "I hadn't had sex since Anthony died. I wasn't thinking about a relationship at all."

"So is this about me? Or about getting involved with anyone?" I didn't want to force Sophie into a corner, but I had to know.

"It's not you, Gage. It's not. I just don't know if I'm ready for this."

"How long has Anthony been dead, Sophie?" I asked, already knowing the answer.

Years. He'd been dead for years, and in all that time she'd been alone. Sophie didn't say a word. I pulled into a parking space in front of the restaurant and turned the truck off before I said, "I know it was bad. And I know you're scared. I can't promise that everything's going to be perfect. I can't promise you a happy ending. But I swear, Sophie, I will make this worth the risk. I swear I will never intentionally hurt you. And I promise if this blows up in our faces, I'll get out of Winters House until you think you can stand the sight of me again. Deal?"

"But you just came home," she protested, her green eyes wide with wonder as they studied my face.

"I didn't say I'd leave Atlanta, but between Charlie and Lucas, Jacob's building, and Vance's place with Magnolia, I have plenty of options if we decide we need some space. I'm not asking you to risk your job, Sophie. I'm asking you to risk your heart."

CHAPTER TWENTY-ONE
SOPHIE

I'm asking you to risk your heart.

Just my heart, that's all.

I managed to stifle a nervous laugh. After Anthony, getting involved with anyone felt like it was risking far more than just my heart. My sanity. My freedom. My life.

After two years as a widow, that should've felt melodramatic. It didn't. I'd been alone all this time for a reason.

Stalling for time, I looked through the front windshield of the truck and saw that Gage had pulled in front of a Middle Eastern restaurant. A few days ago I'd mentioned having a craving for falafel and now he brought me here, because he'd been listening and he remembered. I closed my eyes and tried to think.

Gage was not Anthony. And I was not a victim. Not anymore. I didn't want to lose a chance for something good because I was scared. Getting involved with Gage might blow up in my face. It probably would. But I would regret not taking the chance. I had enough regrets for a lifetime.

I opened my eyes and said, "Let's go have lunch."

Gage dropped his head and pressed his lips to mine. I leaned into his kiss, feeling like I was at the top of a roller coaster, ready to fall. All I could do was hang on for the ride.

After our conversation in the car, lunch was a relief, comfortable and easy. The food was good, the falafel crunchy and spicy. Gage joked that he'd seen enough of sand for a lifetime, but he loved the food over there. He ate enough for two people, but I'd seen how much time he put in in the gym.

We shared sticky, sweet baklava for dessert before Gage led me from the restaurant and down the street to a funky little café with the name Annabelle's painted on the window. Inside, chairs and tables were arranged in a seemingly haphazard pattern, each set hand-painted with a different theme.

An eclectic selection of artwork hung on the walls, everything from watercolors to photographs, to mixed media sculpture, each discreetly tagged with the price and artist information. There was a bookshelf in the back stuffed with paperbacks puzzles and games.

Nearby, two couches and a handful of armchairs surrounded a coffee table where a lively game of Monopoly appeared to be in progress. The line at the counter was at least ten people long, the three baristas on the other side moving in clockwork synchronicity.

Gage led us to the back of the line and wound his arm around my shoulders, pulling me tight to his side. Annabelle's was lively and interesting, and it smelled deliciously of freshly brewed coffee, chocolate, and vanilla, but it wasn't quiet.

Leaning down, his lips brushed my ear as he said, "We went to school with Annabelle, and Aiden actually gave her the loan to start this place when she was still in college. She has the best coffee in town, but her hot chocolate is out of this world. I don't know what she does to it, but there's nothing like it."

"Gage!" A tall, rangy woman with warm brown eyes and long cinnamon colored hair ducked around the end of the counter, a wide smile on her face. She threw herself into Gage's arms. "You're home! Charlie told me you were back. I'm so sorry I haven't gotten over to see you. This time of year it's a mad house around here."

Gage gave her a tight hug and kissed her cheek. I tried not to be jealous. He'd just told me they were old friends. His arm still around her, he turned her to face me and said, "Annabelle, this is Sophie. Sophie, Annabelle of the amazing hot chocolate."

Annabelle's face brightened when she heard my name and her smile grew wider. "So this is Sophie. Charlie says you're a miracle worker. She says you're the only one who can keep her aunt Amelia in line without starting World War III."

Annabelle's enthusiasm was infectious, and I found myself smiling back, forgetting my momentary flash of jealousy. She led us to a cozy table for two in the corner. When Gage tried to pay, she waved him off. "Another time. This is a special occasion. I'm sorry I can't talk, I have to get back behind the counter, but if I don't see you before, I'll see you at the wedding." A quick kiss to Gage's cheek and a shoulder squeeze for me and Annabelle was gone in a swirl of cinnamon-colored hair.

"Is she always like that?" I asked.

"Totally genuine and packed with enough energy for twenty people?" Gage asked with a grin. I nodded. "Pretty much. You'd think it's all the espresso, but she was like that when she was a kid."

Annabelle reappeared just long enough to give us our hot chocolate, a thick slice of red velvet cake, and say she'd have someone bring us a hot cocoa for Charlie when Gage mentioned that was our next stop. I thought I was full from lunch, but Gage had been right, Annabelle's hot chocolate was the best thing I'd ever tasted. This was what chocolate dreamt of – sweet, creamy, and rich with just a hint of bitterness to keep it from tasting like chocolate syrup.

The red velvet cake was almost as good, and I wondered if she baked it in-house. Either way, now that I'd finally been to Annabelle's, I knew I'd be back. I'd been meaning to come here for months—Charlie talked about it all the time—but with Amelia's low sugar diet, bringing her to a place packed with dessert cases was asking for trouble. Since I spent most of my time with Amelia, I'd never been here before.

Charlie's hot chocolate appeared on the table, delivered by one of the baristas from behind the counter. Annabelle was nowhere to be seen as we left. Gage held my hand as he walked me back to the truck, opening the door for me and waiting until I was settled before closing it and rounding the truck to get in himself.

My head spun a little at the sheer normalcy of the afternoon. We were just two people eating lunch together and sharing a slice of cake. Nothing weird about that, right? Except that I couldn't remember the last time I'd been on a date. Not one like this. My dates with Anthony had been formal affairs, dinners in fine restaurants and a chaste kiss at my door.

"Have you seen the new place Charlie and Lucas bought?" Gage asked as he started the truck.

"Not yet," I said. "But the last one they did was amazing."

Just before Thanksgiving, Charlie and Lucas had finished rehabbing a mid-century modern house in the Virginia Highlands, not far from where they lived. Lucas had proposed to Charlie there the day they finished the house, and not a week later it was under contract. I wasn't surprised. I didn't know much about real estate, but I knew what looked good and that house had been beautiful.

I'd heard their newest purchase was a dump. If you went by Aiden's opinion, it was going to collapse on Charlie's head any second, though Lucas had reassured him the foundation and basic structure were sound. When we pulled up in front of the modest Craftsman bungalow, I could see Aiden's point. My opinion must have shown on my face because Gage took one look at me and burst out laughing.

"I'm sure they can fix this, right?" I said, doubtfully. The roof over the porch sagged alarmingly. Most of the front steps were missing, and two of the four windows facing the street were boarded up. The house was a nondescript grayish color that might have originally been green. Or purple. Or blue. Now it was just sad.

"According to Vance, Charlie and Lucas's house was this bad when she bought it. Everyone thought she was nuts, but you've seen it, haven't you?"

I had. Charlie and Lucas's house was a showpiece, every inch of it restored with loving care and a sharp eye for good design. Aiden had commented that she could put it back on the market and make a tidy profit, but Charlie and Lucas had fallen in love putting that house back together. Neither of them would sell it for any amount of money. I found it hard to believe their house had ever been this bad.

"If you say so," I said, willing to give Charlie and Lucas the benefit of the doubt. After all, they knew what they were doing. What I knew about restoring homes wouldn't fill a postcard.

Gage helped me out of the truck, carrying Charlie's hot chocolate in one hand. "She said to go in through the back."

I followed him through the side yard, picking my way carefully across the scrubby grass and around discarded piles of trash. Based on the dented beer cans, damp cardboard, and other junk, it looked like Charlie hadn't gotten around to cleaning up the mess left behind by the former owners.

Charlie met us at the back door, swinging it open and stepping down to the concrete blocks she'd put in place of actual stairs. Her chin length auburn curls were pulled back beneath a beat-up ball cap, and her eyes lit when she caught sight of the paper cup in Gage's hand.

"You brought me Annabelle's!" She jumped over the remaining stairs, meeting us in the grass, and snagged the cup from Gage. "I owe you one," she said, taking a long sip.

"I think it's the other way around," Gage said.

"Whatever." Her eyes drifted down, and she caught sight of Gage's hand holding mine. Raising one eyebrow, she said to me, "So, are you giving Gage a trial run?"

Gage bit back a laugh, and I shrugged a shoulder. "Kind of," I said.

"Good for you. I'd say he's a lot to handle, but you're used to managing Amelia. One of the Winters men is child's play compared to that."

This time, Gage didn't bother to bite back his laugh. I couldn't help but join in. Keeping a handle on Amelia took every bit of creativity and tenacity I had. I still wasn't sure I could manage Gage, but I was going to try.

Gage dropped my hand and put his arm around me. My phone rang in my pocket, and I pulled it out, hearing him say to Charlie, "Do you have that jump drive you were talking about? I finished those reports. When you get a chance, I want to sit down and—"

I stopped listening as I studied the screen of my phone. The number read as UNKNOWN. I hit the button to answer and held it up to my ear. "Hello?" Silence. Something in the background. A voice? I couldn't make it out. "Hello?" I said, again.

Just as I was about to hang up a man said, "Sophie. I've missed the sound of your voice."

The phone slipped from my fingers, striking a broken chunk of concrete at my feet. The plastic case cracked, the noise cutting through Gage and Charlie's conversation.

I heard Gage say my name, felt his eyes on me. I stared down at the phone, imagining I still heard that voice, the way he'd said my name. *Sophie*. Before we got married, I'd loved the way my name sounded when he said it. Almost reverent. Worshipful. Later, it turned my heart to ice.

I heard it again, my name, this time in Gage's low rumble instead of Anthony's smooth, cultured tones. Gage's strong hands closed over my shoulders, turning me to face him. "Who was it? What did they say?"

I looked up at him, eyes wide, not really seeing anything past my shock. It must've been a trick. It had to have been a trick because Anthony was dead. The policeman came to my door and told me Anthony was dead.

"Sophie, who called you?" Charlie asked, gently. I shook my head, not wanting to answer, not wanting to put that horror of a phone call into words.

"Angel, take a deep breath," Gage said, stepping to the side and pulling me back, away from my broken phone and into his arms. I leaned into his strong body, breathing in his scent. Finally, I whispered, "It was Anthony. It couldn't have been, but it was."

Gage's arms tightened around me. Over my head, I heard him say to Charlie, "Call Cooper, find out if he's at Winters House or if he's still at the office. Tell him Sophie got a weird call, we need her phone checked, and the screen is cracked, so she'll need a new one. Find out where he is and we'll meet him."

The door to the house opened and shut as Charlie went in to make the call. Gage rested his chin on the top of my head and rubbed his hand up and down my spine, soothing me. I was such a fucking mess. Just the sound of his voice, two years later, and I was ready to curl into a ball and weep with terror. The worst moments of my marriage poured through my brain in a kaleidoscope of misery and fear.

I leaned into Gage, staring at the scrubby grass of Charlie's yard. Anthony was the past. He couldn't hurt me now. Eventually, my heartbeat slowed and my breathing evened out. Gage must've felt my body relaxing into him because he said, "You okay?"

I shook my head against his chest. No, I was not okay. I'd just gotten a phone call from my dead husband.

"You're sure that was Anthony?" Gage asked, carefully.

I let out a sigh. "Sure it was Anthony's voice," I said. "It couldn't be Anthony. Anthony's dead."

"I feel like an ass for asking this, but are you sure?"

I stepped back a little and looked up into Gage's worried face. "The police said there wasn't much left of the body, but there was enough to identify him. They were sure it was Anthony."

Charlie came back out of the house. She handed something to Gage that looked like a USB drive and said, "Cooper was just leaving the office. He grabbed Sophie a replacement phone and said to bring that one and meet him at Winters House. He'll find out who made the call." Looking at me with warm, concerned eyes, she said, "Cooper will figure this out. That's his job. You'll feel better once you know where that call came from and why."

Gage retrieved my phone and tucked it into his pocket. We were quiet on the drive back to Winters House, both of us lost in thought, Gage's hand holding mine all the way.

CHAPTER TWENTY-TWO

SOPHIE

Cooper Sinclair met us at the kitchen door, his cool blue eyes narrowed on me in concern. We'd met a few times since I'd been living at Winters House. I'd met all the Sinclairs here and there. They were as close as family to the Winters, and they showed up for dinner often when Aiden was around.

Cooper was built like Gage, tall and broad. He didn't look like he spent most of his time behind a desk, though I'd heard him complain about being stuck in the office more than once.

"Let's talk in the library," he said. "Aiden is still at the office, but I filled him in on the security system over the phone. Bottom line, we're installing sensors on most of the first-floor windows, the ones that didn't already have them, and turning on motion detectors in key areas. That's a start until we figure out what the hell is going on."

"You didn't find any sign of a breach in the system?" Gage asked.

"Not so far. If someone got in the house –"

"Someone fucking hit Sophie over the head," Gage

interrupted. Cooper gave him a sober nod. We followed him into the library and sat on the couch, side-by-side.

"However they got in the house, they didn't bypass or breach the system. There has to be a way in we don't know about. Until we find it, the motion sensors will give you an extra layer of safety." Looking at me, he said, "How's your head?"

"Better. It wasn't really that bad." Beside me, Gage growled, a low, almost imperceptible sound. I squeezed his hand. I think he was more upset about my bump on the head than I was.

Cooper shook his head. "I'm sorry. Somewhere, we missed something. It won't happen again."

"It better not," Gage said, his arm tightening around me. Cooper caught the possessive gesture and rolled his eyes. Gage pulled my broken phone from his pocket and handed it to Cooper.

"It's the last call that came in. We haven't tried to turn the phone on, so I don't know how badly it's damaged."

Cooper shook his head in dismissal. "It's good; I can work with this. Sophie, do you care if I have your phone? I can give you a new one."

"No, whatever you need to do is fine."

"What can you tell me about the call?"

"It sounded like it was my husband, which is impossible because he's been dead for two years."

"Do you have any idea who would try to play a trick on you?"

I shook my head, watching as Cooper pulled a mobile phone out of his pocket, powered it on and connected it to my broken phone. Despite the shattered screen and cracked case, my phone powered on at the press of a button. Cooper did a few things on the new phone and set them both on the coffee table.

"We'll find out where that call came from and hopefully who placed it. Do you have reason to believe you might be in danger from anyone associated with your husband?"

I looked from Cooper to Gage, Cooper's eyes curious and Gage's heavy with concern. I hated the answer to his question and how stupid it made me seem. I didn't want to remember the naive woman who'd married Anthony.

"I don't know very much about Anthony's life outside of our marriage," I said. "He kept me isolated, but toward the end, I started to wonder. He came home a few times with blood on his shirt—never very much—and he always had an excuse. And there was the stress." My voice dropped to a whisper. "He was always so tense. Angry. But I didn't actually know what he was doing. Not really. He told me he was an accountant—" I gave a small, helpless shrug. I knew his story didn't make sense, but that didn't mean I knew the truth.

Cooper didn't seem to need more of an explanation. Kindly, he said, "Don't worry about it, Sophie. If he was involved in anything sketchy, we'll find out. Did he leave you anything? Anything someone else might be interested in?"

"Not really. There was some money. Not a lot after the funeral expenses. I got the house, which I sold. His car was totaled in the accident, and there was some insurance money, but if you mean any papers or anything of value, then no. His will stated that all his personal belongings and the contents of the house would go to his brother. It was weird because he'd told me they were estranged, but by the time I knew about the will, Anthony was gone so I couldn't ask him about it."

"Okay, I'll look into that," Cooper said. "I'm going to get out of your hair. I'll be in touch tomorrow to let you know what I find out."

He stood, disconnected my broken phone from the one he'd brought, and handed the new one to me. "I cloned your phone to this one. You can use it just like normal, but we'll be monitoring any calls, so don't say anything you don't want one of us to hear. Unless it's dirt on Gage, in which case feel free to talk away. I can always use the ammunition."

I gave him a weak smile. "I'll see what I can come up with," I said.

"What are the chances this phone call is related to Sophie's hit over the head?" Aiden asked, walking in behind us.

"Thought you were still at work," Cooper commented.

Aiden gave an abrupt shake of his head. "I came home early."

Both Gage and Cooper stared at Aiden for a moment. So did I. Aiden never came home early.

Answering Aiden's question, Cooper said, "It's possible. I tend to think no, but until we figure this out, I don't want to make any assumptions."

"It seems unlikely that we have two separate issues in the same week," Aiden said.

"That's why it's tempting to connect them," Connor said. "But a call from her dead husband is contact aimed specifically at unsettling Sophie. If she's the reason for the break in, then the hit over the head doesn't make sense. Whoever the intruder was, he had her right there, alone in the hallway. Hitting her over the head implies that she was in the way, rather than the target."

"Makes sense," Aiden admitted. "I don't like all this

going on so close to the wedding. The house is going to be filled with guests."

"Evers is working on shuffling things around so we can get more security," Cooper said. "I'm going to head out, but if anything comes up, call me. The new settings on the security alarm will activate automatically at night, so make sure everyone stays put after it's on."

Gage gave me a meaningful look as Cooper let himself out. I didn't like the idea of being trapped in my room after bedtime if I couldn't sleep, but it was better than running the risk of bumping into the intruder in the dark. My head still ached from our last meeting.

"Sophie, I'd like to speak with you in my office," Aiden said.

Pulling my hand from Gage's, I looked up at him and said, "Of course." Gage followed me across the hall into Aiden's office. Aiden looked up to see Gage behind me and said, "I'd like to talk to Sophie alone."

"I'm not leaving." Gage folded his arms across his chest.

"Gage," I hissed. He looked down at me.

"Do you want me to leave?"

That was a difficult question. No, I didn't want him to leave, but Aiden was still my employer. Reading my face, Gage said to Aiden, "Is this business or personal?"

Aiden sat behind his desk and gave Gage a hard look. "Personal."

"Then I'm not leaving," Gage said. He nudged me to one of the chairs opposite the desk, waited until I sat, and then took his own seat beside me. I wasn't sure if I was pleased or annoyed.

"Did you forget our conversation?" Aiden asked Gage.

Gage's expression was stony when he said, "No, I didn't."

"I heard you took Sophie out to lunch," Aiden said.

"What Sophie and I do is none of your business," Gage said, evenly. His voice and expression were perfectly controlled, but I could read the surge of his temper in the way his hand fisted against his leg.

"Sophie is an employee of this family, and she is living in this house," Aiden said, his voice ice cold, "That makes it very much my business."

"Are you firing me?" I interrupted, my stomach sinking. What if he said yes?

Leaning back in his chair, Aiden shook his head, looking from Gage to me. "No, Sophie. It's not your behavior I'm concerned about; it's his. Pursuing you puts you in a difficult position. I've already spoken with him about it once."

Gage lurched forward in his chair, and for a moment I was afraid he was going to swing that clenched fist into Aiden's patrician nose.

Charlie's voice came from the doorway, cutting through the tension. "For heaven's sake Aiden, does she look like she's in a difficult position? You sound like a Victorian father. You have to get past this need to organize everyone's life."

Aiden looked at Charlie with affectionate annoyance. "Charlie, stay out of it. This isn't your business."

"It's not yours either," she insisted.

"Charlie, I don't need you to stick up for me," Gage said, his tone startlingly like Aiden's, affection and irritation rolled up together.

Charlie laughed and sat on the arm of my chair. "I'm not sticking up for you. I'm sticking up for Sophie. She doesn't need everyone interfering in her personal life."

Aiden's back went poker straight, and with an icy look of authority, he said to Charlie, "Sophie is an employee in this household, and when she took the position living here I assured her that she would be treated as a professional. I told Gage to stay away from her—"

"Aiden, whatever thing you and Gage have to work out, it's not Sophie's problem. Stop making this into such a big deal." Twisting on the arm of the chair so she could meet my eyes, Charlie said, "Sophie, if Gage is making you uncomfortable, now would be the time to bring it up."

"I think you have the wrong impression," I said to Aiden.

I was nervous about whatever was going on between Gage and me, but there was no way I'd let our growing relationship turn into a point of contention between him and Aiden. It seemed obvious they had enough to argue about without adding me to the list.

"I'm not sure exactly where this is going," I said, carefully, "but what's between Gage and myself is mutual, and he hasn't done anything he shouldn't."

"Are you sure?" Aiden asked, and I stifled the urge to squirm under that cool, direct gaze.

"I'm positive," I said. "I understand if you feel like it's inappropriate, but—"

"Sophie is going with me to Charlie's wedding," Gage cut in, "so you have two weeks to get used to it."

I looked away from Aiden and turned in my chair to Gage. "I can't go to Charlie's wedding with you," I protested.

"Why not?" both Gage and Charlie asked.

"Because I'm going with Amelia."

"Amelia can take care of herself for one night," Charlie said. "She's not an invalid. And she'd be the first to want you to go to the wedding with Gage."

"That's not the point," I said, exasperated. "She'll head

straight for the sweets and make herself sick. Do you know how often I find contraband in her room? She knows she has to watch her sugar intake, but she's convinced herself that *just once* doesn't count. The problem is that all those little *just once* treats add up. I'm trying to help her control her diabetes with diet, rather than needing insulin, and letting her run rampant at your wedding with no supervision is not going to help."

I turned to Gage. Reaching across the space between our chairs, I took his fisted hand in mine. Rubbing my thumb over his clenched knuckles, I felt his grip ease. "I'd love to go to Charlie's wedding with you, but I can't. I'm sorry."

Aiden let out an aggrieved sigh. "I'll take Amelia to the wedding," he said, sounding defeated and a little amused.

"Don't you already have a date?" Charlie asked. "I thought you were taking what's her name? With the laugh."

"I broke it off. She was starting to get ideas. The last thing I need is to take her to your wedding."

"Thank God, her laugh sounds like a hyena."

"Charlie, I don't need you interfering in my social life."

"Really?" Charlie asked with a laugh. She made a swirling motion with her finger, encompassing all of us in the room, and said, "After this little scene you're going to lecture *me* about not butting into people's personal lives?"

"No, just about not butting into mine." Aiden stood from behind the desk. "Sophie, consider Charlie's wedding your night off. I can keep Amelia out of trouble. It will be a good distraction from having to watch my baby sister get married to Lucas Jackson."

He came out from behind the desk and hooked his arm around Charlie's neck, pulling her in for a quick hug and a kiss to the top of her head before stalking out of the room.

"I thought he liked Lucas?" I asked, my chest warm at the sight of the tears in Charlie's eyes. Aiden could be a hardass, but Charlie always brought out his soft side.

"He does," she said, with a watery laugh. "I think he just imagined me with someone a little... gentler. But I think he also thought I'd spend my life arranging flowers and doing charity work, so he's had to make some adjustments."

"He's interested in Sophie," Gage said out of nowhere.

"What?" Charlie and I both said in unison. I might be a little rusty when it came to dating, but I definitely did not get the *interested* vibe off of Aiden. At all. Aiden saw me as an employee and a female living under his protection. As a romantic interest? Not a chance.

"Gage, no," Charlie said. "I really don't think—"

"Then why is he so concerned with her personal life?" Gage challenged. "He's been telling me to stay away from her since I got back. Sophie and I had barely met at that point, so why bother warning me off unless he was trying to protect his own interests?"

"Gage, you're reading this wrong," I said.

"Then how should I read it?" he asked, his temper flaring. His eyes were hot, blue flame, but he sat very still, as if making a concerted effort to contain his roiling emotions.

"I don't know," Charlie admitted. "I'm not even going to pretend that I understand whatever's going on with you and Aiden. He's missed you all this time. When we thought you weren't coming home, he was a mess, and now that you're here he's being a dick. Sometimes I really do not get the way men think."

Agreeing with Charlie, I said, "Gage, this isn't about me."

He stood up, taking my hand and tugging, so I rose along with him. He pulled me into his arms, and I whispered against his chest, "Really, Gage, if he were interested in me, why would he have said he'd take Amelia to the wedding? He had the perfect excuse to keep us apart."

"I don't know," Gage admitted, rubbing his chin against the top of my head. "Aiden is tricky. Whatever he's doing on the surface isn't necessarily what it seems to be. He's always got a master plan."

"Well, that's true," Charlie said. "What you see isn't necessarily what you get with Aiden, but I still think you're wrong. This isn't about Sophie. It's about you, Gage."

Gage kissed my cheek, and we started toward the door, Charlie falling in step with us. "I don't care what he's up to," he said, "as long as he stays away from my girl."

I shook my head, not bothering to respond. I was with Charlie. I did not get the way men thought.

Whatever was going on between Gage and Aiden, they'd have to deal with it on their own. Between my job running herd on Amelia, a brand-new relationship with Gage, the break-ins at Winters House, and now a phone call from my dead husband, I had my hands full.

Chapter Twenty-Three

Gage

S ophie let out a squeak of surprise as I tugged on her hand and pulled her behind the curtain, drawing her into my arms. Winters House was packed with wedding guests, and we hadn't had a second alone all day.

Charlie's wedding had been planned with only six weeks notice and was on Christmas Eve, but that hadn't stopped most of the guest list from scrambling to attend. She was a Winters, after all. On top of that, her departure from Winters Inc., plus hooking up with a guy like Lucas, had made for some seriously interesting gossip as far as Atlanta society was concerned. She and Lucas had only invited a hundred people, but the house was bursting at the seams.

I'd pulled Sophie into the living room, looking for a quiet corner. The curtains would have to do. As children, we'd hidden in these curtains more than a few times. Reaching from the floor almost to the high ceiling, they were made from layers of heavy, rustling silk. The perfect hiding place—a dark cocoon of privacy—the sounds of the party muffled through the silk.

I needed Sophie to myself for a few minutes. She was my date for the night, but too many wedding guests were intrigued by my return, and it had been impossible to get a moment alone.

Time alone with Sophie had been a constant challenge for the last two weeks. During the day, Winters House had been a hive of activity. Charlie and Mrs. W had every available hand pitching in, and we did whatever she and the wedding planner told us to: rearranging furniture, setting up seating, carrying equipment.

Amelia claimed old age and set up a chair in the front hall to supervise the proceedings, gaining scowls from everyone working, but entertaining us with her comments. Sophie was somehow able to help with the wedding and keep an eye on Amelia at the same time.

When I was a child, both my mother and aunt Olivia had claimed that Mrs. W had eyes in the back of her head. I still wasn't sure about that, but I was beginning to believe that Sophie might. More than once she'd stopped what she was doing, marched over to Amelia's chair, stuck her hand in the pillows propped behind Amelia, and withdrawn a package of cookies or candy bar.

Someday she would make a great mom. Our kids would get away with nothing.

That thought should have shocked me. At least scared me a little. We'd only known each other a few weeks, and we both had things to deal with before we were ready for a commitment like that. Despite all the weddings going on, I wasn't running out to go ring shopping.

Not yet. Not unless I wanted to scare Sophie off. But as every day passed, I grew more convinced that she was it for me.

We slept together every night in her room. I'd tried to

talk her into sleeping in my suite, but she'd insisted she needed to be across the hall from Amelia. Amelia slept like a rock and had never needed her in the night, but Sophie claimed that wasn't the point.

I didn't care. I was happy wherever Sophie was. My room. Her room. I wouldn't mind bedding down on the ground if she were beside me.

We'd both worried that the motion sensors would make our insomnia even more frustrating. It was bad enough not being able to sleep. Being trapped in one room, unable to roam, to get a cup of tea or watch a movie, seemed like a punishment.

It wasn't. The first time I woke from a nightmare of flashing lights and gunshots, Sophie had reached over and stroked my cheek until the iron band around my chest loosened and my heart rate slowed to normal.

She'd murmured my name in her sweet voice, her fingers trailing over my skin, soothing the nightmare away. When I had my head back on straight, I'd pulled her into my arms and thanked her the best way I knew how.

That became our pattern.

Our insomnia was different—I had trouble falling asleep, and Sophie had trouble staying asleep, but we both woke with nightmares. I made love to her every evening after we turned out the light—and sometimes before—until we were both exhausted enough to sleep. When I felt her wake in the dark hours before dawn, I'd reach for her again, chasing away her restless tension with pleasure.

In halting words, her cheeks pink, she'd told me she was protected from pregnancy by a birth control implant, and she'd been tested after her husband had died. If I wanted to, we could forget about the condoms. I wanted to. Fuck, did I want to. Being skin to skin with Sophie, nothing between us, was heaven. It wasn't just the pleasure; it was the intimacy. The trust.

It was too soon to say, but it felt like I was sleeping better. Either way, I'd made an appointment for after the new year with the therapist Cooper had recommended. His patient roster was filled with guys like me who'd seen action overseas and were having trouble transitioning to civilian life.

Sophie had her own appointment after the holidays. To be honest, we were both dreading it, but talking to a shrink was better than waking in the night, mind and body convinced I was back in the worst moments of my life.

Funny how it was so much easier to suffer my own flashbacks and insomnia than it was to watch Sophie do the same. *I'll go if you'll go,* she'd said. If not for that, I have no idea how long it would've taken for me to pick up the phone and call Cooper.

I would have put it off forever if it hadn't been for Sophie. I wanted her to be happy. I wanted her to be free. She would be. I would make sure of it.

There hadn't been any more intruders in the house or another mysterious phone call, but I couldn't relax.

It turned out I was smart to stay on guard. Just the day before, Aiden had pulled me into his office and handed me an unsealed envelope addressed to Sophie, with a local postmark. I'd turned it over in my hands before asking, "What is this?"

"It came in yesterday. Cooper already checked it—no trace, no prints. Mailed somewhere in Atlanta a few days ago."

Inside the envelope was a single sheet of plain, white letter-size paper, the kind sold in reams in any office supply store. The message was written in a slanted hand, the points of the letters dense with ink, as if the author had pressed on the pen too hard.

It read, '*I miss you so much, my darling. Soon, we'll be together again. Forever.*'

"What has Cooper found out about the husband?" I asked, turning the message over in my hands before refolding it and sliding it back in the envelope.

I fought the urge to tear it to pieces. Maybe sensing my thoughts, Aiden reclaimed the envelope and sat down behind his desk, gesturing for me to take a seat opposite.

When I did, he said, "Nothing good. I have no idea how Sophie met this guy, but he was into some bad shit. Among other things, he handled money laundering for the Accorsi crime family. About a year after Anthony Armstrong died, a few of them ended up going to jail, including Matteo Accorsi, the head of the family. Cooper found some information that indicates Anthony may have provided the key testimony that put them there."

My mind raced with the possibilities. "Before or after he died?"

Aiden shook his head. "Cooper is having a hard time finding out, which means anything is possible."

"Shit. Has Sophie seen that letter?"

"No. My gut instinct is to keep it from her, but I wanted to run it by you first."

I thought about the look on Sophie's face when she'd dropped her phone two weeks before. The shock. The fear. The way her skin had turned to ice.

She was a smart, resilient woman. There was absolutely no sensible reason to keep this from her. Whoever the letter was from, she was a target, and she had a right to know.

I still wasn't going to tell her.

Making a quick decision, I said, "She can't leave the house without protection."

"Agreed," Aiden said, immediately jumping on my train of thought.

"I'll disable her car. If she needs to go anywhere, I'll drive her."

"Cooper already has two guys on the house at all times," Aiden said. "Between that and the alarm, she should be safe if she stays here."

"We'll tell her about this later. After the weddings, when things have calmed down a little."

I started to get up, and Aiden motioned for me to stay where I was. Curious, I settled back into the chair and waited. He shot a cautious look at the door before he said, "How does Lise seem to you?"

My younger sister Annalise, Vance's twin, had come home the day before. On the surface, she looked good. She was tan, blonde hair streaked with platinum after spending the last few months in New Mexico, shooting the desert. She'd been all smiles and hugs, but she was too thin, and lines bracketed her mouth.

I shook my head and said, "She needs to slow down. Come home."

"She keeps telling me everything is fine, but she left Taos abruptly a few weeks ago, canceling a show at a gallery that would've been very good for her career. She left them in the lurch, which isn't like her. I think something happened, but she's not talking."

"If she's not talking, how do you know?"

Aiden gave me a level stare.

"The Sinclairs have a guy on her?" I asked, already knowing the answer. With a laugh, I said, "I don't even want to know what they bill you every month."

Aiden shrugged his shoulder. "At least I get the family rate."

"And you don't have the slightest problem with spying on her," I said, already knowing the answer to that question, too.

"I'd do anything to keep my family safe," Aiden said, his voice grave, heavy with truth.

"What does the Sinclair's guy think? How closely is he watching her?"

"Unfortunately, not close enough to know exactly what spooked her in New Mexico. Considering that she's spent the last ten years running from a stalker, we didn't think it was a good idea to watch her too closely and run the risk of scaring her. Riley keeps an eye on her, but he does it from a distance. He went to Taos after she bugged out, but he couldn't find anything solid."

"Riley Flynn? He's the guy the Sinclairs have on Annalise? Is that a good idea?"

"He's motivated," was Aiden's response.

I wasn't sure about that. Riley and Annalise had a history. He had as many reasons to be pissed at her as he did to protect her. And if she found out Riley had been watching her all this time, she wasn't going to be happy.

"You're positive whatever spooked her had to do with the stalker? After all this time?"

Aiden shifted in his seat looking uncomfortable. "It hasn't been that long," he admitted. "We've kept it quiet, waiting for Annalise to tell us herself, which she never does, but every time she stays in one place too long he pops up again, and she runs. We don't know what it was this time, but he usually starts with gifts. Flowers."

"She said she'd be home through the new year. At least a few days after Tate and Emily's wedding on New Year's

Eve. We need to talk to her about this. She can't spend the rest of her life on the run."

"Agreed," Aiden said.

I looked at the envelope Aiden was sliding into his desk drawer and said, "Cooper is going to keep looking into Armstrong?"

Aiden nodded. "We're not going to let anything happen to Sophie."

I didn't like the protective, almost possessive tone in his voice, but if his interest in Sophie meant he'd work harder to keep her safe, I'd let it go. For now.

"I'm coming back to work after the holidays," I stated, flatly. I was done with asking. This time, I was telling Aiden what I was going to do. He may have been running Winters, Inc., but we both owned the same amount of stock. He couldn't keep me out forever.

As I'd expected, his face went blank and hard. With a sharp shake of his head, he said, "Later. We can talk about this later."

"Fine," I conceded.

We had two weddings to get through in the next week. I could wait a little longer. Aiden left without another word.

CHAPTER TWENTY-FOUR
GAGE

The last few days before Charlie's wedding flew by in a blur as every available person rushed around following the increasingly strident orders of the wedding planner. By the time the day arrived, we were all a little shell-shocked. Even after all the preparation, I wasn't ready for the sight of my baby cousin in a wedding dress.

I liked Lucas Jackson well enough. If Charlie had to marry anyone, I'd rather it was Jackson than one of the over-privileged brats she'd dated before him. Those guys had no idea how to handle Charlie. She was smart, confident, and gorgeous. A lot of men found her intimidating, but not Lucas.

If the way he looked at Charlie was any indication, he loved every part of her like crazy. Watching her walk down the aisle on Aiden's arm, in a flowing white dress straight from a fairytale, my heart broke a little. Our parents should have been there. She should have been on Uncle Hugh's arm.

I'd dreamed of them more than once in the past week, all of us more aware of their loss than usual. I'd caught

Charlie alone with Aiden earlier that day, her head on his shoulder, tears in her eyes as he murmured in her ear. I knew without asking that she was missing her parents. Aiden, as he always did, was trying his hardest to fill the gap. To be both mother and father now that they were gone.

I felt a sharp pang of guilt in my heart, watching them. I had a little sister, too. Annalise hadn't been as young as Charlie when I'd left — seventeen to Charlie's ten — but I'd abandoned her all the same. If I'd been around, would she have been running all these years? I'd never know.

I couldn't unmake the past, but the future was mine.

Whatever Aiden said to Charlie must have worked, because she walked down the aisle of the church with a wide smile on her face. Lucas stared at her as if she were a dream come to life, and the kiss he gave her after they'd said their vows hadn't exactly been acceptable for church. I don't think he cared.

Now that we were back at the house for the reception, I was determined to get a kiss of my own. Sophie wasn't so sure. Behind the curtain, she wriggled in my arms, trying to get free.

"Where do you think you're going?" I asked, looking down at her. When I'd picked her up at her bedroom door earlier in the evening, I'd been struck dumb. I was used to her daily uniform of camp shirts and jeans or her white cotton nightgowns. She was gorgeous in either. Everything about Sophie was beautiful.

With her silvery blonde hair piled on top of her head and her curvy body poured into an elegantly form-fitting navy dress, she was a knockout. I'd been struggling all night to keep my hands off of her.

"We can't hide here in the curtains," Sophie protested, leaning back to look up at me.

"Not if you keep wiggling like that," I agreed. The living room wasn't as full as the front hall and dining room. The latter had been converted into a ballroom after we'd hauled the table and chairs into the garage, and most of the guests were there, dancing and drinking and generally having a great time. But we weren't alone in the living room, and if Sophie didn't stay still, we were going to get caught.

Sophie stopped moving, and her eyes went wide as she realized the voices filtering through the thick layers of silk came from people only feet away. Before she could protest again, I dropped my head and kissed her.

I could kiss Sophie for hours. Days. I loved fucking her, the way she went wild when I had her naked, and I was inside her. But with Sophie, just kissing her was better than anything I'd ever had with another woman.

Her mouth fit mine like she'd been born just for me, her soft full lips parting in welcome. The stroke of her tongue against mine made my knees weak. She was a lot shorter than me, an issue we usually solved by getting horizontal. Not a workable plan behind the curtains, but I was a good problem solver.

Her dress had a slit up one side, and I took advantage, running my hand over her hip until I found the place where the fabric parted. I slid my hand beneath, pulling the dress to her waist and lifting her in my arms. Bracing her back against the wall, I let myself fall into the kiss, taking her mouth over and over.

She slid her arms around me with a barely audible moan, one hand gripping my shoulder and the other buried in my hair as she pressed her body to mine. Those soft, full breasts pillowed against my chest, and I thought about later, when I would lay her across her bed and strip off all of this dark blue silk to bare her soft curves to my hands and mouth.

I hitched her up against me tighter, grinding my now hard cock into the heat between her legs, her whimper of pleasure driving me a little out of my head. I curled my hand over her ass, letting my fingertips dip into her pussy and she cried out.

I froze as, behind us, a woman said, "Did you hear that?"

Sophie went stiff in my arms. I tore my mouth from hers, and pressed my lips to her shoulder, both of us breathing hard and trying to hide it.

Annalise's voice, laden with amusement, said, "I didn't hear anything. You must be mistaken."

"No, I'm sure I heard something. Is there someone behind the curtain?" the woman asked, torn between curiosity and outrage.

I didn't mind being caught making out with Sophie, but Sophie would be appalled. Unfortunately, in our current situation, there wasn't a lot I could do if someone decided to cross the room and whip back the heavy curtains.

Annalise, somehow keeping her laughter at bay, came to the rescue.

"Oh no, I'm sure there's not," she said. Then, after a short pause, "Is that someone tapping a champagne glass? I think they might be getting ready to cut the cake."

High heels clicked on the hardwood as Annalise herded the woman out of the living room. I risked a peek to confirm we were alone before pulling back the curtain.

"We almost got caught," Sophie hissed.

I kissed her temple and murmured, "I won't let you get caught, Angel."

She gave a little sigh and leaned into me as we left the

living room. It turned out Charlie *had* been cutting the cake —good timing—and we stood at the door of the dining room-turned-ballroom to watch. Annalise sidled up beside me.

I looked down with a grin and said, "Thanks for the save."

She elbowed me in the side, leaning across me to send a wink to Sophie and said, "Anytime big brother. I like your girl. I don't care if you get embarrassed, but I wanted to save Sophie."

"That's the new family theme," I said, pretending to complain. "Everyone wants to save Sophie, and no one cares about me."

"That's because she takes such good care of Amelia. And so far she's kept Amelia from burning down the house. That's a major accomplishment."

Sophie leaned around me to catch Lise's eye. "Amelia's the most fun I've had in years," she said. "Even if I had to disarm a prank just this morning. I usually help her, but we all put our foot down. No pranks for the weddings. Especially not if they involve plastic frogs."

We all looked up as Lucas fed Charlie a bite of the cake, popping it into her mouth and laying a sweet kiss across her lips. On either side of me, Annalise and Sophie both let out a sigh. Annalise said in a wistful tone, "She looks so happy."

"I think she is," I said.

"I love him with her," Annalise said, fervently. Surprised by the emotion in her tone I looked away from Charlie and Lucas to see her watching our youngest cousin, her eyes filled with love, affection, and maybe a little envy. She went on, "He's strong, and Charlie needs someone strong. She needs someone she can depend on. Someone who will have her back when things get hard."

"Charlie does a good job of watching her own back," I said.

Annalise let out a long breath and said, "I know. Charlie has always been stronger than anyone gave her credit for. She's quiet about it, but when things get hard, she doesn't fold. She doesn't run. She'll be a good match for Lucas."

I heard what she didn't say. "You're not weak, Lise."

Her chin dropped and she looked at the ground. "Not weak," she agreed, "but not brave, either."

"You should come home," I said, knowing it was a waste of time.

She shook her head, a little sadly, I thought. "I want to. I'm thinking about it, but I don't know if I can."

"You can't run for the rest of your life, Lise."

"I don't know if I can stop," she said.

A new song started, and I took her hand, turning to Sophie. "You don't mind if I dance with my sister, do you?"

"Of course not. I'll be right here."

I dragged Annalise, over her protests, onto the dance floor. I was an awful dancer, but Annalise wasn't, so we evened out. I glanced over her shoulder to see Aiden at Sophie's side and scowled. He ignored me.

I was keeping my peace for now, but he and I were going to have to deal with each other. About the company. About Sophie. About a lot of things. After the weddings.

Following the line of my gaze, Annalise said, "I don't know what's up with you two."

I shook my head. "You run away from home, and everyone welcomes you back with open arms. I join the army, and when I finally decide to come back, Aiden isn't speaking to me."

"It's not fair," Annalise agreed. "I could give you a

bunch of reasons why, but it's still not fair. Do you want me to talk to him?"

"No, sweetheart. Aiden and I will come to terms on our own, one way or another. I'm back, and I'm not going anywhere. Aiden will have to deal."

CHAPTER
TWENTY-FIVE
SOPHIE

I don't know what woke me, the sound of breaking glass or the blare of the alarm. It must have been the alarm, but as I struggled to wake, I imagined I'd heard glass break, the thud of footsteps.

I'd been deeply asleep, caught in the beginnings of a nightmare. Anthony chasing me through the endless halls of Winters House, my heart pounding in fear and his fingertips grazing my shoulder as he reached for me.

I was still untangling dream from reality when Gage rolled out of bed, yanked on his boxers, and pulled a gun from the bedside table. He held the weapon as naturally as if it were a part of him. After so many years in the army, it probably was. He stopped at the door to look over his shoulder and said, "Stay there."

The hell I would.

I wasn't foolish enough to follow him down the hall. I didn't have a weapon, and I wasn't trained in self-defense or any of the other things the security guards and Gage undoubtedly knew how to do.

But Amelia was right across the hall, and the alarm

would have woken her up. I had to get over there and make sure she stayed in her room because, while I might have been wise enough to stay put, Amelia was daring enough not to.

Knowing she wouldn't be able to resist her curiosity for long, I quickly changed into the clothes I'd been wearing that day, glad I hadn't stuffed them into the hamper. Gage had dragged me into my room only seconds after Amelia had gone to sleep, stripping me efficiently at the side of the bed before drawing me under the covers and keeping me awake for hours.

My cheeks warmed at the memory. I shook it off and buttoned my shirt. Shoving my feet into slip-on sneakers, I went to the bedroom door and cracked it an inch, peering into the hall.

At the far end, by the library and Aiden's office, I saw lights and movement, heard voices through the din of the alarm. The hall itself was empty. I crossed to Amelia's door, arriving just as she was drawing it open and preparing to slip out.

"Don't even think about it," I said, sliding my arm around her shoulders and turning her back into her bedroom. She came with me easily enough.

"What's happening?" She asked. "Is everyone all right?"

"I don't know," I said, as soothingly as I could, given my own nerves. I led her to the oversize armchairs in the sitting area of her bedroom and urged her down. "I'll make you some tea."

"I don't want any tea. I want to know what's going on," she said querulously, sounding her age for the first time since I'd known her.

She might not have wanted tea, but the normalcy of it would soothe her. I went to the bookcase on the other side of the room where Amelia had an electric kettle, two mugs, and a box of tea.

As I heated water and chose a teabag filled with soothing herbs and flowers, I reflected that if I'd had an electric kettle and tea in my room, I wouldn't have had to wander to the kitchen in the middle of the night and probably never would have gotten to know Gage. At least not the way I did, alone and in the dark of night.

Even without our secret meetings, I was pretty sure we would have ended up where we were eventually. There was something that drew us together, something primal. Living at Winters House, there was no shortage of attractive men around. I wasn't blind, I could appreciate their good looks, but they weren't Gage. They weren't mine.

The alarm finally cut off, the sudden silence oppressive. Amelia looked to the door and then to me. "Can we open it? I want to hear what's going on."

I dropped tea bags into mugs of hot water and carried them to the armchairs, placing them on the table between them before I sat opposite Amelia. "No," I said, gently. "I locked the door, and we're not opening it until Gage or Aiden tells us to."

"I don't like being shut up in here," she complained.

"I don't like it either," I admitted, bobbing my teabag up and down in my mug, watching the hibiscus flowers stain the water red. "But we don't know if it's safe out there, and we don't want to get in their way."

"You're right; I'm just terrible at waiting."

"Tell me something I don't know," I muttered into my tea, my lips curving at Amelia's laugh.

It was an eternity before a light knock sounded on Amelia's bedroom door, followed by the handle turning and releasing. At the door, I heard Gage's low rumble, tight with a thread of tension as he said, "Sophie, tell me you're in there. "

"I'm here," I said as I hurried to unlock the door. "Is everyone all right?"

I opened the door to see Gage on the other side, in one piece and seemingly unharmed. Reassured that he was okay, I relaxed a little. His gun was nowhere to be seen, but I didn't doubt he had it on him.

"Everyone is fine. Aiden wants us in the dining room."

"Why did the alarm go off? Was someone in the house?" Amelia asked from behind me.

Gage shook his head as he ushered us out of the room. Not in denial, I realized, when he said, "In the dining room."

"But—" Amelia protested. Gage wrapped his arm around her shoulders and kissed the top of her head.

"Sweetheart, I know the suspense is killing you, but just give it a minute, and we'll tell you everything. Lise is freaked out, and this will be easier if we're all together."

I slowed as we passed the library, glancing over my shoulder to see two men in dark clothes at one of the windows taping thick plastic over the empty space where the window glass had been. Before I could come to a stop and look more closely, Gage caught my hand in his and tugged me along to the dining room.

Aiden waited just outside the door, his arms around Annalise, speaking in her ear in low, soothing tones. Whatever he was saying, it wasn't working. Her blue eyes were wide with shock, her face pale, hands shaking.

As we sat around one end of the table, Gage leaned into me and asked, under his breath, "You okay?"

"I'm fine," I said, mostly telling the truth. I was somewhere in between Amelia and Annalise. Now that Amelia could see for herself that her family was safe and well, I could tell by the gleam in her eyes that she was more curious than alarmed by whatever had happened. Annalise, on the other hand, looked ready to bolt.

Gage sat between Amelia and me. I suspected Aiden would have taken the head of the table, but he sat opposite us, next to Annalise, and took one of her trembling hands in his. She curled her fingers around Aiden's and held on, tight.

"Cooper is sending more security," Aiden began. "They should be here any minute, so don't be alarmed if you see more of the Sinclair team in the house. We're going to search the lower level. Whoever got in didn't know about the motion alarms and set them off when he or she tried to enter the hall. They broke the glass in the library window to get out, but they didn't have time to cover their tracks."

"What does that mean?" Amelia demanded. "Cover what tracks?"

"Did you catch him?" Annalise asked in a thin voice.

Shaking his head, Aiden said, "No. We saw someone running across the back lawn when we got to the window. One of the security team went after whoever it was, but they had too much of a head start. And we don't know that it's a man. We don't want to make any assumptions. We made that mistake with Marissa Archer when she was leaving the pictures. We might've caught her sooner if we hadn't assumed the person on the security tapes was a man."

"Cover what tracks?" Amelia repeated.

"The hidden door in the library leading to the hall outside the theater room downstairs was open. However the intruder has been entering the house, we think they're getting in down there. We're going to start looking tomorrow."

"This is an old house," Gage said. "The rooms on the lower level have been repurposed more than once, but there used to be a furnace, a coal chute, who knows what else. We'll figure out how they're getting in and seal it off."

A quick double knock sounded at the door to the dining room, and we all turned to see a man in a Sinclair Security uniform standing at the door, holding a wooden box.

Aiden gave him a questioning look, and he said, "We found this outside the broken window. It had fallen open, and the contents were scattered in the dirt. We think this is what the intruder was after, but when he dropped it, it opened, and he had to abandon it if he wanted to get away. We put everything back in the box and thought you might want to take a look."

Crossing the room, he handed the box to Aiden and turned to go.

"It's possible this is what the intruder has been after from the beginning," Gage said, studying the box on the table in front of Aiden. A little taller than a shoe box but about the same dimensions, it was made of dark wood, with brass hinges and a brass clasp. There was a lock on the front. It looked as if it had been smashed in, I was guessing by the intruder.

Aiden lifted the heavy lid of the box, folding it back carefully and drew out a creamy sheet of paper with smears of dirt on the front. His eyes scanned the scrawling, hand-written note. When he was done, he set it on the dining room table and pulled out a second, seemingly identical folded sheet of paper.

When he reached for the third, Annalise ran out of patience and snapped, "Aiden!"

CHAPTER TWENTY-SIX
SOPHIE

Aiden's dark brows pulled together in concentration. He looked up at her and gave a tiny shake to his head. She shifted in her chair, I thought repressing the urge to get up and snatch the box away from her older cousin. Aiden dug to the bottom of the box and drew out one more letter, this one on gray paper larger than the first few notes. He scanned it and returned it to the bottom of the box.

"So far, they're all addressed to your mother," he said, looking from Annalise to Gage. "No signature."

"From our father?" Annalise asked, reaching for one of the letters Aiden had left on the dining room table. Aiden moved it out of her reach before he answered.

"It's not his handwriting. Not my father's either. The date on the letter from the bottom was July 1980. Before Anna started dating Uncle James. The letter on the top was from a year after they got together."

"What did they say?" Gage asked.

"They appear to be love letters," Aiden said quietly as shock settled over the room.

Beside me, I felt Gage go utterly still. This was his mother they were talking about. I knew from Amelia that shortly before I'd been hired, they'd discovered that Anna Winters had borne a child and given him up for adoption before she'd married James Winters. They'd been looking for the missing child ever since.

Finding the box should have answered questions instead of creating more. Had Anna been the one to carefully pack up all those letters? What were they doing in the library? And how had the intruder known where to look?

Gage studied the box sitting so innocuously on the table and said, "I don't remember seeing that box anywhere in the library."

"Neither do I," Aiden said. "But there's more hidden in there than just the door to the lower level. My dad told me there were secret compartments."

"Where?" Annalise asked. "Why didn't I know about this? Did you know?" She asked Gage.

Gage gave a guilty shrug. "Uncle Hugh said there were three, but Aiden and I only ever managed to find one. Could the box have been in another? Who would've known where to look?"

"Where is it? Where's the secret compartment that you found?" Amelia asked.

Both Aiden and Gage remained silent, and Amelia scowled at them, muttering, "You don't have to tell me, I'll figure it out."

I didn't have to wonder what our next project would be. Maybe searching for the hidden compartments would keep Amelia out of trouble.

"What if this is him?" Annalise asked. "What if this is the missing baby?"

"You think our intruder is Anna's missing son?" Aiden asked.

"There's a logic to it," Gage said. "Just because we can't find him, doesn't mean he doesn't know who he is, or who we are. We have no idea what he's been told or how he was raised. He could hold a grudge or have an agenda we know nothing about."

"It could be the father," Amelia cut in. "None of the documents Charlie found revealed the identity of the baby's father. We know it couldn't have been James, but James knew about the baby, or that paperwork wouldn't have been so easy to find. That box of letters just proves my point. If Anna was trying to hide them, she would've burned them or torn them up, not put them in a box. I'd bet either Hugh or James had that box, not Anna. She never favored the library when she was in the house. Anna loved the living room. More light, she always said." A shadow crossed Amelia's face, and I reached out to squeeze her hand.

Across the table, Annalise propped her heels on the edge of her chair, bringing her knees to her chest, and wound her arms tightly around them, turning herself into a defensive ball. "So basically we have no idea who it is. It could be my missing half-brother; it could be my mother's lover—"

"It could have something to do with that phone call," I cut in.

Gage and Aiden exchanged a look I couldn't decipher. They knew something. I sat up straighter in my chair and leaned forward, looking between them.

"The break-ins started after I moved in. Not long before I got that phone call. This might not be about your family at all. This might be about me."

"You'd been living here for months before anything

happened," Aiden argued. "I think it's unlikely this is related to your phone call."

Before I could say anything, Gage jumped in. "It's not about you, Sophie. If the intruder had anything to do with you or Anthony Armstrong, why would he want a box of my mother's old love letters?"

I couldn't argue that logic. The timing just seemed odd.

"It could be my stalker," Annalise said in a stark, flat voice.

"No." Aiden and Gage both answered, together. Aiden continued, "The timing doesn't work, Lise. The break-ins started well before you came home and they don't follow the pattern. There was no card, no note, no flowers, no gifts."

"Maybe he's escalating," she said.

Aiden gave her a sharp look. "Did something happen you haven't told us about?"

"I didn't say that," Annalise hedged.

"It's not the stalker," Aiden said.

Annalise settled back into her chair, her expression unconvinced. "I should leave," she said.

"Don't even think about it," Aiden said. "Tate is getting married in two days. You can wait two days."

Annalise gave a noncommittal shake of her head. Aiden packed the letters back in the box and stood.

"The house is secured for the night. We have extra security outside, two in the library, and two downstairs. The window will be repaired tomorrow. I suggest we all try to get some sleep. Lise, I'd like you to move up to Gage's room. It's less exposed than your bedroom at the front of the house."

"I thought you said the house was secure," she said.

"It is," he said gently, "but I think you'll sleep better upstairs. The only way to Gage's room is the main staircase, and that has sensors all over it. Jacob's suite is the only other room near yours, and it's empty. You won't be able to relax down there, and I know you don't want to sleep with Amelia."

"My snoring isn't that bad," Amelia muttered.

"We can hear you across the hall," Gage said, easily. My cheeks burned at his open admission that he was sleeping in my bed every night. Everyone knew it, but knowing it and talking about it in the open were two different things.

"Gage," I hissed under my breath.

"Angel," he said, trying to hide his laugh. He reached out and took my hand, running his thumb over my knuckles. I couldn't bring myself to lift my gaze from the surface of the dining room table. I was too embarrassed.

"I'll move my things upstairs," Annalise said, taking the attention off me. I shot her a grateful look, and she returned it with a kind smile.

We all stood, and Gage turned to me, saying quietly, "Walk Amelia back to her room and stay with her until I come get you. I'm going to help Annalise move her things upstairs and grab what I need. Wait for me to get back before you go to your room."

"I thought you said the house was safe."

"It is. Just humor me, okay?"

I walked Amelia back to her room and busied myself rinsing out our tea cups and throwing away the used tea bags. So many secrets. I'd been living with the Winters family for over six months, and I still couldn't keep track.

Maybe I was paranoid, but I was sure Aiden and Gage were keeping something from me. Something about that phone call or Anthony. I didn't need any more intrigue. I had enough of it trying to keep up with Amelia. I'd managed to keep her from pulling any pranks at Charlie's wedding, but she was planning something for Tate's. I knew it. I just couldn't figure out what it was.

She'd snuck off a few times, and I'd caught her staring out the window with a secret smile playing across her lips. After half a year together, I knew the signs. She had something up her sleeve.

Trying to use our time alone to my advantage I said, "If you're planning a joke or surprise for Tate's wedding, please don't. This is not the time. Everyone is too on edge."

"That's exactly why this is the time," Amelia said. "Trust me. I'm not going to scare anyone, but we need to relieve a little tension around here. Everyone is way too pent up."

"Amelia, did you see Annalise? She looked like she was about to jump out of her skin. And Gage is doing better than he was when he came home, but he's still not ready for surprises. If you're going to do something, at least tell me what it is."

Amelia pressed her lips together and shook her head. "No, you can't keep a secret. You're going to have to trust me."

"I love you," I said, "but when it comes to this, I don't trust you as far as I can throw you."

"Hmph," she grumbled as she let me tuck her into bed. "That's not very far. You have T-Rex arms."

I looked down at my arms and back to Amelia. "I do not! My arms are a completely normal length."

"Compared to the rest of you, maybe. On a normal size person, they'd be tiny."

It was the middle of the night. I was not prepared to argue Amelia's circular logic. I knew she was just trying to distract me from our conversation about whatever she was planning for Tate's wedding. Gage opened the door before I could figure out how to get her to talk.

I left Amelia in bed and followed Gage across the hall to my room. His hands were on the buttons of my shirt seconds after he turned the lock on the door. I batted them away and took a step back.

"What aren't you telling me?" I demanded.

"A lot," he said, surprising me with his honesty. "But nothing you need to know."

"I'd rather judge that for myself," I said.

His hands went for my buttons again. "I know you would. You're just going to have to trust me."

"Why does everyone keep saying that?" I muttered. "I don't want to trust you; I want to know what's going on. I want to know what you and Aiden aren't telling me."

"Trust me," Gage murmured in my ear, slipping my shirt over my shoulders and undoing the clasp of my bra with a flick of his fingers behind my back. "I'm not going to let anything happen to you, Sophie. Just trust me. Let me take care of you."

I let out a sigh, giving in as his hand covered my breast and his lips touched mine in a slow, lazy kiss. He backed me toward the bed, helping me step out of my jeans. I was on my back a second later, his hard, hot body over mine, his hips nudging my thighs apart, the head of his hard cock sliding against me, rolling over my clit in slow circles.

I forgot to argue. I forgot how much I trusted him, and how much I didn't want to. I forgot everything but the rising sea of pleasure and his long, drugging kisses.

I'd remember in the morning. That would have to be good enough. For now, I didn't want to fight. All I wanted was Gage.

Chapter Twenty-Seven

Gage

"I do."

Tate barely waited for the officiant to finish saying, "You may kiss the bride," before he scooped Emily into his arms, bent her back and laid a kiss on her mouth that was borderline inappropriate for a wedding.

Emily didn't look like she minded.

My new sister-in-law glowed with joy, the wide smile on her face matching Tate's. Their wedding couldn't have been more different from Charlie and Lucas's the week before. Aside from two close friends, the only guests were family.

Our uncle William had an out-of-town emergency, and while Mrs. W and Abel weren't strictly relatives, we considered them family just the same. They excused themselves to get dinner set up, and Emily dragged Tate off to take a few pictures with Annalise, who was acting as the official wedding photographer. I took advantage of everyone's distraction to sneak a kiss from Sophie.

She wore the same elegant navy blue dress she had to Charlie's wedding, but this time she'd left her hair down, at my request. It flowed over her shoulders, the silvery blonde waves as soft as silk. I couldn't keep my fingers off it. If she'd been wearing white, she would've been the perfect picture of the angel I always called her. I looked down at her, framing her face in my hands and slid the pad of my thumb over the dark circles beneath her eyes.

She hadn't slept more than a few hours at a time since the break-in, waking abruptly after snatches of broken sleep, moaning and murmuring in plaintive tones. I hated seeing her so vulnerable. I'd asked her to trust me, and I knew she was trying, but trust came hard for Sophie.

It would have been easier if we'd caught the intruder. We'd made a little progress. The library window was fixed, and the Sinclair team had discovered how the intruder was entering the house – a long abandoned coal chute that fed into a closet at the back of the gym. Aiden and I had debated sealing it up, but at Cooper's recommendation, we'd left it as is, adding only a silent sensor to alert us if the chute was used. The next time this fucker tried to get into our house, we'd have him.

None of that was helping Sophie to sleep at night. Who knows, I might have been in the same shape if she wasn't waking me up so often. As it was, I'd had fitful nightmares myself, flashes of finding my aunt and uncle dead in the library, sometimes seeing Sophie in their place, blood spilled across her pale skin, her green eyes blank and glazed with death. None of us would relax until we caught whoever was breaking into the house.

Annalise had finally conceded that it was unlikely the intruder was her stalker, but she was still jumpy, hyper-alert and on edge. I doubted she would stick around more than a day or two now that Tate and Emily were married.

Sophie let me pull her down the hall to the wine room.

Tate, Emily, and Annalise were occupied with photographs in the living room, Mrs. W and Abel in the dining room, while the rest of the family was sharing drinks at the temporary bar set up in the front hall. It was the perfect time to sneak off for a few minutes.

I wasn't the only one with that idea. I pushed open the heavy door of the wine room and was greeted by a startled gasp and a low chuckle. Vance had Magnolia pressed against the back wall, her dress hiked halfway up her leg, his hand on the back of her thigh and his mouth on her neck. Her dark red hair spilled over both of them, matching the embarrassed flush on her cheeks.

Over his shoulder, Vance said, "Get a room. I'd get one, but your girl is using mine."

He had a point. While we all had rooms in the house, Sophie had taken his, and Amelia had moved into Holden and Tate's. Sophie's hand firmly in mine, I tried to tug her down the hall, toward her bedroom but she dug in her heels.

"Not in the middle of the wedding," she said.

"Technically the wedding is over, and the reception hasn't started yet," I reasoned. Lively music sounded from the front hall, and I knew I'd lost my window. As expected, Sophie raised an eyebrow at me.

"I'm pretty sure that's the reception starting right now," she said, "and I have to keep an eye on Amelia. She's up to something; I just can't figure out what."

I gave in, but not before backing her into the wall outside the wine room and kissing her senseless. Her eyes were hazy and her lips swollen when I finally raised my head. "Now we can go to the reception," I said, my lips against her ear, loving the way she shivered in my arms.

I could have urged her down the hall just then and locked us both in her bedroom. A few more kisses and

Sophie would be more than willing to be late to the party. I didn't do it. Sophie wanted to go to the reception. She wanted to keep an eye on Amelia. So that's what we'd do. I'd have plenty of time alone with her later.

I kept an eye on Amelia as we got our drinks and joined my cousin Holden and his new fiancée Jo by the French doors overlooking the terrace behind the house. Holden had proposed to Jo not long after Tate and Emily had gotten engaged, though they were waiting to get married. They hadn't decided what kind of wedding they wanted. Considering we'd just had two in a row, and Jacob and Abigail were planning the wedding to end all weddings, Holden and Jo just wanted to enjoy being engaged for a while.

I listened to Sophie asking Jo about her work and studied Amelia, across the room. On the surface of things, she looked innocent enough, but there was a smugness to her happy smile that set me on edge. Sophie was right, Amelia was up to something.

Mrs. W appeared in the doorway of the dining room to tell us all it was time to eat. Tate had insisted she be a wedding guest and she, in turn, had insisted that she oversee the festivities, considering that it was only family. They'd both gotten their way, and after directing us all to our places, she took her own seat at the table. The seat beside her was empty, reserved for Abel, who Tate had also insisted join the party. Uniformed waiters, hired for the evening, carried in plates through the butler's pantry and set them before us.

Sophie sat beside me on the left. Amelia sat to her left, close enough to keep watch on, though as far as I could tell she wasn't interested in anything other than her soup.

We were just finishing the main course when Sophie saw it, tucked discreetly beneath her placemat. A note in heavy white vellum, folded in half. She was teasing it out from beneath the placemat when I caught sight of the note in her fingers, the curious crease between her eyebrows.

"What's that?" I asked, instantly suspicious.

"I don't know," she said, turning the note over in her hands before unfolding it.

Meet me in my office when Gage is asleep.

I need to see you alone.

A

I knew that handwriting, the arrogant slash of that A.

That fucking bastard. I fucking knew it this whole time. The way he warned me away from her. The way he looked at her. I risked a glance at Sophie, her wide, shocked eyes barely registering through my surge of fury.

"Gage," she stammered, "I don't know what this is. I swear, I don't know why –" She looked up at Aiden, at the head of the table, and back at the note. "I don't understand."

I shoved to my feet, tipping my chair over behind me and tore the note from her hands. "I do. And I'm fucking done."

I stalked down the room to the head of the table, a tide of rage rising in my chest. He could ignore me. He could put me off. He could punish me for leaving and shut me out. I'd resigned myself to that, was even okay with it.

Going after Sophie? Fuck, no. Sophie was mine, and this was a step too fucking far. I reached Aiden's chair in a few long strides that seem to take forever and reached down, my fist closing around the knot of his tie. I hauled him up, knocking his chair back. I only took a moment to register the shock on his face before I planted my fist in the middle of it.

CHAPTER TWENTY-EIGHT

GAGE

Aiden went down hard. His back hit the floor, and his skull bounced on the carpet. Then he was up, lunging for me. I met him halfway, arm raised and ready to strike. He hit me with a shoulder to the gut and took me to the floor. Smart move. Aiden had wrestled in high school. He wasn't trained in combat like I was, but on the ground, he had a chance.

My awareness dissolved into swinging fists, kicking feet, and grappling arms. Aiden didn't have my skill, but he was driven by rage, all his pent up resentment and anger and unspoken emotion flooding out through his clenched fists as we rolled. He pinned me, getting in a good strike to my temple before I scissored my legs and threw him off, kicking him hard in the back.

I got him in a choke hold for a few seconds, managing to get enough breath to growl out, "Keep your fucking hands off Sophie," before he twisted free and I took another fist to the jaw.

An unexpected strike to the shoulder had me looking up to see Sophie standing above us, her arms crossed over her chest, a furious look on her face. "You two are complete idiots. I'm not going to watch grown men act like children."

She strode from the room as I stared after her. Aiden let out a roar and lunged at me, catching me distracted, his fist connecting with my cheekbone.

We'd fought before. We'd grown up side-by-side and shared a room most of our childhoods. But we'd never fought like this. Over a decade of pain and anger, of betrayal and disillusionment, of grief and love, spilled through me. Somewhere in the middle of it, I realized I wasn't even mad anymore.

Sophie didn't want Aiden. She was mine because she wanted to be mine, not because I declared it so. Aiden couldn't take her from me. Only Sophie could do that. If I hadn't been on such a hair trigger lately, I never would've gone for the bait.

Bait.

The word exploded in my head in a flash of understanding. God dammit. *Amelia.* Aiden hadn't written that note. I went limp and fell to my back just as icy water splashed over us. Shocked and sputtering, I looked up to see Mrs. W standing over us in the same posture as Sophie had, arms crossed over her chest, foot tapping, glower firmly in place. An empty water pitcher dangled from one finger.

"You boys are too old for this nonsense," she said in a steely voice. "This is Tate's wedding, not a circus. Go sit out back on the patio and cool off. Don't think about coming back in this house until you've worked out your differences, do you understand me?"

"Yes, ma'am," we said in unison. Aiden and I dragged our bruised bodies out of the dining room, ignoring the amused laughter of the rest of the family. I pushed my way through the French doors to the terrace and sat on the top step, the icy slate freezing my ass through my suit.

Georgia had been unseasonably cold over the holidays, but the frigid air felt good on my bruised and rapidly swelling face. Unwilling to completely give in I said, "You still have a pussy left hook."

"Fuck you," Aiden said, without heat. "Why the fuck did you hit me?"

I shrugged and winced at the unexpected pain in my shoulder. "Sophie found a note from you under her place-mat," I said.

"I didn't write Sophie a note. Why the hell would I do that?"

"Yeah, I figured that out while we were beating the shit out of each other."

"Amelia."

"Bingo," I said.

A strangled laugh erupted from Aiden's throat, and he shook his head, pushing his hair back with the heel of his palm. "She told me if we didn't work things out she'd deal with us her own way."

I let out a strangled laugh of my own and felt hot liquid warmth run from my split lip to my chin. Fuck. If my face looked anything like Aiden's, we were both a mess.

His dark hair was tangled and matted with sweat, falling over his forehead and almost hiding the swelling around his left eye. I could feel my own eyelid swelling to match his. By morning we'd have twin black eyes. And split lips. People had always said we looked alike.

I braced my elbows on my knees and stared down at the slate between my feet. Letting out a long breath, I said, "I'm sorry I left. I should've stayed. I should've manned up and stayed and helped you. I know you hated me for it. I know why you can't forgive me, and I understand."

Beside me, I felt Aiden go still, and then his eyes on me. I couldn't look up. I couldn't stand to see the accusation, the blame in his eyes.

"What the fuck are you talking about? I don't hate you. What do you mean I can't forgive you? I'm fucking pissed you took so long to come home. And I'm pissed you almost got yourself fucking killed, but—"

I shot to my feet and faced him down, finally ready to take the judgment I was due.

"I didn't save them," I shouted at the top of my lungs, the words tearing from my heart in raw pain and the sheer relief of draining a wound that had never healed. "I didn't save them. I was here. I was up in my room fucking sulking because I was grounded, and I didn't save them."

My knees folded abruptly as if pulled by a string, and I sat back on the step, swamped with guilt and grief. Beside me, Aiden sucked in a breath and let it out.

"You had your headphones on," he said, quietly. "They were in the library. You couldn't have heard anything."

"I should've known," I said. "I was *here*. I was upstairs. They died, and I didn't save them."

"It wasn't your fault, Gage," Aiden said, his voice a low rasp. "Is that why you didn't come home? Because you thought I blamed you? How could you think I would blame you?"

"Why *wouldn't* you blame me?" I asked. "I blame myself. If I'd heard something, if I'd gone downstairs, if I hadn't been sulking in my room like—"

"Like a teenager? Which is what you were. A teenager. Not super Gage special forces soldier. You were eighteen and unarmed. If you'd been downstairs, you probably would have died with them. Did you ever think about that?" Aiden asked.

"Maybe," I conceded.

I had thought about it, but that logic had never felt like absolution. Maybe Aiden was right, and I would've been killed along with my aunt and uncle. But maybe if I'd been there things would've changed. We didn't know what had happened to them, only that they'd been shot in the library in a crime almost identical to the one that had taken my parents lives so many years before.

In both cases, the deaths were written off as murder/suicides and dismissed, but we knew someone had killed them. We just didn't know why. Without answers, I couldn't stop wondering how I might have changed things.

"I'm sorry I've been an ass since you've been home," Aiden said. "I want you to come back to the company. I do. I just—" he stopped and swallowed hard. "I understand why you left, Gage. It was hard here without you, but I understood. You found them. You walked in the library in this house, and you found them dead. I get why you needed to get away. I thought you would come home after a few years, but I figured you just needed more time. And then they told us you were missing and probably dead and—"

Aiden's voice choked off. I tried to speak and found my throat was locked shut.

We sat there in silence, fighting to get our emotions under control. Finally, Aiden reached out and punched me in the shoulder. Pain exploded, far out of proportion to his strike. I must've landed on it wrong when we'd hit the floor in the dining room. Shit, we were immature assholes, even in our thirties.

"I should've come home a long time ago," I said when I thought I could speak again. Fighting off the tightness in my throat, I said, "I should've known you wouldn't blame me. I just... I couldn't stop dreaming about them. I still do."

"Gage," Aiden said, "it's been twelve years. You can't let it take over your life like this."

"I know," I interrupted, "I know. It's not just that, it's the last six months, and everything I did, everything I saw the years before that. It's a lot of shit all rolled up in my head so I can't sleep, and I'm on edge all the time—"

"Yeah, no shit," Aiden said, and I laughed. "You were always Mr. Cool, and now you're jumping me at a wedding?"

"Yeah," I said. It wasn't funny, not really, but I laughed anyway. "Cooper set me up with someone to talk to. My first appointment is next week."

I shook my head and looked out over the back lawn into the moonlit trees behind the house. On the other side of those trees, through the dark woods, was my parents' house, sitting empty and abandoned. I shook my head again.

"I can't tell you how many times I've sat like this with guys dealing with the same shit and told them all the right things. There's no shame in it. It helps to talk to someone. Don't just bottle it up and ignore it. Then it's me, and I'd rather go without sleep than admit I can't handle it on my own."

"You always were a stubborn fuck."

"You going to let me come back to work?"

"Whenever you want," Aiden said with a hint of a smile. It might've been a grin if his mouth hadn't been as torn up as mine.

"I've been studying up with Charlie," I admitted.

"I know," Aiden said, surprising me. "She tore me a new one, told me what a royal asshole I was, and how hard you've been working. The stuff on the jump drive came from me, not Charlie. Once you get through that, you're probably ready to start easing your way in."

"Sounds like a plan," I said.

We sat there in the dark for a few minutes before Aiden said, "So what's up with you and Sophie?"

"I'm in love with her," I said, liking the way the words sounded when I spoke them out loud. Trying it again, I said a little louder, "I'm in love with her."

"I hope she's in love with you," Aiden said, slowly rising to his feet, moving as carefully as an old man with achy joints. I'm pretty sure I looked exactly the same as I stood up beside him. "She was pissed as hell when she stormed out of the dining room."

Sophie was still pissed as hell when I knocked on the door of her room. She swung it open from beneath my rapping knuckles and glared up at me, her usually sweet face twisted into a scowl, her green eyes fiery with anger.

"What do you want?"

Looking down into those burning emerald eyes I could only think of one thing to say. "I love you, Sophie. I love you with everything I am and everything I will be. I'm sorry I acted like an adolescent and tried to beat up my cousin in the dining room, and I'm sorry if I embarrassed you with my behavior. Will you please let me in so I can show you exactly how sorry I am?"

Tears filled her eyes, turning the green fire to cool smoke. She blinked, and they ran down her cheeks. Reaching up, she traced a finger over the tight, hot skin on my cheekbone.

"You love me?" she asked, wonder in her voice.

I caught her hand in mine and kissed her fingertip. "I love you," I said again.

The tears flowed faster down her cheeks, her eyes

flicking back and forth as she took in the wounds on my face, her heart in her eyes.

"I love you too," she whispered.

"Can I come in?" I asked.

She stepped back and opened the door to let me into her room. Her pale eyebrows knit together as she studied my stiff gait and she said, "You need a hot shower and an ice pack. Or two. Maybe an ice *bath*."

I shut the door behind me and turned the lock.

"All I need is you."

CHAPTER
TWENTY-NINE
GAGE

I let Sophie lead me to the shower, murmuring over my bruises and split lip, her busy fingers unbuttoning my shirt as she walked backward, alternating between scolding and sympathizing. I ignored most of it. I'd already had my scolding from Mrs. W, and I was more interested in getting Sophie naked than in her sympathy.

I worked on her zipper as she turned on the hot water, peeling all that elegant, navy silk from her smooth, creamy skin. I loved her body, loved the way she was made. So soft and round in all the right places. The curve of her ass. Those full breasts. Everything about her was warm and welcoming.

Including the way she gasped when I ran my hand down her spine, cupped her ass, and dropped my fingers between her legs. I urged her over the tile threshold and under the steamy spray, watching as the water darkened her silvery hair, plastering it to her face. It stung my split lip but felt good on my bruises.

I didn't object when she urged me to switch places with her. Especially since she poured citrus scented body wash

into her hands and rubbed the soap all over my skin. I'd
stand there all day if Sophie wanted to scrub me down.

She started out briskly efficient, but when she turned
me around to face the water and went to work on my shoulders, her stroking hands slowed.

Her breasts pillowed against my back as she leaned
close, sliding her hands over my chest, stroking me in long
swipes, fingers dropping teasingly close to my cock. Her
nipples were two hard points when her hands took my
length in her slick, soapy grip.

She squeezed once, and I had to fight to keep my knees
from going weak. One hand pumped my cock, and the other
dropped to cup my sack. I groaned her name. "Sophie."

Just when I thought I couldn't take it anymore, she
leaned back and pulled my hip, turning me to face her.
Water cascaded over both of us, rinsing the soap from my
body as Sophie dropped to her knees and took the head of
my cock in her mouth. I tipped my face back into the spray,
eyes closed, oblivious to the stinging pain of the water on
my lip, to my aches and bruises, as the sweet suction of her
mouth chased it all away.

Her hand closed over my ass, fingers digging in, pulling
me closer, taking more of me. Her tongue fluttered against
the underside of my cock, sending shivers up my spine.

Before I completely lost it, I pulled her to her feet and
turned us around, reaching behind me to sweep bottles of
shampoo and body wash and who knew what else off the
deep bench on the far side of the shower. Plastic clattered to
the tile, and I sat, pulling Sophie onto my lap facing me.

She blinked at me, clearing the water from her eyes, and
I watched them flare wide as I sank two fingers into her
tight, hot pussy. She fell forward, her breasts against my
chest, her mouth sucking at my neck as I pumped my

fingers in and out, my cock straining, needing to take their place.

Spreading her knees wide, I lowered her, filling her sweet pussy in slow, torturous increments. She was gasping for breath by the time I sank to the hilt inside her. Her mouth lifted from my neck and she breathed, "Gage, Gage."

The tight quarters of the bench didn't give Sophie much room to move, but she didn't need it. My hands closed over her ass in a tight grip, and I rocked her against me, grinding her pussy down hard, lifting her barely an inch before bringing her down again. And again. And again, until she went flying into orgasm. Her body clamped down on my cock, and I followed her, spilling into her in gasping shudders.

When we thought we could move again, we dried off, and I carried her to her bed, sliding us both beneath the covers naked. Now that we'd taken the edge off in the shower, I could take my time. Settling myself between her legs, I did just that.

We slept late the next morning, mostly because I woke Sophie more than once, reaching for her in the dark, needing to touch her. To be inside her. Something about my confession of love and hers in return had unlocked any restraint I still had. I wanted to imprint my body onto hers, to fill her with me so deeply I became a part of her and she a part of me.

If it'd been up to me, we would've stayed in bed all day. But Sophie, being Sophie, insisted on meeting Amelia at the breakfast table as usual. Unlike Sophie, she let me hold her hand all the way there. I guess she was done trying to hide our relationship. Fighting over her in front of the whole family made hiding pointless anyway.

Aiden was already there, the newspaper spread out in

front of him, his face a kaleidoscope of greens and purples and blues, bruised and swollen. I took a long look and said to Sophie, "Do I look that bad?"

She only arched an eyebrow at me and shook her head. I was taking that as a *yes*. She busied herself with Amelia, and I looked up to see Aiden sliding me a folded section of the newspaper. He tapped the headline, an article about developments in steel production.

"What do you think about that?" he asked.

I picked up the paper and began to read, quickly absorbed by the subject matter. Only a few days before I'd been studying up on both the process and the company in question as Winters Inc. had been considering going into business with them. I didn't look up until a plate slid before me at the table.

Cold oatmeal. Ugh. Why did I have cold oatmeal when I smelled bacon?

I looked around the table to see another bowl of cold oatmeal in front of Aiden. His coffee cup was empty, and mine had never been filled.

Both Sophie and Amelia were digging into plates of fluffy scrambled eggs, partnered with small mountains of bacon and hot bowls of creamy cheese grits. Steaming cups of coffee sat in front of them.

Shit. Neither of us had apologized to Mrs. W for our fight the night before. Sophie looked up and took in my plate and Aiden's, then looked back to her own and Amelia's. She shook her head and said under her breath, "Serves you right. Both of you."

"You're not going to share with me?" I asked.

Picking up a piece of bacon and taking a delicate bite from the end, Sophie shook her head again. "That wouldn't be fair," she said. "Amelia doesn't have enough left to share with Aiden. You'll just have to take your punishment and then apologize. I can't believe you both got into a fist fight in the middle of the wedding."

Looking a little bit ashamed of himself, Aiden said, "It wasn't in the middle of the wedding, it was at the end of dinner."

Both Sophie and Amelia ignored his excuse. Sophie slanted Amelia a look and said, "You deserve cold oatmeal, too. That was not funny."

Amelia's shoulders began to shake. She swallowed hard to clear her throat before her laughter got the better of her, and she choked. Through her giggles, she said, "It was hysterical. The look on Gage's face? I thought he was going to explode before he even stood up. Maybe you three didn't think it was funny, but the rest of us haven't had that much fun in years. They used to go after each other like that all the time when they were boys."

Sophie looked from Aiden to me in fascination. "You did? What did you fight about?"

Aiden and I both shrugged. "Nothing, really," I said. That stuff was impossible to explain to women, especially a woman like Sophie. Sometimes we just needed to let off a little steam. Most of the time whatever had seemed important at the first punch wasn't a big deal by the time we were done.

Sophie would've told us to sit down and talk out our differences. A good fight was more efficient. Aiden and I suffered through our cold oatmeal and went together to apologize to Mrs. W for our behavior. Just as she had when we'd been kids, she accepted our apologies with starchy formality and a warning to see it didn't happen again.

The house was quiet the next few days. Tate, Emily, Charlie, and Lucas all left on their respective honeymoons.

Annalise left abruptly after an unexpected and mysterious delivery of flowers to the gatehouse. Despite the extra security, Annalise had taken one look at the arrangement of gardenias and violets, turned bone white, and gone to pack her bags. No amount of arguing had changed her mind.

An hour after the flowers arrived, she was gone. Sophie had taken the arrangement, vase and all, and carried it to the kitchen with shaking hands, shoving it deep in the trash. She wasn't as bothered by the flowers as Annalise, but it was close. When I asked her about it, she just shook her head, lips pressed tightly together, and refused to discuss it. Things had been so good I let it go.

Aiden had gone back to work, but for the next few weeks, he decided I would stick with him. We split our time, working from his home office in the mornings as he put me through a crash course on the company, and in the corporate headquarters every afternoon where I shadowed him, taking notes and getting up to speed. We hadn't decided what my official position would be, and I didn't care.

Like Aiden, I'd interned at the company through high school, learning from the ground up, earning minimum wage and working my ass off. And like Aiden, I'd loved every minute I was there. It wasn't just the business; it was all the memories tied up in the place. Knowing my grandfather had sat at Aiden's desk. Remembering the way I'd perched on my father's lap in the office that would someday be mine.

The company wasn't just about money and power; it was history and family. To Aiden and to me, Winters Inc. was just as much the heart of us as Winters House. Being back healed something inside of me that I'd damaged all those years ago when I'd left.

A few days after Annalise took off, Aiden and I sat behind his desk in Winters House, poring over a pair of spreadsheets, when an alert sounded from the front gate. Aiden punched a finger at the screen of his phone and put the guard on speaker.

"What is it?" he asked.

"Someone here to see Mrs. Armstrong. Says he has information and a delivery from her husband."

For a second, I didn't know who he was talking about. I never thought of Sophie as *Mrs. Armstrong*. I hated hearing the title of another man's wife attached to her. The most primitive part of me bristled at the thought.

Aiden looked at me with a raised eyebrow. I nodded, and he said to the guard, "Let him through."

CHAPTER THIRTY
GAGE

Without discussing it, neither of us went to tell Sophie she had a visitor. We waited as a sleek, low-slung sports car came through the inner gates and parked in front of the doors. A tall, slender man with dark hair and olive skin unfolded himself from the car.

He was dressed with elegant precision, his suit custom tailored, his shoes shined to a high polish, not a hair out of place. With a look of cold calculation, he scanned the court-yard before he climbed the steps to the front door.

Aiden opened the door at the first knock. I looked into the icy depths of the man's dark eyes, and a chill ran down my spine. I'd seen that look before. This was a man devoid of compassion. Of pity. A man without the capacity for love or simple human kindness. This was a man who knew only greed and destruction.

He opened his mouth and said, "I'm Anthony Armstrong. I'm here to get my wife."

From behind me, I heard a soft intake of breath. "Anthony?"

Fuck. Sophie. I didn't want her anywhere near this guy. The second I'd realized who he was, it took everything I had not to beat the life out of him.

I loved Sophie with every breath in my body, and this man had made her life a misery. He'd tried to destroy her. She'd been afraid he'd kill her. My muscles locked down, as a fine, almost imperceptible tremble shook me from head to toe. I would not lose my temper. I would control my anger, my rage.

Hurting Anthony would not help Sophie. Not in that moment. She needed me to think. She needed me to hold it together. I closed my eyes and took a deep breath, forcing my emotions to settle before I looked at Sophie.

She stood beside Aiden and me, her eyes wide with shock, skin pale. As I watched, she started to shake. Ignoring Anthony, I stepped back and went to her side, pulling her into my arms and wrapping her in a tight hold. She pressed her cheek to my chest, still staring at Anthony with those wide, terrified eyes.

In a soft tone that pretended to soothe, Anthony said, "Sophie, darling, I know this is a shock. If we could go somewhere to talk... Everything is over now, and you can come home."

Aiden shifted to block Anthony's entrance to the house. "I'm afraid I can't invite you in. Sophie isn't going anywhere. Since we were all under the impression that you died in a car accident two years ago, we can start with you explaining your presence on my doorstep."

"You're not going to let me in the house?" Anthony asked, incredulous.

I got the impression people rarely told him no. He'd met his match in Aiden. I tightened my arms around Sophie. Everything inside me wanted to deal with the vermin on our doorstep, but I wouldn't leave Sophie alone with Anthony so close. Aiden didn't need my help. Sophie did.

"No," Aiden said, "I'm not. Explain yourself, or get off my property."

"Sophie, they wouldn't let me tell you," he said smoothly, his eyebrows coming together in a frown as he took in his wife's face pressed to my chest, her arms wrapped tightly around my waist.

Forcing the expression from his face, he gave her a coldly gentle smile and went on, "I've been in protective custody. I testified against my former employers, and the prosecutor wanted me off the street until the case was closed."

"I thought you were dead," she whispered.

"I know, darling, I know it was hard, and I'm so sorry I hurt you like that. Testifying was dangerous, and it seemed safer for everyone if I appeared to be dead. Telling you would've put you at risk."

"That case ended over six months ago," I said. "Where have you been since then?"

Hot rage flared in Anthony's eyes as he met my gaze, then disappeared so quickly I wondered if I'd imagined it. In the same cool, gentle tone he said to Sophie, "We wanted to make sure the dust had settled before I came back to life."

"Who is we?" I asked, suspicious. "You and the prosecutor? You and the US Marshals service? I assume that's who had you in protective custody."

"Of course," Anthony said. Turning his attention back to Sophie, "You should never have had to go back to work, sweetheart. Damien was supposed to see that you were provided for. Taken care of. He's been dealt with, and now it's time for you to pack your things and come home."

At those words, Sophie shook harder, her breath tight

and short. Warm tears soaked through the front of my shirt, and I realized she was crying. I'd seen her wake from nightmares about this man, seen the fear his memory evoked, but I don't think I truly understood how bad things had been until I felt her fall apart in my arms.

"Sophie isn't going anywhere with you," I said, slowly and deliberately. "Sophie's home is here. With me. *We* are her family. She's getting a restraining order, and then she's filing for divorce. You can contact her through our lawyers. Aiden will get you the information."

I didn't wait for Anthony's response. I swung Sophie into my arms and carried her down the hall to the library where she and Amelia had been reading before Anthony arrived. Amelia looked up in surprise, then shock, when she saw Sophie in my arms and heard the sounds of her quiet weeping.

"Tell Mrs. W we need a tea tray," I said, "Tell her to make it strong and sweet." Amelia hesitated, clearly wanting to ask what was wrong. "Now, Amelia," I said, working to keep my voice gentle.

With a worried glance at Sophie, Amelia left. Sophie raised her head off my chest and tried to climb out of my arms. I sat on the couch and pulled her closer, stroking her hair back from her tear stained face.

"Angel, it's okay. He's not going to get to you. You never have to see him again. You're safe from him, I promise."

She drew in a shuddering breath and said, "I have to leave. He's going to come back, and I have to leave. I can't stay, I can't let you protect me like this. I can't, I can't—"

"Shhh, Angel. It's going to be okay; I'm not going to let anything happen to you."

"You deserve better than this. Better than me. I stayed

with him. I let him hurt me. I'm not strong enough for this. For you."

"Sophie, no." It was like she didn't hear me. She closed her eyes and sobbed so hard her body shook with it. It felt like she cried for hours. Amelia returned with the tea tray and waited patiently until Sophie finally ran out of tears.

I hadn't wanted to leave her while she was crying, but I needed to talk to Aiden. I needed to make sure Anthony Armstrong was gone. I settled Sophie into the couch and stood. Crouching in front of her, I wiped the tears from her cheeks with the pads of my thumbs and tried to get her to meet my eyes. Her green gaze was dull and fixed on the carpet.

"I need to go talk to Aiden," I said, softly. "We won't let him near you again, do you understand?"

All I got was a tiny nod. I kissed her gently and straightened. Amelia slid beside her and pulled Sophie close, tucking Sophie's head against her shoulder and stroking her arm.

"I won't be long," I promised and slipped from the room.

Chapter Thirty-One

Sophie

I wanted to call Gage back, to beg him to pull me into his arms again, to promise one more time that he could keep me safe. My worst nightmare had come to life the moment I saw Anthony at the front door of Winters House.

Worse than the beatings.

Worse than the fear that he'd kill me in a fit of rage and bury my body in the woods.

I'd had two years of freedom. I'd found love. I was happy. And then suddenly he was there, telling me to come home with him in that calm, icy voice I knew too well.

I felt that voice deep inside, freezing me, chilling my heart and stealing it from Gage. I couldn't love Gage. I couldn't be with him. He deserved so much better than a woman who had married a monster.

A woman who had stayed with that monster after he'd unmasked himself.

I thought I'd forgiven myself for that. Maybe I did forgive myself, but I was still a frightened, broken thing. Anthony had hurt me, and I'd stayed, too weak and afraid to leave him. Afraid he'd kill me. Afraid he'd go too far in his rage and bury me in the cold earth in the woods behind the house.

I should have run. I should have taken the risk. I'd faced pain so many times, but when it came down to it, I was too afraid of dying to reach for freedom.

Gage deserved so much better than a woman paralyzed by fear. He deserved so much better than a shattered mess. One sight of Anthony and I fell to pieces. Gage had survived six months as a prisoner of war. He'd never given up. Gage had escaped.

I'd never asked him how many times he tried to get away, but I'd bet it was more than two. He'd fought for himself. He deserved a woman who could do the same.

Amelia's gentle strokes on my arm centered me after my endless crying fit. I hated that she'd seen me weeping like a child. I lifted my head from her shoulder and sat up, scrubbing at my face with my palms.

"Drink this," she said, pushing a teacup into my hands. I sipped lukewarm, overly sweet tea.

Without thinking, I said, "I need to leave. If Anthony's alive, and we're still married, I can't stay here. I can't be with Gage. I have to leave."

"Don't be foolish," Amelia said in her best no-nonsense voice. "You need to stay exactly where you are. We're your family, and this is your home. Gage loves you. I know you love him."

"He deserves better than me," I said, needing to get it out, to hear the words spoken aloud and make them real. "He fell in love with me because I was here and I'm convenient, but he's so much stronger than I am. I'm so scared. All the time. I thought I was getting past it, but one look at Anthony and I fell apart."

"Sophie," Amelia said, trying to soothe me. I wasn't having it.

"No. You don't understand. He hit me, and I stayed. He beat me and kicked me like a dog, and I stayed. How can I ask Gage to love a woman like that?"

Amelia handed me a cookie and said, "Eat this. You need sugar in your brain. You're not making any sense."

"I'm making perfect sense," I snapped back, her brusque manner sparking temper that should have been extinguished by all my tears.

"Rubbish," she insisted, pushing the cookie into my hand. "Eat. If I can't have it, I don't want to see it go to waste. Perfectly good shortbread. She knows that's my favorite."

The familiar grumble brought me back to myself a little bit more. I straightened, taking a bite of the cookie. Salty, buttery, sweet shortbread melted over my tongue. I was the only one who knew that Abel baked shortbread because it was Mrs. W's favorite dessert, and he'd been sweet on her for years. I hadn't yet figured out if she returned his feelings.

At the thought that I might have to leave Winters House without ever knowing, new tears sprung to my eyes. I blinked them back. No more crying. I had to figure out what to do.

I nibbled the rest of the cookie, took a sip of tea, and tried to make sense of my roiling emotions. A part of me wanted to run out of the room and find Gage, to burrow into his strength and love. To let him protect me as he'd promised he would.

I couldn't. I was still trying to process seeing Gage and Anthony standing almost side by side. They were so different. Anthony's elegant, smooth façade covered the heart of a monster. Gage was so strong, body and mind, his heart loyal and true.

How could a woman who'd chosen the monster deserve the hero?

There was a weakness in me, a weakness had led me to marry Anthony, had convinced me to give in, to stay when I should've kept trying to run.

"Stop it," Amelia said in a sharp voice.

"What?" I asked.

"Whatever you're thinking, stop it. I can see it in your eyes. You're doing his work for him, you know."

I stared at her, baffled. "What are you talking about?"

"Your husband. You're doing his work for him. He wants you scared, so you'll do what he says and go back to him. And here you are, convincing yourself that you somehow deserve less because of him. It's not true, and you know better."

"Amelia," I said, "It's not—"

Impatient with my protests, she cut me off. "What would you tell me? If our places were switched, what would you tell me?"

"It's not the same, Amelia. It's complicated."

"It's always complicated, Sophie. I know you have more backbone than this."

"Because I won't let you have your cookies?"

"Because you've survived everything he did to you. He used you. He tried to grind you into nothing, and you survived.

I shook my head. The shortbread turned to sawdust in my mouth, and I put the rest down on the tray. "You don't understand. I didn't leave. I stopped fighting, and I didn't leave. I gave up. I was afraid."

"Bullshit," Amelia proclaimed in a crisp voice. "You

survived. You've already told me. You tried to leave twice, and the second time he caught you, he almost killed you. So you decided to survive and then fate handed you a way out. You underestimate yourself, Sophie. You think that strength is fighting, is kicking and screaming and yelling, or imposing your will on another the way he did to you. But sometimes strength is in enduring. It's waking up every day and facing the pain, knowing you'll do it again and again, for as long as you have to. There are a lot of ways to give up, Sophie. You didn't choose any of them. You kept yourself alive long enough to escape."

"If he hadn't died, I'd still be there," I said, choking a little at the thought. I wanted to believe Amelia was right. I wanted to see myself the way she saw me, as strong and brave.

"Maybe," she said. "Maybe you would. Maybe you'd still be waiting for that chance. Or maybe he would've been arrested when they got someone else to testify against those people he worked for. You don't know. We'll never know what might've happened; you only have what *did* happen. And what *did* happen is that you took a job with us, at Winters House. And you fell in love with Gage, and he fell in love with you. There is no way on God's green earth that boy is going to let you leave this house while the man who hurt you is out there. I promise you that."

"I'm married," I said, and the words felt heavy in my mouth, sticky with despair. I was married. I was committing adultery with Gage, and I hadn't even known it. I was tied to Anthony, and I'd been dragging him into our bed. I swallowed hard in revulsion at the thought.

"Aiden has an excellent divorce lawyer," Amelia said, handing me another piece of shortbread. "He needed her to get free of that viper he married."

"How long does it take to get divorced?" I asked, turning the novel thought over in my mind. Divorce. Anthony was alive, and we were still married, but we didn't have to stay that way.

"I have no idea, but we'll find out."

I ate the second cookie mechanically, thinking hard. Amelia's voice interrupted, "Do you love him?"

"No!" The denial erupted from my mouth before I had time to think. "No, I don't think I ever loved him, but not now. Not after the first time he hit me."

Amelia reached out and squeezed my hand. "Not Anthony, silly girl. I meant Gage. Do you love Gage?"

"Oh," I said, stupidly.

Gage. I didn't have to think about that. The first night we met, he'd scared the heck out of me when he grabbed me in the dark. I remembered the way he'd smelled my neck, and a tiny smile curved my lips. He'd been all raw energy, strung tight, and yet he'd apologized and walked me to my room. If I hadn't fallen for him that first night, I'd been well on my way after we'd shared that horrible tea. I was head over heels by the time he kissed me, tasting of chocolate cake and Gage.

So sweet and so strong.

Fierce and gentle.

How could I not love Gage?

"Hmph." Amelia made a sound of dismissal in the back of her throat and reached for a cookie. Out of reflex, I smacked her hand. She scowled at me and said, "You were so lovestruck, staring into thin air, I figured you wouldn't notice if I snuck a cookie."

"I always notice when you sneak cookies, Amelia Winters."

"You are so head over heels in love with him you can't

even answer a question when you think about him. How can you possibly consider walking out of this house? You'd tear him apart."

"He deserves better," I said again, though every time I repeated them, the words felt a little less true.

"Maybe he does," Amelia agreed, surprising me. "Isn't that for him to decide? This isn't about what he deserves; it's about what he wants. And he wants you. That boy has suffered through so much already. I never thought I'd see him happy again, the way he has been with you. Don't take that away out of some misguided idea that you're doing what's best for him."

"I—"

I didn't get a chance to finish my thought. The door to the library opened, and Aiden entered, followed by Gage. They each took one of the armchairs opposite the couch and sat. Aiden glanced to Gage, who spoke first.

"Armstrong's story checks out. Cooper's been looking into him, and he's got a contact with the marshals. Armstrong walked away from protective custody, and they've cut him loose. No one knows exactly what he's been doing for the last six months. Aiden talked to Stephanie Marks. She handled his divorce, and he said she's the best. She's on her way here. She'll get started, including what you need to file for a restraining order."

Aiden leaned forward and said, "We need you to stick to the house until we have a better idea what Armstrong is up to. I know you two enjoy getting out and taking walks, but I need you to put a hold on that just for a while."

I nodded, not sure what to say. The practical part of my brain kicked in. "Amelia has a doctor appointment tomorrow. I need to drive her—"

"I'll take care of it," Aiden said. "Mrs. W can bring her if I can't."

I looked at Amelia to see how she was handling the idea of a doctor appointment escorted by Mrs. W but, oddly, she looked unperturbed. They seemed to have forged a fragile peace over their meddling. Mrs. W had been sternly disapproving of the fight in the dining room, but just as firmly in support of the note that had started it.

"How long does it take to get a divorce?" I asked, looking between Gage and Aiden. Gage looked to Aiden, and he shook his head.

"It depends. If both spouses agree, then it's fast."

"I don't think he'll agree," I said, darkly.

Aiden gave a sober nod. "He did not like my sending him away. Stephanie is very good, but you may have to be prepared to ride this out. If he refuses the divorce, you'll have to go to court, and that takes time. I'll use what influence I have to speed it up but—"

"I don't expect you to—"

"Sophie, you're family. We have the power to make this easier for you, and we're going to use it. Don't argue."

"I'm not family," I protested. "I—"

"Aiden, Amelia, I need a minute alone with Sophie," Gage said, his eyes locked on mine, as serious as I'd ever seen them. I found it impossible to look away. I heard the others leave, closing the door behind them.

"I'm married," I whispered, feeling tears prick the back of my eyes again. I didn't want to be married. I wanted to be free. I'd thought I was coming to Gage free.

"I don't care," Gage said. "I love you. That's all I care about. That's all that matters."

"Okay," I said. "Okay."

Gage stood and crossed to me, leaning over and

scooping me off the couch. He sat, settling me into his chest and kissed the top of my head.

"Don't take off on me," he said in a low voice. "I know you're scared to death and I know this is messing with your head. It's messing with mine too. Just knowing that guy is alive and breathing after what he did to you... Angel, it's taking everything I have not to hunt him down and tear him apart."

I tried to sit up, pulling against his arms. "Gage, you can't do anything like that. You can't—"

"I know. I know, because I want to spend the rest of my life with you, not rotting in jail for murder. So I'm ignoring my instincts. We're going to do this the right way. We're going to get you free of him. We're going to figure this out step-by-step. We can handle it, as long as we stay together, okay?"

I relaxed, pressing my forehead into his neck and absorbing the heat of his body against mine. I took his hand and played with his fingers, the simple intimacy grounding me.

"I love you," I said. "I'm sorry I freaked out. He... I saw him, and it was like a nightmare, but I was awake and I just... I just lost it."

"I know, Angel. I know."

"I'm scared," I admitted. "I could put it behind me when I thought he was dead, but knowing he's still out there..."

"He's not going to get to you," Gage promised.

I knew he meant it, but I couldn't help my fear. Anthony's ghost had haunted my dreams, kept me from sleeping in the two years since his death. The sudden knowledge that he was alive, that the ghost was real...it was too much.

"He came back for me. He's not going to let me go."

"He can't have you," Gage said. "You belong with me."

We sat there on the couch until the divorce lawyer arrived, not really talking, just being there. Together. Gage stayed while I talked to Stephanie Marks, holding my hand the entire time.

She was brusque and efficient, but the fire in her eyes when I explained my situation was comforting. I tried to ask Gage about her fee and he pressed a finger across my lips.

"No."

"But—"

He shook his head and pressed his finger harder.

"No, Sophie. I promise I won't hunt down your soon to be ex-husband and kill him in cold blood. In return, you agree to let me take care of your attorney's fees."

When he put it like that... I did the only sensible thing and nodded my head.

CHAPTER THIRTY-TWO

SOPHIE

T he next twenty-four hours were anti-climactic. I was on the edge of my seat waiting for my phone to ring, for a knock at the door, but there was nothing. Anthony had disappeared as mysteriously as he'd appeared back in my life.

Stephanie Marks filed the paperwork for the restraining order, and it was granted almost immediately. I suspected Aiden's influence. She'd explained that the paperwork itself was as good as useless, but if he violated the order, it would only help my case in the divorce. Useless or not, the restraining order made me feel better.

Mrs. W drove Amelia to her appointment since Aiden and Gage had a meeting at the office they couldn't easily reschedule. Gage didn't want to leave me alone in the house, but I reassured him that I'd be fine.

The guard at the gate had strict instructions not to allow anyone on the property until they returned. There another guard on the property, and the alarm was set.

I was safe in the house and I was going to be brave. That

included not asking Gage to sit by my side. Anthony was alive. I was going to have to learn to deal with that.

The house was quiet with everyone gone. I tried to read a book but couldn't keep my attention on the page. Finally, I gave up and curled up on the couch in the library in front of the fire, listening to the hiss of the gas logs and watching the dancing flames.

My phone rang, discordantly loud in the quiet room. I glanced at the screen before I answered and froze. Unknown number. My thumb hovered over the red 'call' button, debating what to do as it rang in my hand over and over.

My heart trying to pound its way out of my chest, I punched my thumb at the button and hoped for the best.

"Hello?"

"Sophie," Anthony's familiar cool tone sounded in my ear. "You were so unfriendly yesterday, I almost didn't recognize my own wife."

"I have a restraining order," I said, surprised at how calm I sounded. My breath was strangled in my chest, but my voice was level when I said, "You're not allowed to come near me, or call me, or contact me in any way."

"You're my wife," Anthony said, unruffled. "No one can tell me I can't call my own wife. Now, I've got a problem, and I think you can help me with it. I have an unwanted guest. I'd like to trade her for you."

A cold ball of horror gathered in my chest as I heard Amelia's voice echo in the background over the phone. "Don't listen to him, Sophie. Stay where you are and don't listen to him. Don't you dare—"

The smack of flesh on flesh sounded over the phone and Amelia fell silent. I knew that sound, knew it too well. I squeezed my eyes shut, trying to think.

Anthony said, "I don't have any interest in harming the old woman, but I will if I have to. You have an hour. I'll text you the address. Don't be late or I'll slit her throat."

He hung up. A few seconds later my phone chirped with a text message. An address I didn't recognize. I sat staring at my phone, frozen in indecision. Panic told me to run for the car keys and go after Amelia. Every muscle in my body strained to leap off the couch and move, but I stayed where I was.

If I showed up there by myself, not only would Anthony get me, he would almost certainly kill Amelia. If I did nothing, he would kill Amelia. I was reaching for my phone when it rang, startling me so badly I almost fell off the couch.

"Hello?"

A familiar voice said, "Sophie, Cooper. We caught Armstrong's call. I've got a team on the way to that address. We'll get eyes on Amelia. You stay put for now."

"He said if I'm not there in an hour, he'll kill her," I said. "Are your guys going to get her out?"

"Uncertain at this point," he said, his tone businesslike as if he weren't discussing the life and possible death of a woman he'd known since birth. "We're going to get eyes on her and assess the situation. I'm headed in your direction. Gage and Aiden will meet me there. The address isn't far. We have time for a game plan."

All I could say was, "Hurry."

I paced the front hall, the minutes after Cooper's call stretching, distorting, until every heartbeat felt an hour long. The clock was ticking. Anthony had Amelia. He hadn't mentioned Mrs. W.

I didn't know where he'd grabbed Amelia. From the car? From the doctor's office? Had he hurt Mrs. W? I didn't know. I didn't know anything. I was walking in circles in the front hall of the house, alone, and I didn't know anything.

Anthony had Amelia.

Just the thought of it had nausea rolling in my stomach. Amelia. She was my job, my patient, but in the last six months, she'd been more a mother to me than anyone since my own had died when I was a teenager. I wouldn't let Anthony hurt her. I could live with a lot of things, but not that.

The front door finally opened, and Cooper strode in, his eyes scanning the room. "Aiden and Gage aren't here yet," he said, stating the obvious. "They should be right behind me."

"He wants to trade me for her," I said. "We can't let him hurt her."

Cooper gave a brusque nod. "I heard the call. We'll have a report from my team in the next five minutes. The address he gave wasn't far."

"You have a plan?" I asked, crossing my arms over my chest and hugging myself.

"I have a few options in mind," he said. I'd only met Cooper once before, and I'd thought he was all business then, but I saw now I'd been wrong. Cooper was a cipher, his face betraying nothing. If he was worried about Amelia, it didn't show. When I looked at him, all I saw was focus.

The door swung open again, and Aiden entered, followed by Gage. I was momentarily struck dumb at the sight of Gage in a suit. I hadn't quite gotten used to it yet. He was handsome enough in a T-shirt and cargo pants. In a custom-tailored grey suit and starched white shirt, he made my heart skip a beat.

For the shortest second, I forgot my fear and almost

smiled. Then he was at my side, pulling me close and dropping his head to mine. "We'll get her back, I swear, Sophie."

Cooper's phone rang, and he answered it with a quick, "Report." He stood in the middle of the carpet in the front hall, motionless, his entire being concentrated on the words pouring into his ear. I heard him say, "Anything you can do to improve the line of sight?" Then, a minute later, "Okay. Okay. No, not yet. We don't want to spook him while we still have time. Hold your position."

Cooper hung up the phone and slid it into his pocket. "He's got her in a building that used to be a garage, out by the airport. There are empty lots on either side, wide open in three directions. The two front windows are papered over, no visibility. He's got cameras on the outside, so we can't get close enough for a good view through the uncovered windows on the sides, but one of my guys was able to get to a small window in the back without being seen. He verified that Amelia is tied up and gagged but uninjured."

"Did he get eyes on Armstrong?" Gage asked. Cooper shook his head.

"Briefly. Armstrong's smart. We can't get a line of sight on him. A few quick glimpses. Enough to see that he's armed, but not long enough to get our own shot. We can't take him out unless he moves. With those cameras live, our options are limited."

"What about your guy at the back?" Gage asked.

"The windows are too small for entry, and anything we could introduce that might disable Armstrong would endanger Amelia."

"Then what do we do?" I asked. He'd said he had options in mind. I wanted to know what they were.

Cooper studied me for a long moment, then turned his

dark gaze to Aiden and Gage. I got the feeling he was weighing their mood before he spoke.

"I have an idea that might solve all of our problems," he said, slowly. "But I don't think you're going to like it."

Gage went still. Aiden narrowed his eyes on Cooper and said, "What is it?"

"We put a vest on Sophie, wire her, and send her in. She draws Armstrong into position, and we shoot him."

Gage exploded. "No fucking way. Are you fucking insane? We're not sending Sophie in there. No fucking way, Cooper. Think of something else."

Aiden jumped in with his own protest. "Unacceptable, Cooper. We can't put Sophie at risk."

"He has Amelia," I said. "He'll kill her. He's not bluffing. Anthony doesn't bluff. He told me he'd slit her throat and he meant it. We're running out of time."

"Sophie, no," Gage said.

I stepped back, pulling myself from his arms and looked him in the eye. "I can do this, Gage."

"No," he said again. "I swore to you I would keep you safe from him."

"I'll be wearing a bullet proof vest," I said, looking from Gage to Aiden, who was shaking his head.

Gage let out a bitter half laugh. "You think a vest is going to do you any good when he shoots you in the head? And forget about armor piercing bullets. A vest is barely safer than nothing at all. No. It's too dangerous, Sophie."

"He's not going to shoot me," I said.

"You don't know that," Gage shouted, and I flinched.

He wasn't angry at me. He was scared. We were all scared. And he liked the idea of me walking into a room with an armed madman about as much as I would like it if he offered to do the same. I took a deep breath and let it out.

"I do know that, Gage. Anthony had guns when we were married. There was always one nearby, but he never once threatened me with a weapon. If he's going to kill me, he'll do it with his hands, not a bullet."

"Sophie, no," Gage said, his eyes searching my face, anguished and furious.

"If I can get him to move into the right spot, your guys can shoot him?" I asked Cooper.

"Yes," he confirmed, sending a wary look at Gage.

Gage let out a frustrated growl and stepped back, his fists clenched at his side. Without another sound he turned on his heel and stormed out the front door, slamming it so hard it shook in the frame.

Aiden looked at us both. "Sophie, I think this is a shit idea. I'm not going to try to stop you but—"

"Aiden, we don't have time for this," Cooper reminded him.

"I know. Give me a minute with Gage." He looked to me, then to Cooper. "Get her suited up. I'll get Gage on board, and then we'll go." He walked out the front door, leaving me alone with Cooper.

"For the record," Cooper said, "I don't like this idea much better than they do. But we need some help to take him down. And if anyone else goes in there, he'll shoot on sight."

"I can't let him hurt Amelia," I said. "I can live with a lot, but I can't live with that."

"Then let's get to work," he said, scanning me from head to toe. I wore a long sleeve button-down, jeans, and a pair of white canvas sneakers. "Go change into a sweater. Something thick and loose fitting. Be fast."

I took off down the hall to my room, unbuttoning my shirt as I ran. By the time I got back to the front hall,

Aiden and Gage had returned, and Cooper had a long black duffel bag open on the floor. He pulled out a stiff black thing that I guessed was the bulletproof vest and handed it to Gage. "Get this on her. The wire is already attached."

Without a word Gage crowded me into the corner of the front hall, shielding my body from view with his bigger frame and said, "Pull your arms out of your sleeves, and lift up your sweater."

I did as he instructed and stood still, letting him fasten the vest over my shoulders and around my torso with efficient motions that told me he'd done this more than once.

I opened my mouth twice to say something. Anything. No words came out. Gage couldn't seem to look at me.

When he was done, he tugged my sweater back into place and turned to join the others. I followed, surprised to hear him say, "I'm taking the shot."

"Gage, I've got a guy in position –"

"I'm taking the shot, Cooper. You're not sending her in there and leaving me sitting in a van two blocks away. Fuck that. I'm taking the shot. You don't have a single guy on your team better than me."

"You're not a sniper," Cooper argued.

"You don't need a sniper. You need a guy who can take a shot through a window at medium-range without endangering hostages. What the fuck do you think I've been doing for the last ten years?"

Cooper lifted his chin in the direction of the stairs and said, "Change out of that rig and grab what you need. The clock is ticking. Meet us in the car."

Gage flew up the stairs. I barely had my seatbelt on when he came out the front door and slid into the backseat of Cooper's oversize SUV beside Aiden. He'd changed into a muddy green, long-sleeved T-shirt, khaki cargo pants, and was carrying a gun.

Gage didn't say a word as he buckled his own seatbelt. Cooper had me sitting in the front so he could spend the drive giving me instructions, most of which revolved around not getting myself killed.

Aiden and Gage sat in the backseat in silence, the weight of their disapproval pressing on me. My chest ached, worse every time Gage refused to meet my eyes in the rearview mirror. I didn't know if he'd forgive me for this.

If I were in his shoes, I'd be furious. I don't know if I'd understand. I'd like to think I would, but the idea of Gage putting himself in danger turned my stomach. I understood why he was angry, why he might not forgive me, but I had to do it.

I couldn't let Anthony hurt Amelia any more than he already had. Maybe he would shoot me. It was possible, but I was pretty sure that wasn't his plan. I doubted he'd guess I'd called for help. Anthony would think I'd done as I was told, too scared and too stupid to defy him.

I was scared, but I wasn't stupid. And I was done with doing what I was told.

Amelia had been right. I'd endured, and I'd waited for a chance. My patience had been rewarded, and I'd gotten that chance when Anthony had played dead. I wasn't giving it up.

If Anthony wanted me back badly enough to kidnap Amelia Winters, he wasn't going to stop. This had to end now, and I wouldn't let it end with Amelia's death. Not if I could help it.

My hands were shaking, and I felt sick to my stomach, but I knew what I had to do. I looked down at the tablet Cooper had shoved into my hands. On it was a rough sketch of the garage, showing the lines of sight from the windows and Amelia's position.

The rear window, where Cooper's guy kept watch on Amelia, was the only one without a camera. Probably because the approach was blocked by another building and the window was high on the wall. Anthony must have assumed no one could get up there anyway.

Gage would. As I studied the sketch, I saw exactly where I needed to move Anthony so Gage could take his shot.

We got there with thirteen minutes to spare. Cooper stopped the SUV two blocks away, behind a midsize tan sedan. A man dressed in black combat gear got out of the sedan and walked to the driver side door of Cooper's SUV.

Cooper rolled down the window and accepted a set of keys and the man in combat gear jogged off. Cooper handed me the keys and said, "We can't approach from the front. We're going to leave you here. Get in the sedan, count to a hundred, and drive up two blocks. The garage will be on your right. Number fifteen eighty-two."

I nodded and took the keys, unfastening my seatbelt. I turned to face Gage before I got out. His eyes finally met mine, and their remote expression chilled my aching heart.

"I love you," I whispered.

He didn't answer. Tears pricked the back of my eyes, and I blinked, forcing them back. This wasn't the time. I could fall apart later. First, I had to save Amelia and hopefully, myself.

Chapter Thirty-Three

Sophie

I climbed down from Cooper's tall SUV, going through his instructions in my head as I walked calmly to the beige sedan and climbed behind the wheel. I counted slowly, hearing the SUV pull back into the street and drive away.

I reached one hundred and turned the key, my heart pounding but my hands steady.

The engine turned over smoothly, and I drove down the street. Exactly as Cooper had said, number fifteen eighty-two was on my right, an abandoned garage, the bays closed, the front windows papered over, weeds growing through the cracks in the parking lot.

I parked the sedan and left it unlocked, gripping the keys tightly in my hand. Knowing I was being watched, I straightened my spine and marched to the front door.

It helped knowing that Cooper's men were somewhere nearby. That Gage might already be in position. A car passed on the street behind me, reminding me that while the area wasn't heavily trafficked, neither was it deserted.

Anthony would want me inside the garage. Maybe I could use that to get Amelia out.

I knocked on the door. No answer. I pushed the heavy glass door open and propped it with my foot, keeping the other foot outside, squinting into the dimly lit room. With the glass door and front windows papered over, the only light came from the bare bulbs hanging from the ceiling and the small, square window high on the back wall. Amelia sat duct taped to a folding chair in the center of the room.

Anthony stood a few feet behind her, pointing a gun at the back of her head. When she saw me, Amelia's expression shifted from scared to irritated. I was sure that if Anthony hadn't taped her mouth shut, she would've started yelling at me. As far as I could tell, she was unharmed except for swelling on the side of her cheek.

"Come in, and shut the door," Anthony commanded. I shook my head.

I held up the car keys and tossed them into the parking lot. They landed with a click of metal on pavement and skidded across the cracked surface, the winter sun catching the grooves and flashing in my eyes. I looked at Anthony and said, "Let her go, and I'll come inside."

"You come inside, and I'll let her go."

I couldn't pull off casual. I was too scared, and Anthony could smell fear like a shark could smell blood. I shrugged anyway. Now that I was inside, the layout wasn't exactly like the sketch Cooper's men had sent him, but it was close enough.

Amelia was just inside target range, and, standing behind her, Anthony was out of sight. If he moved toward me, he'd be right where Gage wanted him.

"I'll let her go when I'm ready," Anthony said. "Step

inside and shut that door or I'll slit her throat right in front of you."

His free hand slipped into the pocket of his dress pants, and he withdrew something long and black. Pressing a button on the side, a blade snicked up, the metal gleaming in the light from the bulb over Anthony's head. I stepped into the garage and let go of the door.

"I don't understand why you're making this so difficult, Sophie," he said in his cool, even voice.

He stood there in dark dress pants and a tailored shirt, his shoes immaculate, not a hair out of place, and threatened to kill Amelia right in front of me. How had I been unable to see the monster lurking inside his polished exterior?

Two months he'd courted me, and I'd never realized what he was.

"You don't understand why I'm making this difficult?" I asked. "Are you serious?"

Caution screamed at me to be quiet. Not to aggravate him. Not to set him off. I didn't have a choice. I needed him to come for me, and following his orders wouldn't do the job.

"Sophie," he said, his voice patient but his eyes hard, "your place is at my side. I need you to come home."

"We don't have a home. I sold it when you died."

Anthony waved the knife in dismissal. "Damien wasn't supposed to let you sell the house. He had some idea he'd take over for me. He wanted you out of the way, and he was too squeamish to kill you."

"What happened to him?" I asked, aware every word we said was being recorded.

"He won't be a problem," Anthony said.

"Did you kill him?" I asked, pushing harder.

Anthony smiled, a slow widening of his mouth that telegraphed satisfaction and said, "Among other things."

My stomach rolled with nausea. Time to get us back on track. "I'm not coming home with you. I'm filing for divorce."

Anthony's eyes narrowed. "You can't divorce me. You're my wife."

"That's what divorce means," I explained slowly as if he were a child and not a full-grown man holding a knife in one hand and a gun in the other. "I'm your wife now, and after we divorce, I won't be your wife anymore."

"I won't allow it," he said as if that simple statement ended the conversation.

"I don't care," I said.

I turned and crossed the room, keeping distance between myself and Anthony but trying to draw him away from Amelia. My new position put me too close to Gage's line of sight, but it worked. Anthony turned away from Amelia and dropped the hand with the gun to his side. He closed the knife and slid it back in his pocket.

"Let Amelia go," I said.

"No. Someone will find her after we're gone."

"I'm not leaving with you."

"Yes, you are. I have a new house, on the side of a mountain, surrounded by trees. You'll be safe and protected there. We can be alone, just you and me. I've missed you, Sophie. You don't know how I've missed you."

"I haven't missed *you*," I said, trying to rattle him enough to make him forget where he was in relation to the back window. Anthony went on as if I hadn't spoken at all.

"You bring me peace. You can't imagine what it's been like the last two years, staying away from you, pretending I was dead, surrounded by people who didn't care about me.

The stress, it was so intense, so much worse without you. I need you. You're the only one who takes it away. I tried with other women, but none of them were you."

His voice was wistful, almost sweet. I fought the urge to throw up. I brought him peace because he worked out his stress by beating me half to death.

A rush of anger displaced my nausea, and I heard myself say, "You don't want a wife, you want a punching bag. You want a victim. You're only happy when you hurt someone weaker than you. I'd say you need help, but you're beyond help. You're a monster."

Anthony's handsome face twisted into a snarl and he took a jerky step closer. Not close enough. I moved my foot back, and the gun swung up.

"Don't run away from me, you little whore."

I froze in place. He kept the gun aimed at me and went on, his calm façade cracking as his eyes burned with fury. "I'm dead not two years, and already you're fucking some guy? Letting him touch you, letting him soil you. You were supposed to be clean. Pure. You can't take it all away from me if you're dirty."

I was getting dizzy trying to follow his twisted logic. It kind of made sense, the way he'd dressed me in those virginal nightgowns, barely touched me sexually, insisted I stay away from men, from people. Isolated and alone, existing only to serve him. I shuddered at the memory and took a step back without thinking.

Anthony's hand jerked to the right, and he squeezed the trigger. Chips of concrete flew off the wall. I heard myself scream.

"I said don't move," he shouted, spittle flying from his lips. I'd never seen Anthony so unhinged. Even when he was hitting me, he'd always been in control.

"You're ruining everything," he said, the hand holding the gun shaking, thrusting forward, punctuating every word. "I bought us a house. I have money put aside. So much money. I took it all and then I testified against them. We'll have everything. You just have to come home."

"I'm not coming home," I said quietly. "I'm never going anywhere with you again. You can kill me if you have to if that's what it takes to get away from you."

Anthony went still. The gun dropped to his side. "You love me," he stated, flatly, as if it were the only truth he knew.

"No. I hate you."

He looked at me with incomprehension. "I had to do it, sweetheart," he explained. "It was the only way to get it out of me. And after, I felt so calm. I need that back. I tried with other women, but it didn't work. Only you take the dark away. Only you can give me peace."

I fought the urge to tell him he was crazy. Completely, totally, insane. Did he really think I was going to come back to him?

"How many people did you hurt in the last two years?" I asked. I had to know. I wanted to make him say it out loud, to admit what he was. He cocked his head to the side and studied me for a long moment before answering.

Did he know about the wire?

If he did, he'd kill us both.

Finally, he said, "I didn't hurt anyone, Sophie. It's never me. It's the darkness." His voice lowered to a hoarse whisper. "Without you, Sophie, the darkness was hungry."

"Then why did you leave me?" I asked, taking a tiny, sliding step back, drawing Anthony forward, just a little. Caught in memories of the things he'd done, he barely noticed as we shifted a foot in the wrong direction. Then another.

"I thought I could feed it other ways, just for a while," he said, in that same hoarse whisper. "But it took longer than I planned and it got to be too much."

"Is that why you left the marshals?" Another small slide back. Almost there.

Anthony gave a dismissive shake of his head, seemingly unaware he'd stepped forward to match my careful retreat. "I got away from the safe house when I needed to. But it wasn't the same. Those other women, they weren't you. They couldn't make it happy. Couldn't take it away like you did."

"What did you do to them?" I asked, conversationally, sliding my foot back another step. "The same as you did to me?"

"No, Sophie, no," he said, tracking me, stepping closer, almost in Gage's line of sight. His voice was entreating, just short of begging. I'd never heard so much emotion from Anthony. "I'd never touch them like I touched you. They weren't clean, weren't pure. They only made the darkness hungrier. It needs you."

I suppressed a shiver. I had no idea what that meant, but I had a terrible feeling he'd done far worse than beat them with his fists and feet. I didn't want to hear any more. I couldn't do it, couldn't play a game with this monster of a man.

"Do you want me back?" I asked, softly.

Anthony nodded, slowly.

"Then come and get me," I invited. I held out my hand as if waiting for him to take it.

Anthony carefully placed his gun on the floor and walked toward me, his dark eyes relieved, his face relaxed.

Just as his fingertips brushed mine, his body jerked to the side, the sound of a gunshot and breaking glass echoing through the empty room.

He hit the floor and rolled, groaning. I heard a voice shout, "Sophie, get out."

I ran for Amelia, pulling frantically at the duct tape binding her to the chair. The voice shouted, "Sophie, move. We've got Amelia covered. Clear the room, now."

I did as I was told, standing and bolting for the door. I heard a shuffle behind me, one shot, then another. A cannonball hit me in the back, and I went down, my shoulder and the side of my head smacking into the concrete floor.

I couldn't get air in my lungs.

I scrabbled at the floor, sweaty palms slipping, my chest heaving for air, my back burning with pain. Feet rushed by me. Shouts echoed against the concrete walls.

Then Gage was there, his hands patting me roughly, yanking up my sweater, tugging at the Velcro of the vest and smoothing over the unbroken skin of my back. He pulled me into his lap, gathering me close, and pressed his forehead to mine.

"Don't you ever fucking do that again, Sophie. Do you hear me? He fucking shot you."

His arms tightened around me, squeezing out what little breath I'd managed to suck in.

"The vest?" I whispered.

"Did its job," Gage confirmed, "but you scared the hell out of me. No more confrontations with armed madmen."

I let out a shaky breath. "Agreed."

I opened my eyes and peeked over Gage's shoulder to see police officers surrounding a groaning Anthony. In a low voice, Gage said, "He's going to jail for a long time, Angel. He's not going to bother you again."

I let my eyes slide closed and pressed my face to Gage's chest. "Are you still mad at me?" I asked.

His arms went tight again, and he said with a growl, "I'm fucking pissed at you, Angel. You almost got yourself killed. It's going to take a long time for me to forget him pointing that gun at you."

I had a feeling it would take me a long time to forget that, too.

"Do you still love me?" I asked, hoping I already knew the answer.

"Always, Angel. Always."

EPILOGUE: PART ONE
GAGE

Sophie handled Anthony Armstrong with a steely nerve I hadn't expected, but the aftermath was messy. Not his arrest. Thanks to Sophie, they had him admitting to murder and repeated spousal abuse, on top of the charges of kidnapping.

With an irate Mrs. W as a second witness, at least to the kidnapping, he wasn't getting away with anything. He'd snatched Amelia from the parking lot outside her doctor's office, leaving Mrs. W tied up in her sedan with a bump on the head, but fortunately no serious injuries. Between her testimony, the camera in the parking lot, and Sophie's wire, there was plenty of evidence to send him away.

Anthony went straight to prison, and after his disappearing act on the marshals, the judge wasn't inclined to grant bail. Her divorce was proceeding—complicated slightly by Anthony's uncertain legal status—but it was proceeding. It was the rest that was hard.

Neither of us slept much the week after Anthony shot Sophie. Her back was black and blue, and her cheek bruised from her fall, but her body was otherwise undamaged. Her mind, on the other hand, struggled to process everything that had happened.

At night, she barely fell asleep before she jerked awake, gasping and crying out in fear and pain. I was there, every time, drying the tears on her cheeks and holding her until she slept again. I had my own bad moments. I'd been doing better since I'd been home, feeling more grounded, less on edge, but seeing Sophie go down after that gunshot had knocked me off balance.

I tried to hide it from her, but the few times I fell asleep I was forced to watch the same scene play out in my mind, only this time Sophie wasn't wearing the vest. This time Amelia was dead, her throat slit, and Sophie bled out on the floor.

It was a good thing we'd scheduled those appointments. We needed them. By the time we went, Sophie was looking forward to hers. I'll admit I was still reluctant. I didn't want to talk to some stranger about all of the shit swirling around in my head, especially after Sophie's close call. It was too personal.

I didn't have a choice. Sophie needed help. She needed sleep. And when I'd suggested I might postpone my own meeting with the therapist she'd squeezed my hand and said, "I'll go if you go." *Fuck.*

So I went. It wasn't that bad, in the end. I was never going to be buddy-buddy with the guy. He asked way too many questions, made me explain too much, but it turned out he'd done two tours himself, mostly in Afghanistan, and he'd seen a lot of shit firsthand. He'd also worked with a lot of guys who had the same problems I did, and he assured me that if I stuck with it, things would get better.

Sophie and I both went in twice a week. It wasn't a miracle solution. That first month, Sophie's nightmares didn't improve at all. I think they may have gotten worse, though we were so sleep deprived it was hard to judge anything. By the end of those first weeks, her skin was so pale I could see the blue veins beneath, and she had dark circles under her eyes.

Gradually, something inside her settled, began to ease, and she started sleeping for longer and longer stretches, waking less often with her breath caught in her throat. And when she started to sleep, so did I.

By the third month after Anthony's arrest, we were back to where we'd been before the day he'd taken Amelia. Still waking in the night, but mostly chasing off the nightmares with sex. If I had anything to be grateful for in Sophie's horror of a marriage to Anthony Armstrong, it was that he hadn't seemed interested in her sexually.

I didn't want to imagine what a man like that could've done to her, the way he could have destroyed her natural sensuality. He'd left that part of her untouched, and it was mine from the beginning.

We were in a waiting game. Anthony was doing everything he could to fight the divorce. Out of delusion, or spite, we didn't know. It didn't matter. He had money, so was immune to bribery. I'd tried that avenue more than once.

The only thing he wanted was Sophie, and she was the one thing he couldn't have.

Cooper Sinclair had told us to be patient. His guess was Anthony would never see trial. He'd testified against the Accorsi crime family after stealing from them. He was in solitary confinement for his own protection, but Cooper was positive it wouldn't be enough. He'd violated his agreement with the marshals when he'd taken off, and they'd washed their hands of him. So we waited.

I was working full time at Winters, Inc. by then, slowly

moving out from under Aiden's shadow and finding my own place in the company. I still didn't have an official title, but I didn't care. We all owned equal shares in Winters, Inc., which made titles kind of irrelevant.

What mattered was that I was home, things were right with Aiden, and I was moving forward with my life. I'd never regret my years in the military—the last six months aside—but living in Winters House and working with Aiden, I finally felt like I could put my demons behind me.

I just needed one more thing. A wife. Not just any wife, I needed Sophie. She refused to discuss the future until she was divorced from Anthony. My girl was sweet, but she was stubborn as hell. And old fashioned. Not only did she refuse to talk to me about getting married, she wouldn't move into my room.

She said it was inappropriate for her to move bedrooms, never mind that I slept by her side every night. As long as she was legally married to another man, she wasn't moving in with me. Like I said—stubborn.

Finally, four months after Anthony Armstrong was arrested for kidnapping Amelia and trying to shoot Sophie, Cooper got word that he'd been found by a guard with his throat slit, despite his seclusion in solitary. It might have been the original locked room mystery, but no one wondered who'd killed him. Testifying against one of the biggest organized crime families in the Southeast, after stealing a chunk of their cash, was a death sentence. I was only surprised we'd had to wait for so long.

I wasn't quite sure how to tell Sophie. I wanted to celebrate, but I knew she wouldn't find that funny, no matter how relieved she'd be that her tormentor was dead. After a detour with Cooper to verify that Anthony wasn't going to come back to life this time, I headed home.

I found Sophie in the library with Amelia. I have no idea what they were up to, but from the guilty look on their faces and the scramble to hide what looked like dark fabric in a shopping bag, I guessed I'd find out soon enough.

Amelia had dialed back the pranks in the first few months after the kidnapping when Sophie and I were exhausted and jumpy, but now that we were better she was back to her old tricks.

Just the week before she'd talked Sophie into putting bubble wrap beneath the hall carpets, so they popped with every step. To be honest, no one really minded that one. I even caught Mrs. W doing a little dance down the hall by the kitchen when she thought no one was looking, each step punctuated by cheerful little pops.

Sophie's eyes brightened when she saw me come in. She was off the couch and in my arms before I'd cleared the threshold, her sweet, sultry scent filling my lungs as I kissed her temple. I wanted to kiss her mouth, but not with Amelia looking on, an avid grin spread across her face.

Stepping back, I said, "I need you to sit down, Angel. I have some news."

Sophie's eyes darkened, and she bit her lower lip, sitting obediently and waiting, braced for bad news. I hated that the life she'd lived left her assuming that any news was automatically bad. Now that Armstrong was dead, that was finally going to change. I sat beside her and took her hand.

"Anthony was found dead in his cell this morning." Sophie just stared at me, disbelieving. I went on, "Cooper got us in to see the body, Angel. He's dead. It's not a trick."

"He's really dead?" she whispered, taking a quick, deep breath. "You're sure?"

"I'm sure," I promised.

She still looked unconvinced. I could understand why.

The last time someone told her Anthony was dead, he'd knocked on our door two years later, very much alive. After going through so much, my Sophie was afraid to hope it was really over.

She blinked and took in another quick, deep breath. She was fighting tears. I wished she'd just let go, but she had this idea that crying made her weak. She couldn't have been more wrong. Sophie was one of the strongest women I knew.

I pulled my phone from my pocket and brought up the last pictures I'd taken. It was gruesome and totally against regulations, but I'd known what I'd need to set Sophie's mind at ease. Without a word, I handed her my phone, a picture of Anthony's dead body filling the screen.

He lay on a metal tray that had been pulled from a wall of similar trays, his skin grey with death, his eyes closed. His neck gaped in an open wound, bloodless and dark, like an obscene grin beneath his chin. Sophie cradled my phone in both hands, staring down at the picture.

Amelia leaned over and took a quick look, grimacing and saying, "Couldn't have happened to a better man."

I expected Sophie to scold her, but she remained silent, still staring at the picture of her dead husband. She stared so long I started to wonder if I'd done the right thing in showing her Anthony's body. Just as I was about to reach for my phone, she clicked the screen off and handed it back to me.

"You saw him? You took that picture yourself?"

I knew what she was asking. She'd been fooled once, the last time by the police. She had to be sure. So did I, which was why I'd asked Cooper to call in a favor and get us a first-hand look at Anthony's dead body. I slid my phone into my pocket and wrapped my arm around Sophie, pulling her tight to my side.

"I took the picture myself. He's dead, Sophie. Ice cold and very, very dead. They said he bled out in his cell. He's not coming back this time."

Sophie let out a long breath and slumped against me, winding one arm around my waist and holding me tight. It felt like we'd been waiting forever for her to be free. Divorce had been one solution, but this was much better. Finally, Sophie's nightmare was over. For good.

"If you two don't have other plans," I said, "I was thinking we could go get a hot chocolate at Annabelle's and stop by to see Charlie and Lucas's project. Charlie said the kitchen is done and we need to see it before the painters cover it up."

Sophie straightened and smiled. "Sure, just let me change."

I caught her hand in mine before she could leave. "You okay, Angel?"

Sophie gave me an absolutely brilliant smile and said, "I've never been better."

As soon as she was out of the room, I turned to Amelia and said, "I have a plan, and I need your help."

Epilogue: Part Two

Sophie

"Sophie, while you're up, would you get my book from the library?"

Amelia was comfortably ensconced in her bed, covers tucked to her chin. I looked at her suspiciously. She never read in bed. When the lights went out, so did Amelia.

"Which book?" I challenged.

"The mystery. The one about the knitting club and the murder."

That described any number of mysteries Amelia had read lately, but I thought I knew the one she meant. Helpfully, she said, "I left it on the table closest to the fireplace."

"You can read it in the morning," I said, wondering what she was up to.

"I want to finish that chapter now. I won't be able to sleep until I know whose body they found behind the yarn shop."

I sighed. I didn't believe her for a second. There was no chance Amelia was going to stay up late to read a book. She loved her sleep too much. But Gage was at a dinner meeting with Aiden, and I was at loose ends, not tired enough to sleep myself, so I might as well do what she asked and let her plan play itself out.

"Okay, be right back."

I headed into the hall, braced for a surprise. None came. Soft lights illuminated the wood floors and cream walls, and outside in the courtyard, the fountain was still lit, the flowing water gleaming in the darkness. The house was quiet with Mrs. W at her cottage, Abel in his apartment, and both Gage and Aiden out to dinner.

The house needed life. It needed children. Gage had been trying to convince me to have my birth control implant removed. He wanted a family with me. He wanted babies. As much as I loved to imagine having Gage's children, his dark hair and serious blue eyes looking back at me from a little boy or girl, I didn't want to take any chances. I wasn't getting pregnant while I was still married to Anthony.

It hit me again that Anthony was dead. This time, I was really, truly a widow. Just the thought of Anthony's dead body put a spring in my step. Maybe I was morbid, but after he'd come back from the dead once, nothing comforted me like seeing evidence that he was gone for good. I was free.

A light was on in the library. I'd been sure they were all turned off when we left earlier. My steps slowed as I approached the door with caution. Amelia couldn't have planned anything elaborate. I was with her all evening. I'd know if she were up to something big.

Still, I entered the library on alert, my eyes scanning the room from one corner to another, looking for anything out of place. The room was empty, the pillows fluffed, blankets folded, and Amelia's book exactly where she'd left it, on the table by the fireplace.

As I crossed the room to retrieve the book, thinking I was too suspicious, the fireplace clicked and flickered to life, the flames filling the room with warm light. I jumped a little and spun around, but the room was still empty. Just as I was getting my bearings, the lamp on the far side of the couch turned on, the abrupt glare blinding me for a second.

I blinked a few times, and my eyes adjusted, the lamp coming into focus. A shadow marred the white silk shade, a dark circle topped with a fat dark triangle.

A ring.

Why was there an oversize ring on the inside of the lamp?

I'd understood the bugs. Those had even scared *me* a little, and I'd been the one to tape them in place. But a ring? I walked closer, curious. The ring was the diameter of a dinner plate and a little lopsided.

I was starting to doubt Amelia was behind this. She was a stickler for perfection in her pranks, and she could cut a better circle than that.

Walking closer, I peered beneath the shade, reaching inside to take down the silhouette of the ring. A sparkle caught my eye, and I froze. Tied to the inside of the shade, dangling in front of the light, was a ring. A diamond ring.

My hands shaking a little, I tugged on the thread securing the ring, and it tumbled into my hand, the stone catching fire in the light from the bulb. I turned it over, studying the simple gold band and the large, brilliant diamond.

"It was my mother's," Gage said, from across the room. Startled, my hand closed over the ring, and I looked up to see him in the hidden doorway, watching me.

"The ring," he said, clarifying. "It was my mother's. My

father gave it to her a few months after they started dating. He always said he knew the moment he saw her that she was it for him. I never really knew what he meant until the night I met you. I held you in my arms, and I knew I never wanted to let you go."

I stared at Gage in shock, my mouth hanging open, the ring clutched tightly in my hand. The diamond cut into my palm, but I didn't care.

I was never letting go. Not of the ring, and not of Gage.

"I didn't want you to," I admitted. "I knew I should, knew I could lose my job, but I didn't care. You were in my heart from the beginning."

Gage crossed the room and took my hand, gently pulling my fingers back from the ring. Taking it, he turned my hand over and said, "Sophie, will you marry me? I want to have a life with you. A family. I want to spend the rest of my life making you happy."

"Yes," I whispered. "Yes, I'll marry you." A tear streaked down my cheek as he slid the ring on my finger, and I barely registered Gage nodding to someone at the door. Turning, I caught a flash of Amelia's satisfied smile and Aiden's grin before the door shut, and we were alone.

"You got Amelia to help you prank me with a ring?" I asked, looking between Gage's face to the diamond sparkling on my hand. The ring was a simple solitaire, but it wasn't plain. The diamond was too big, had too much fire, to ever be plain. It was perfect, mostly because it came from Gage.

"It seemed fitting," Gage said, drawing me into his arms.

"You got it wrong, then." At Gage's confused look, I explained, "Pranks are always a little mean. A joke at someone else's expense." I held my hand out between us.

"This is the best thing that's ever happened to me. You're the best thing that's ever happened to me."

"Then it's not a prank; it's a surprise."

"You gave me your mother's ring," I said, looking at my hand on his shoulder, the way the big diamond sparkled against the dark blue of his suit. I knew how much it meant that he'd not just asked me to marry him, he'd asked with *this* ring. His mother's ring.

"She'd love you wearing it. Both of them would have loved you. You're smart and stubborn, and just the sound of your voice makes my heart beat faster."

"Gage," I whispered, more tears spilling over my cheeks. I didn't want to cry, but my heart was so full I couldn't hold it in.

"When I came back to Winters House," he said. "I was a mess. I wanted to get my life back, and I had no clue where to start. Then you were here, and I knew that whatever else happened, as long as I was with you, everything would be all right. I'm still a mess, but if we're together, I'll get through."

"Always. You'll always have me," I promised. "And you're not a mess. Neither am I. We're just two people, doing the best we can."

"Angel," Gage whispered, and his mouth took mine. I understood why Amelia had shut the door when Gage backed me to the couch, his hands on the belt of my robe. "Have I ever told you how much I love this robe?"

"*This* robe?" I asked, a little breathless from his kiss. I looked down at the bulky, waffle-weave white cotton in confusion. Gage peeled it off to reveal a white, silk, knee-length slip. It wasn't terribly revealing, but it was sexier than my normal white cotton. His eyes dilated, and he drew in a breath.

"*This* robe," he confirmed, dropping it to the floor and examining me in the white silk. "It covers everything, and only I know what you're hiding underneath." With one finger, he traced my shoulder, sliding under the narrow strap of the slip and flicking it off to fall to my arm. The silk slid, hanging on the tip of my breast.

Gage nudged it all the way down, baring me. He stared down, his eyes hot and intent, a mix of love and lust that had me melting. I went to work on his tie, tugging at it. I still hadn't gotten the hang of stripping him out of his suits, but I was getting faster. His jacket was on the floor, his shirt mostly open, when he stepped out of his suit pants, pulled my underwear over my hips and dragged me to the couch.

I was on his lap, straddling him, while we were both still half dressed. Neither of us cared. His thick cock was right there, pressing between my legs. I'd worry about our clothes later. I rose up on my knees and shifted over him until the head of his cock touched my sex. Sinking down slowly, I let out a long groan against his neck.

Nothing felt as good as Gage. Inside me, filling me. He was a part of me, my heart, and when he made love to me, I felt him in every bit of me, body and soul.

Gage loved for me to be on top, but he couldn't help taking over. His big hands closed over my hips, and he fucked his cock up into me, grinding into my clit, making me cry out his name.

We didn't last long. I meant to. I tried to hold out, but the way Gage held me against him, whispering in my ear how much he loved me, was too much. I came in a rush that took me by surprise, my body squeezing his until he followed me with a hoarse shout.

As soon as we had our breath back, Gage stood, setting me

EPILOGUE: PART TWO

on my feet. Carefully, he pulled the strap of my slip back up over my shoulder and wrapped me in my robe, loosely belting it at my waist. He didn't bother with his suit jacket, but put his pants back on, even stopping to straighten the pillows.

My heart squeezed with love. I knew Gage wouldn't care if we left our clothes littering the library, but I might die of embarrassment if I knew Mrs. W had found them in the morning. Gage took my left hand, raising it to his lips, and kissed the ring he'd placed on my finger.

"Soon," he said, in his low rumble. "I don't care if it's big or small, but I want to marry you soon."

"Here," I answered. "Next month when the peonies are blooming in the garden. Just family. I don't want a big show. I just want you."

"Done," Gage said. "I'll get Mrs. W on it tomorrow, first thing. You get Amelia, Charlie, and Maggie to help you find a dress." He paused and tugged the lapel of my robe. "Or just get married in this. As long as you're there, waiting for me, it'll be the best day of my life."

My eyes misted with tears and I didn't see him move as he scooped me into his arms and strode for the door. The hall beyond was empty, the house quiet. When Gage turned for the stairs, I let out a little sound of protest.

He silenced me with a firm kiss and said, "Not tonight, Angel. Tonight, you sleep with me."

I didn't argue. I'd resisted sleeping in Gage's bed because I hadn't wanted to come to him there as another man's wife, no matter the circumstances. But now I was my own. Anthony was gone, and I'd pledged myself, heart and soul, to Gage.

He carried me up to his suite, our suite, and didn't put me down until we were in the bedroom. I watched him strip

317

off his suit with hungry eyes, and knew we wouldn't sleep all night.

This time, for the best reason of all. Love.

**Turn the page for a sneak peek of Annalise's story,
Engaging the Billionaire**

SNEAK PEEK
ENGAGING THE BILLIONAIRE

PROLOGUE
Annalise

He lay in the hospital bed, eyes closed, his chest rising and falling with every breath. He was alive. That was something.

Life had taught me to expect the worst. When I'd been summoned to the emergency room my head had been filled with disaster. Death. My stomach was already twisting, my heart sick with grief. But Riley wasn't dead.

He was unconscious and his arm was broken, but so far that was it. The nurse told me he'd woken once, to ask for me, and was simply sleeping. I was having a hard time believing her. I'd been sitting by Riley's hospital bed for hours, holding his hand, waiting.

If this was normal sleep, he would have woken. Wouldn't he?

The white bandage wrapped around his head was a jarring contrast to his tanned skin and dark hair. Riley couldn't be hurt. Riley was strong and smart. Riley was everything. Since the day we'd met, he'd taken over my life. It seemed impossible that anything, even a pickup truck and a drunk driver, could slow him down.

The nurse came back in, narrowing her eyes at the sight of Riley, still asleep.

"Shouldn't he be awake by now?" I asked.

She spared me a sidelong glance as she checked his vitals and made notes on the chart. "Not necessarily. The doctor can tell you more when he does rounds, but your boyfriend has a concussion and a broken arm. So far, that's it. No internal bleeding and his brain isn't swelling. I would have expected him to be up by now, but I don't think there's cause to worry."

She patted my shoulder as she left. I didn't think you were supposed to go to sleep when you had a concussion, but it seemed ridiculous to question the nurse. I knew nothing about head injuries and she was a medical professional. If she wasn't worried, I shouldn't be either. I knew that. It didn't seem to make a difference. I wanted Riley to open his eyes.

His dark lashes fanned against his cheeks, hiding the green-flecked hazel of his eyes. I loved Riley's eyes. They were the first thing about him to capture my attention.

I'd been watching him for two months before we officially met. He sat three rows ahead of me in Intro to Psychology. Three rows up and just enough to my right that I could stare at his profile when I was supposed to be paying attention in class.

One day, as he stood to grab his backpack, he'd looked up and his eyes met mine. Warm, light hazel framed by the kind of long lashes men never appreciated and women envied. A strong blade of a nose, dark hair a little too long, and the hint of a tattoo peeking up from the collar of his gray T-shirt.

He was prime eye candy for a girl like me. He wasn't too pretty. None of that highly polished, pampered look I'd been over by the time I hit my teens. I'd grown up around rich boys with their expensive haircuts and overpriced watches. Designer clothes didn't do it for me. The way that gray T-shirt stretched over his arms definitely did.

He slung his backpack over his shoulder, locked those hazel eyes onto mine, and winked. My heart stopped in my chest. By the time I'd recovered, he was gone. I'd never looked forward to a class as much as I did the next session of Intro to Psych. He was there, in the same seat he always took — three rows up and four to my right.

The class went by in a blur. I took notes, but later I realized none of them made sense. I spent most of my time studying the curve of his ear, the way his hair was a little too long in the back, curling up over the collar of his T-shirt, this time a faded navy blue with the logo of a classic rock band on the front.

His jaw, the side of it I could see, was clean-shaven and strong. His shoulders were broad and his left arm was just muscled enough to be sexy. I could tell you I didn't sketch the edges of his tattoo, visible below the T-shirt sleeve, but I'd be lying.

That time, when he winked at me, I had just enough composure to smile back. I leaned down to grab my own backpack, and when I looked up he was gone. Again.

We played that game for another week, and suddenly it seemed like I saw him everywhere. Checking his mail at the student union, waiting in line in the cafeteria. Every time I caught sight of him my heart sped up.

I thought about approaching him, planned on it, but

when I had the chance I chickened out. My mystery man was older than the rest of us, at least by a few years. He had a detached air about him that was intimidating, even to me.

I'm not easily intimidated. Not by most people. I'm Annalise Winters. Yes, one of those Winters. The Winters family of Winters Incorporated, heir to a company whose value dwarfed most country's GDPs. I'd been born a billionaire.

Most people thought that made me lucky. In some ways it did. I didn't have to worry about tuition. I'd never had to worry about paying bills or going hungry. I had a beautiful home and a sweet, tricked out SUV my oldest cousin had gotten me for my high school graduation.

But I don't know that 'lucky' was a good description of my life. I also had two dead parents, victims of a murder/suicide that had drawn relentless media coverage, a clusterfuck that had only gotten worse when the aunt and uncle who raised me died in an almost identical crime when I was seventeen.

The scandal had been irresistible. The legitimate news, gossip columns, people I'd grown up thinking were my friends—they were all obsessed with the downfall of the Winters family.

Money could insulate you from a lot of problems, but it couldn't fix everything. Not the stuff that really mattered. By the time I started high school I knew how to keep my guard up, knew how to be cautious. I'd learned the hard way not to trust easily. Threats could hide anywhere. Even in the hazel eyes of a cute boy in class.

So, I'd watched him and I'd let my heart beat too fast when he winked at me, but that was it. I wasn't looking for a boyfriend. I was just trying to be normal for a while. Normal never lasted long for me.

A few weeks after that first wink, I'd turned around and bumped right into him, almost spilling my coffee all over another one of those faded, well fitting t-shirts.

"Whoah," he'd said, reaching out to steady my arm. His strong fingers closed over my elbow and my heart fluttered.

"Sorry, sorry, I didn't see you there," I babbled.

His fingers firmly gripping my arm, he led me away from the line at the coffee shop. "It's my fault. I was standing too close. To tell you the truth, I was trying to figure out what perfume you're wearing."

Up close, I could see that his hazel eyes were flecked with specks of green and gold. My brain struggling to catch up, I said, "It's not perfume, it's lotion."

"Good to know," he said, the side of his mouth quirking up in a half smile that made my knees weak. "I'd offer to buy you a coffee but—" he gestured to my coffee with his own. "Looks like you've already got that covered. How about a walk?"

"Okay," I said, my head spinning a little as I let him lead me out of the coffee shop and into the street. We'd fallen into step together, exchanging names, though I only gave my first. I didn't want to tell him who I was.

Not yet.

I had my own reasons for being gun shy about relationships, reasons that had nothing to do with my family. But I didn't want to tell Riley who I was until I decided if he'd be worth the trouble.

It didn't take long to figure out that Riley Flynn was worth the trouble, and I ended up spilling more than I meant to about my personal life by our third date.

I found out that he looked older than the rest of us because he was. He'd taken off after high school and back-packed around the country before settling down for his freshman year. He'd taken the news about my family in stride, seeming disinterested, though he'd shied away from meeting them. I didn't care.

I was living on campus for my freshman year and I was more than happy to keep Riley all to myself. My oldest cousin, Aiden, was technically head of the family now that his parents were dead, and he'd come home to take the reins of Winters Inc. My oldest brother Gage had taken off and joined the Army the year before, only a few days after our aunt and uncle had been killed.

My twin brother, Vance, was also in his freshman year at Emory and I guessed everyone figured he was keeping an eye on me.

Not exactly.

Vance was keeping an eye on coeds and parties. His sister? Not so much.

That was fine with me. I was tired of living behind gates. I wanted to pretend to be a normal college student, with a normal life. I wanted to get serious about my photography and study art. So far, everything had been working out perfectly. I should have known it wouldn't last.

I watched Riley sleep in the hospital bed and tried to tell myself that people got into car accidents. It wasn't good, but it was normal. It happened. It didn't mean Riley was going to die. If it were that serious, they wouldn't let me in his room. The nurse would've seemed more on edge. Everything was fine.

I must have squeezed Riley's hand too hard, because his fingers flexed over mine and he let out a low groan. Those thick eyelashes fluttered against his cheeks and his eyes opened, bloodshot and swollen, but the familiar green-flecked hazel soothed my worries. I felt my own eyes flood with tears and Riley smiled weakly.

"Hey, hey, it's okay," he said. "I'm okay."

"You wouldn't wake up," I said. Riley squeezed my hand again. He knew me, knew what I was thinking. Knew how I feared more loss. More death.

"I'm awake now, and I'm fine."

I swiped a tear from my eye and nodded. He squeezed my hand again.

"Lise, look at me," he ordered. I did. His pupils were uneven and his words were a little slurred, but he was still Riley. "I'm okay," he said. "Everything is okay. I'm not going to die on you."

"Promise?" I couldn't help asking.

"Promise." His eyes slid shut and he murmured, "Just need to close my eyes."

I pressed the button to call for the nurse. By the time someone showed up, and I let her know Riley had woken, he was fast asleep again. The nurse was unconcerned, both that he'd woken and that he was back to sleep.

I tried to reassure myself that this was another sign everything was okay. She adjusted something in the IV attached to his arm, murmured to herself, and left the room. I settled back into my chair by his side to wait.

Alarm bells woke me from a light doze. Running footsteps, flashing lights, and I was pulled from his bedside, his hand torn from mine. I knew better than to interrupt. People in hospital scrubs leaned over him, their voices urgent, the words coming fast and unintelligible.

I didn't know what was happening, I only knew that it was bad.

I did what I always did when things were bad. What all of us did when things were bad. I called Aiden. He was there twenty minutes later, bullying the nurses with his implacable authority, insisting I be allowed to stay by Riley's side when they were done, demanding to know what was happening.

He shoved a cardboard cup of tea into my hand and made me sit in a chair in the waiting room on Riley's floor.

"As soon as he's stabilized, they'll let you back in, though they're not happy about it," he said.

"What happened? He was fine. He was sleeping and then—"

"A mixup with the drugs," Aiden said, shaking his head. "The nurse misread the dose on his morphine. They don't know where she is, but they'll question her as soon as they find her. What's important is that they caught it in time and he's going to be okay."

"They messed up his medicine? How does that happen? I thought he would be safe in the hospital—"

When I heard the alarms, saw the flashing lights and the rushing nurses I'd assumed it was something to do with his concussion. It never occurred to me that they might accidentally kill him.

I wanted to bundle Riley up and take him home to Winters House. Except Winters House had never been particularly safe either. There was nowhere in my life that was safe. Nowhere death couldn't follow.

"After all this, are you going to bring him home for dinner?" Aidan asked, nudging my shoulder with his. My cheeks flushed. I hadn't dated a lot in high school. Between my family's notoriety, my aunt and uncle's deaths my junior year, and other stuff, I just wasn't that interested.

Riley was the first boy — man — to catch my eye. What we had was so perfect I hadn't been willing to bring it into the mess that was the rest of my life. But maybe it was time.

"Is it all right if he comes home to Winters House when they let him out? He has an apartment off campus but—"

Aidan wrapped his arm around me and pulled me into a hug. "Of course it's okay. Now that I know what's really going on with you two, I'd rather have him where I can keep an eye on him."

I made a disgruntled sound low in my throat, and rested my cheek against his chest. Aiden was overprotective. If I thought he was bad with me, I just had to see him with my little cousin Charlie. She was twelve, still shaken from losing her parents, and Aiden hovered over her as much as his responsibilities would allow.

He was only twenty-two, barely two years older than me, but he was the one who held us together. He'd left college after his parents died and came home, finishing school in Atlanta and taking his father's place at the company and at home.

He read to Charlie at night and made sure Vance and I got our college applications in on time. He'd been the one to insist I live in student housing when I suggested I should stay home and help him with the kids. He'd given up everything so we could have normal lives.

I'd tried to argue, but no one argued with Aiden. He just stared you down and steam-rolled over you.

I hadn't fought him that hard. Both Vance and I felt guilty about running off and leaving Aiden with the kids, but as much as we'd wanted to help, we'd wanted to get away even more. And it wasn't like we'd gone far. All the Winters went to Emory, right in Atlanta, so we were close if he needed us. Only Aiden had gone out of state to school, but he'd ended up leaving Harvard and finishing at our father's alma mater in the end.

We'd gratefully acceded to his demand that we be normal college students. Or as normal as we could be. But now, seeing Riley in a hospital bed, all I wanted was home.

It felt like hours before they let me back in Riley's room. I imagined he looked paler, more worn. Aiden left to make whatever arrangements he was going to make, after reassuring me that Riley would be released in a day or two.

I took my place beside Riley's bed, twining my fingers with his, rubbing absently against his callused thumb, and waited patiently for him to wake.

I opened my eyes the next morning to see a nurse enter the room, her face blocked by a huge arrangement of mismatched flowers. My stomach tightened at the sight of the flowers and I asked, "Where did those come from?"

"They were left at the desk," she said, setting them on the table across the room. "Odd arrangement. I'm not sure I like it much, but I'm sure whoever sent it meant well."

I was sure they didn't.

I waited until the nurse left the room after reassuring me that Riley would wake soon. I had a sick feeling that it no longer mattered. Not for me. Trapped in a nightmare I thought I'd escaped, I pulled my fingers from Riley's and stood.

The few steps across the room seemed to take forever.

The nurse had called the arrangement odd. It was a generous description. The flowers clashed, discordant and ugly together, but the sender hadn't been going for pretty. The flowers were a message, one he knew I could decode.

My mother had loved flowers, had taught me their language, but experience had forced me to understand what they really meant. The clash of yellow and pink blooms told me exactly what had happened to Riley.

Yellow Hyacinth for jealousy.

Rhododendron for danger.

And most terrifying, the deep pink blooms of Begonia — a warning of future misfortune.

The car crash was no accident. Neither was the over-dose that had almost killed Riley.

The flowers were a threat and a warning.

Numb, I picked up the arrangement and carried it from the room. I didn't look at the card until I was in my car. It had been a year since I'd seen those precise block letters. A year since he'd sent me flowers.

I'd convinced myself it was over. Convinced myself he'd moved on, or forgotten about me, or died. I'd been so sure I was free. Safe. I never would have let myself fall in love with Riley if I thought he was still out there. Still watching.

I turned the card over in my fingers, knowing I had to read it. Knowing that once I did, my path was set. I'd have to write a note of my own to Riley, one that would make him hate me. Hate would keep him far from me. Hate would keep him safe.

A hot tear slid down my cheek as I tugged at the seal of the small white envelope. I'd been arrogant. I wanted Riley so badly I'd convinced myself I could have him. That arrogance had almost gotten Riley killed.

I understood what the flowers were saying; Walk away from Riley, or the next time he'll be dead.

I didn't need to read the card.

I opened it anyway, my fingers shaking.

TELL HIM GOODBYE, OR I'LL DO IT FOR YOU

The Rebel Billionaire

The Billionaire's Secret Kiss (Novella)

The Billionaire's Angel

Engaging the Billionaire

Compromising the Billionaire

The Counterfeit Billionaire

THE BILLIONAIRE CLUB

The Wedding Rescue

The Courtship Maneuver

The Temptation Trap

ABOUT IVY LAYNE

Ivy Layne has had her nose stuck in a book since she first learned to decipher the English language. Sometime in her early teens, she stumbled across her first Romance, and the die was cast. Though she pretended to pay attention to her creative writing professors, she dreamed of writing steamy romance instead of literary fiction. These days, she's neck deep in alpha heroes and the smart, sexy women who love them.

Married to her very own alpha hero (who rubs her back after a long day of typing, but also leaves his socks on the floor). Ivy lives in the mountains of North Carolina where she and her other half are having a blast raising two energetic little boys. Aside from her family, Ivy's greatest loves are coffee and chocolate, preferably together.

VISIT IVY
Facebook.com/AuthorIvyLayne
Instagram.com/authorivylayne/
www.ivylayne.com
books@ivylayne.com

Printed in Great Britain
by Amazon

26205002R00188